AXEL

CORPS SECURITY, BOOK 1

HARPER SLOAN

Axel
Copyright © 2013 by E.S. Harper.

ISBN-13: 978-1-4909468-1-8
ISBN-10: 1490946810

Cover Art Designed by MGBookCovers
Photographer FuriousFotog
Model Steffen Hughes
Editing by Mickey Reed
Formatting by Champagne Formats

You can contact Harper Sloan here:
authorharpersloan@gmail.com
www.facebook.com/harpersloanbooks
www.authorharpersloan.com

AXEL PLAYLIST

It is my personal belief that music can turn any ordinary situation into something magical. I have ALWAYS been a huge fan of losing myself in a song. When I was writing Axel, there wasn't a second that my iTunes wasn't rocking away. There were songs that I had to set on repeat a few times because they just made me feel the scene at a whole new level. Especially when I needed to step into psycho. SO—this is my Axel playlist. Some songs mean more than others, some just made me smile, and some made me feel.

Ed Sheeran- Lego House
Ben Harper- Walk Away
Rihanna- Stay
Tim McMorris-Overwhelmed
Fall Out Boy- My Song Know What you Did in the Dark
Macklemore & Ryan Lewis-Can't Hold Us
Christina Aguilera-Just a Fool
Incubus-I Miss You
Dave Matthews Band-Crash Into Me
Lady Antebellum-Need You Now
Rascal Flatts-Stand
Zedd-Clarity
Miranda Lambert-Over You
P!nk- Try
Maroon 5-Sad (particularly the version Amber Carrington sang on The Voice)
Train-Marry Me
Taylor Swift-Mean
Emeli Sande-Next to Me
Gavin Degraw-More Than Anyone
Coldplay-Fix You
Christina Perri-A Thousand Years
NSYNC-Gone
Disturbed-Down with the Sickness
Eli Young Band- Crazy Girl
will.i.am ft. Miley Cyrus- Fall Down

Author Warning:

As a reader myself, I know how important it is to be aware of 'hot button' issues that could trigger painful memories for some. Axel is a story about love. The greatest love that you could find in a lifetime, the undying kind. But, Axel and Izzy didn't have an easy road and unfortunately to tell their story, I had to tell the story of Izzy's hard times. There is a scene that shows the darker side to a bad marriage. There is a scene, however brief it may be, dealing domestic violence. I feel it is my job to advise the reader of this violent episode. With that in mind, please note that this is not a book that focuses on that violence but the strength within Izzy to overcome and the love between her and Axel.

This book is intended for a mature reading audience and isn't suitable for readers under 18. Brash language, sexual hotness, delectable alpha males, and adult situations are all over this book—you have been warned! **wink**

Enjoy! I hope you fall in love with Axel, Izzy & their story! ☺

DEDICATION

To my daughters
M, T, & A
I love you three little ladies to the
moon and back!

PROLOGUE

GOD...PLEASE LET him be late. Traffic? Boss needed help? Hell, at this point, I would even pray for his shoe being untied. *ANYTHING* to give me just five extra minutes.

Taking a frustrated breath, I remember that I gave up pleading to the heavens years ago. Ten years to be exact. The day *he* walked out of my life. The day the sun stopped shining and my world turned gray. The day my dreams turned into nightmares. I miss my dreams, I miss the sun, and I miss *him*. So fucking much, even though I know I shouldn't. After all, what good does it do to miss a ghost?

Come on... Come on.... I silently beg the light to change. Why is it that, the only time I'm running late, every single light catches me? "Fuck! Just fucking change!" I just know if I am not home in the next ten minutes all hell will break loose. *Finally*, as soon as the light turns green, I slam on the gas. All I need to do is hurry and everything will be fine.

Right?

I roll into the driveway at 5:45, throw the car in park, and rush into the house. Thankfully I had enough foresight when I left earlier to start the slow cooker. "Okay, Okay..." I mutter to myself while rushing around the kitchen island to the table. If I don't hurry... Nope, I can't go there. *There* would cause me to lock up in fear, and cutting it this close, I can't lock up.

"Deep breath, Iz... Just breathe," I remind myself, setting the bowls of chili down. As quickly as I can manage, I set the table, making sure the glasses are spot free and the silverware is perfectly aligned. I am *not* going to make those mistakes again. Rushing back to the kitchen, I make sure I've washed and dried all the cookware and signs of my slow cooker use. I have just enough time to make sure that my 'face,' as he so lovingly calls it, doesn't look like I just rushed my duties.

At 6:05 on the dot, I hear the garage door rolling up. *Breathe.* A few moments later, he walks in. Of course he would never run late. God forbid he would make it home a minute past his normal scheduled time. The world might end, the sky might fall, and pigs might start flying.

No, not my husband; he is never off his game.

"Good evening, Isabelle. How was your day?" he asks while unloading his arms of his coat, briefcase, and keys. He makes sure his coat is hung perfectly; wrinkles wouldn't dare mess with him. Even they know not to poke the bear. After he disposes of his cell, wallet, and other pocket shit, he finally looks up at me with his cold, dead eyes.

Permission to speak has silently been granted.

"Good evening, Brandon. Things were normal as always today. Did some laundry, ran the errands you asked me to do, and got home around three. I know you said your parents are thinking of coming this weekend, so I wanted to make sure I had enough time to get the spare room situated before I started dinner."

Lies. All lies… Just enough to hopefully make him think I wasn't out.

"Hmmm," he states while rolling his sleeves up. "So"—he looks up with his evil smirk and those dead eyes—"that wasn't you I just saw speeding down Oak Street like the bats of hell were on your bumper, Isabelle?"

Fuck. Me.

"Brandon, I swear it's not what you think," I squeak out. Shit, this is going to be bad. "Dee stopped by. She's in town and just wanted to say hi, catch up a little. I haven't seen her in six months—"

His smile stops me cold. Immediately, I start backing away. *Oh shit, I know that look.*

"Now, now… Isabelle. What have I told you about Denise? Hmm? If I remember correctly, it was something along the lines of you are not to talk to, call, or take calls from her, and you are definitely not to FUCKING SEE HER!"

He's stepping closer now. Frantically, I look around for an escape, but he's blocking my only exit.

"You have been told, and I would have thought you learned this lesson six months ago. Isn't that how long you said it's been? What do I need to do for you to get it through your dumb fucking head? Jesus Christ, you're a stupid fucking bitch." His eyes are so cold as he steps right into my space. "What part of you being mine—and only mine—did you not understand the last time I was forced to explain this to you? I will not share you with fucking anyone. Do you hear me, Isabelle?" He sneers my name like its very presence on his tongue disgusts him. I've hit panic mode now. He has me backed into the wall, no escape in sight. "No fucking person in this goddamn world is allowed you. Only. Fucking. Me!"

He continues berating me, his eyes bugging out and his spit hitting me in the face. "You're nothing but a stupid fucking slut! Isn't that right, Isabelle? I should have walked the other way that night at Fire. I should have known a bar slut from a mile away. But no! It's all your fault my dick wouldn't walk the other way."

He rears back and slaps me hard across my cheek. I squeeze my hands into fists, digging my nails into my palms to keep from screaming out. I can feel the blood running down my neck from the cut his ring must have caused on my jaw. I may be stuck, but I'll be damned if I will let him break me.

"What did I fucking say, Isabelle? NO DENISE! No afternoons chatting like little fucking bitches. You're to be here, cleaning my fucking house, cooking my fucking dinner, and spreading your fat fucking thighs for my dick!" He reaches out and grabs a bowl of chili, throwing it with all his strength against the wall. I watch chunks of meat, beans, and sauce run down my happy yellow walls. "And what in the fuck is this shit? I told you, you fucking bitch, I wanted lasagna. Does that look like lasagna?"

I should have seen it coming, but my attention was still focused on my happy yellow walls and the globs of dinner rolling down. I was just turning back to him when his fist hit my temple, momentarily making my vision blur. At least that seems to have knocked some sense into my sluggish brain. I dart to the right, quickly trying to escape the second fist I know will soon be following. Too late—always too late—I catch the second one in the ribs, knocking the breath right out of my lungs. Brandon grabs my thick hair, and with a twist of his wrist, I'm right back at his mercy.

Mercy I know he doesn't have.

Throwing me into the hallway with what feels like the strength of ten men, he's quick to follow with a kick to my stomach. "You stupid bitch. You just can't listen. I own you, all of you. No one else. No one else touches what is MINE. Especially not fucking DENISE! I warned you what would happen. No, I promised your dumb ass what would happen if you went near her again." Kick—Slap—Punch—Kick. "You're never going to learn are you?" He's panting with exertion, and it's taking everything I have not to let the blackness overcome me. Even if I know numbness would be following quickly.

I lose track of how long he stands over me, screaming and beating, alternating between his feet and his fist.

Freedom—that's all I crave now.

I close my eyes and pass out.

WHEN I wake up, the house is dark. Every bone, muscle, and hair on my head hurts. I can't take a deep breath without wanting to die. I can feel wetness on various parts of my head and body. *Fuck.* It's never been this bad. I can't hear anything out of my left ear. What the hell happened to my ear? Fuck, I need to move. Clutching my arm around my middle, I slowly climb to my feet. I take a look around out of my very swollen eyes and see that dinner is still sitting on the table. The broken bowl, chili dried to the wall, and even the spotless cups are sitting there mocking me. With a slow and silent step, I glance into the living room. No sign of Brandon. Shuffling—more like dragging myself to the kitchen, I see that his keys are gone. Holy shit! He's not here. Never, not once in six years, has he left me alone in the house after a 'lesson.'

I walk along the wall, holding on for support until I reach my purse, unzipping the side zipper; I reach in and take out my phone—the phone Brandon doesn't know I have. I'm not allowed to have a phone, and he disconnects the house phone and takes it with him when he leaves. I can barely see enough to turn the phone on. I slide my finger across the screen and unlock it. Finally, after a few wrong buttons, I place the call.

"Hello? Hello, Iz? Iz, are you there? Is everything okay? IZ??" I can hear her. She's practically screaming. But I can't get the words out. She knows I wouldn't be calling this late. Hell, she knows I wouldn't call at all.

I take a shallow breath and rasp out the only word I need to bring my salvation.

"Help..."

Then the blackness pulls me under.

CHAPTER 1
Izzy

I HAVEN'T ALWAYS been this weak person…this broken woman. I used to dream, and when I did, I dreamt big. I had plans, plans of a future so bright it would blind you. I can still remember the day those dreams, those grand plans, and that future as bright as the sun went poof.

I just didn't know it at the time.

At the time, I thought everything would be okay. After all, what seventeen-year-old girl doesn't think she's invincible?

That, coincidently, was the same day I decided fate hated me. No, she didn't hate me… She loathed me. People say that karma is a bitch, but I have news for you. Karma doesn't have anything on fate when she is after blood. Not a single thing.

I wish I knew what it was that set fate on the path of my doom. Maybe it was just being born? I like to think I was at least okay there. My parents loved me, they prayed for me, and I was everything to them. So, no, I don't think that was the day.

Or it could have been the day I stole Maggie Jones's pudding cup. But Maggie was a bully, never nice, and always stuffing her face, so I like to think I did her a favor.

I once stole a chocolate bar from the grocery store, but seriously? Fate would have been after every little teenage shit if that were the case. Point fingers all you want, but where I come from, it's like a rite of passage.

No, I think fate decided she hated me the day I walked into Dale High School freshman year and my path collided with Axel's. It would make sense that the reason she hated me was the reason for all my pain. The reason I'm convinced fate will never shine in my favor again.

Why would she? She took it all away. Wiped out every single thing I have ever loved in one swift kick.

One day, I might figure it out, the reason fate hates me, Isabelle West. But until that day, I damn sure will be careful with my dreams and my plans, my heart and my soul.

Fate might hate me, but that doesn't stop me from hoping that one day she forgets about her favorite chew toy. When that day comes, I hope karma has some fun with that bitch fate.

2 YEARS LATER

I CAN feel the sun warming my skin. I love this blissful state between sleep and just waking up. It reminds me of being numb. You haven't hit the switch to turn on your mind, giving it permission to process and remember. You are just there. I love waking up feeling the sun warming my skin; it reminds me that I am alive. Alive and surviving.

I sigh and roll over in bed, laughing when I see the stupid body pillow dressed like a man with an oddly lifelike face drawn on the top. Dee insisted that I needed it in my life. Her theory was that if I didn't want a man at least I wouldn't sleep lonely, whatever that meant. I stopped trying to understand all that is Dee years ago. She has been my best friend for the last eleven years. She is the sister I never had and I know without a doubt in my mind that she would always have my back.

We met when I was eighteen and pissed at the world. She was bopping all over the room during freshman orientation, smiling at everyone who would look at her. She took one look at me and decided that we would be the best of buds. I think she saw the broken soul inside me and with her infectious happiness decided she would be my medication. She was by my side with every up and every down—and trust me, there were a lot of downs. She was my biggest cheerleader and supporter, and she singlehandedly brought light back into my life.

She picked me up when I had fallen, dusted me off, and helped me heal.

She did it again two years ago. No questions asked. She dropped everything, ran to my rescue, and helped me heal again.

We had lost that 'sisterhood' for a little while when I was married to Brandon. It wasn't easy, but I was able to keep in touch with her with stolen calls and secret meetings. I knew she worried. She knew things weren't good at home, but Dee, being Dee, came with a smile and the knowledge that if I needed her she would be there.

And she hadn't lied; she dropped everything and ran with one word.

I know she feels somewhat guilty for introducing us. It's unjustified, but it is there. I can see it sometimes in her eyes when we would be spend time together with a few bottles of wine between us. She hides it well, I will give her that, but I know my girl, and with a heart that big, she can't help it.

I met Brandon when I was twenty-one, carefree, and looking to numb my world with drinking and parties.

He was the first man I gave a second glance to after Axel. It had been almost four years and I was ready to try and love again.

Oh, how blind I was.

Brandon was, on the outside, perfect. He was a few years older than me, and had already graduated from the University of North Carolina and established himself within his father's accounting firm. He was successful and quickly on his way to even bigger things. He wasn't overly tall, just shy of six feet, with a lean runner's body. Sandy brown hair and brown eyes. He was the perfect boyfriend, showering me in romance, extravagant vacations, and gifts, always showing up to take me on surprise trips, doing all the little things we always think makes a man perfect. Six months after we met, that perfect boyfriend became my fiancé, and four months later, I became Mrs. Brandon Hunter.

Then the Brandon I had met and fallen in love with slowly changed. Gradually, he began distancing me from my family, friends and most importantly, Dee. He knew, of all the bonds I had, that hers was the strongest. I became a prisoner in my own life. I know my grandparents worried, but he was slick and always came up with the perfect reason we couldn't come, or when the rare occasions came that we did, he was always called home for some reason. Dee was harder for him to brush off, but he did. Or at least he thought he did. He was good; I'll give him that—the master of control and manipulation.

And he downright terrified me.

The beatings didn't start until we had been married for about two years. I went to see Dee when I was supposed to be picking up his dry cleaning. I missed my best friend, and I had honestly thought I could be in and out before he noticed. But Brandon Hunter noticed everything.

They weren't bad at first, a slap here and there for whatever offense he deemed beat-worthy. Eventually though it didn't take much. I could sneeze, and if he didn't like it, I was sporting a black eye the next day.

He had played his hand right and I was well and truly stuck. Cut off from those I loved and so terrified of his wrath, I wasn't going anywhere.

Those were the years I prayed and prayed for Axel to find his way back to me. Every single horrible day I was at the receiving end of Brandon's fist, I tried to take myself to another place. To a place where Axel was, ready to take me away and be my hero. But I eventually had to face the facts; my hero was gone.

Closing my eyes, I think back to the time my life was the happiest. Twelve years ago to be exact.

"I can't believe this is our last night together for six months, I'm going to miss you so much, baby." I look up into his bright green eyes. God, I love his eyes. I think I would be happy to just sit here and look at his handsome face for hours.

Get lost in him.

How will I make it without him?

This boy I love more than anything.

I lay my head back down on his warm chest, feeling his strong heart beating under my ear.

I've known this beautiful boy since I was fourteen, and Axel has been the love of my life for the last three years. Not a day has gone by without him in it. How am I going to go just one day without him, never mind six months?

"Babe, quit. It will be over before you know it and I will be back to get my girl," I hear him rumble under my ear. He knows exactly what is running through my mind.

We've been lying here in his tiny twin bed for hours, just getting lost in each other. I know he hates being in this house.

His foster family isn't a bad foster family. Well, as far as they come, I guess. He might as well be a meal ticket for them, but they leave him alone. I get the impression that they are counting down the seconds before he leaves for basic training and they get his body out and a new one in. They wouldn't want their check to be short—greedy assholes. His foster parents have never liked me. I don't think I will ever understand why, but Axel thinks it's because I have been around the last three years, taking up space and eating their food. Who knows? I just can't wait for him to be free of them.

I can't believe my beautiful boy is leaving for the Marines tomorrow. Marines… God, Ax is really leaving. I haven't let myself think about what could happen to him when he leaves. Axel was born a fighter, a survivor. Nothing would happen to him, and I just had to believe that.

He starts to shift under me, sliding out from under my body and rolling onto his side to face me. I look into his bright, twinkling eyes again, smiling up at him. He really is perfect. Thick, messy black hair is sticking up in disheveled waves from me running my hands through it. His strong cheekbones and powerful jaw always remind me of how ruthless he can be. I run my finger down his perfectly straight nose and then run it along the thick lips I love to get lost in, tracing first the top and then the bottom. His lips twitch, and that lazy grin I love so much pops onto his face.

"What are you thinking about, Princess?"

"God, Ax, just about how much I'm going to miss you. You promise to come back to me?" I ask him, the tears coming back into my eyes, and the melancholy that has been a constant presence since his graduation Friday night returns.

"Just try and keep me away," he says, leaning in to take my lips in a toe-curling kiss. His tongue licks my bottom lip, and then he catches it in between his teeth, lightly biting down. I open my mouth *to let him in and capture his moan down my throat. Pushing his shoulder, I roll him underneath me, feeling his already hard cock nestle within my wet core.*

"Mmmm, babe, already?" he groans.

"Always, Axel. I'm always ready for you," I say as I lift up and help guide him inside my body.

As I begin to move with a perfectly mastered rhythm over his lean, hard body, I think to myself how hard it's going to be to drop my boyfriend off at the bus tomorrow knowing that it's going to be six long months before I see him again.

Little do I know, the last time I look into these eyes will be when he turns around to wave while walking up the steps to the bus, the bus that takes my heart with it.

A heart that never returns to me.

LIKE I said, I haven't always been this weak woman. I don't think anyone wakes up and says, "Hey, today I think I will be weak, broken, and completely fucked up!" I certainly didn't. I think I have worked hard to become who I am today. With the help of Dr. Maxwell—and Dee, of course—I have slowly become the me I once was.

It hasn't been easy, and I still have my moments. I can't hear my full name without it taking me back to the dark years with Brandon. I started taking the steps to finalize our divorce about six months ago. The same time I had finally healed enough to start moving on. I started my own web design company, something I have always loved to do, and it seemed like the perfect choice. I felt comfortable being able to work out of the house Dee and I shared. Safer.

Brandon isn't making things easy for me. One would think with a clear, black and white police report and hospital records showing what the marriage to him did to me that I wouldn't have any issues with a quick divorce. But no…nothing ever came easy for me. I've been fighting with him the whole time—through lawyers, of course. I haven't actually seen him since the day I was released from the hospital two years ago.

That was also the day that Dee and my duo became a trio.

The day I met Greg.

Where Dee is my sister; Greg is my brother.

Bonds so tight they would be almost impossible to break.

Greg is our protector, whether we want him or not. He looks out for us and doesn't shy away from Friday nights spent in watching chick flicks and eating junk food.

I met Greg the day I was released from the hospital after a week stay, healing from Brandon's final beating. Dee was there to pick me up. She pulled up in a minivan with the back loaded up full of boxes. Looking back now, I can laugh, but the look on her face when I asked her why she had the boxes was priceless. She looked me dead in the eyes with the fiercest expression she could muster and said, "Girl, if you think I will leave you here with that piece-of-sorry-shit husband, you are nuts. Nope, no way. We are packing you up and hitting the road. The world is our oyster or something like that." She then explained that she had the local sheriff meeting us there to make sure Bastard Brandon didn't try anything. Dee was ready for anything. She told me not only would the law be there to look over things, but she had one of her friends meeting us there. She didn't get into detail, and I didn't care. I wanted it over.

When we pulled up to the house I shared with Brandon, he was of course there and raging mad. I sat in the passenger's seat shaking like a leaf. Dee came around and helped me out, using her tiny body as a shield. I kept my eyes down until they met two huge booted feet in my path. Following those boots up thick thighs, a rock-solid chest, and powerful arms, I looked up into thunderous blue eyes. He was a huge man, easily a foot over my five foot three. With his expression, I immediately shrank back, hoping it hadn't been noticeable, but nothing escaped this man's eyes. He carefully schooled his expression and tucked me under his thick arm by throwing it over my shoulders.

As he guided me into the house, he softly said, "Don't you worry, baby girl. We've got you now." I don't know what it was, but when I met Greg that day, all it took were those words to instantly set me at ease.

An hour later, we had six years of my life boxed and loaded.

I left it all, only taking my clothes, important documents, pictures from my childhood, and small treasures I had hidden away from my life before Brandon.

I haven't looked back since.

I may feel alive, but today I'm alive with one bitch of a hangover. Looking at the clock, I shake my head at the time. How the hell did I sleep this late? That's right—Dee. Dee is how I slept this late. Crazy chick got home last night and thought we should spend the evening with Jack. One of these days she is going to remember that, Jack and I, we are not friends. Never have been, never would be. Nights spent with Jack always bring me to the same spot—hung over, and pissed off. Damn, Dee. She better have breakfast ready this morning, er... afternoon.

What did I let her talk me into last night? The last thing I remember is Dee coming home from work with a big-ass brown bag in her arms, screaming "Liquor delivery, bitch!" I guess that's what happens when you have been friends with someone for so long. She knew I needed her, and damn it, I needed Jack. So her announcement was met with red-rimmed eyes, ratty sweats, and a best friend on her third carton of ice cream.

She knew me, and she knew I would be hurting this weekend. So instead of letting me drink myself stupid alone, she grabbed two glasses and proceeded to get wasted with me. Helping me forget, helping me numb my mind, and just being there.

Walking over to my desk, trying to clear the fog from last night's bender, I look down at my desk calendar and triple-check the date. Yup, it's still August 8th, my thirtieth birthday. Also the twelve year anniversary of what is still the worst day of my life. Getting into the shower, without the aid of Jack, I can't stop my mind from wandering back in time.

"GRAM!" I screamed at the top of my lungs. "Gram, oh my God, GRAM!! There's blood, so much blood, Gram! What do I do? Why is there so much... Why is there any?" I've reached complete hysterical breakdown proportions with my wailing.

This can't be happening! There is no way God would be so cruel to take this too!

I crash down onto my knees, doubling over and curling into myself, screaming and praying...praying and screaming. Sobbing big, huge, gasping sobs.

Pop's voice finally reaches my grief-filled mind, picking my small frame up and carrying me out to his truck. "Here we go, my little one. Buckle up and have no worries for your beautiful heart. Pop's got you now."

Shaking my head, I come back from that horrible day. My eighteenth birthday is still, twelve years later, marking all the birthdays that follow with heart-stopping pain. *One day*, I promise myself. One day I will be able to wake up on my birthday and smile. I can't wait for that day.

Feeling slightly more human than I did a half hour ago, I throw my fluffy robe over my naked skin and take off to find my best friend.

I walk into the kitchen and smile down at the note from Dee.

Yo! Made you some grub. Eat...and shower because I bet you smell like yesterday's shit. I had to run into the office, but be ready... I'll be home around noon. We have some serious shopping and pampering to do! That's right, not getting out of it! LOVE-me!

Picking up the salad from the fast food joint up the street, I plop down with a smile. *Made me some grub, my ass. More like drove two seconds away and paid someone else to do it.* Leave it to Dee. Busy as always on a Friday before a long weekend but still making sure I eat and take care of myself. Times like this remind me of how lucky I am to have her in my life; I really don't know what I would do without her. She has saved me from myself more often than I can count. Knowing she will be home in an hour is just more proof of that. She knows I need her this weekend, so she is closing up shop half a day early.

I finish up lunch and then tidy up the kitchen. I return to my room to collect some laundry and get some housework done before Dee gets home, anything to try to keep my mind free of bad memories.

I know she means well, but I would much rather stay home and just be alone.

I understand why she wants to keep me busy, I really do, but I just don't think I will be able to do it. Another year of going through the 'normal' motions. Another year missing him, missing them, missing everything.

A quick peek at the clock has me picking up my speed. Little Miss Happiness should be floating in soon; I at least need to be ready before the rainbows and glitter start fucking with me.

I'm deep in my closet, trying unsuccessfully to find something to wear today when I hear her…singing. Laughing to myself, I let a smile crack my face. Dee can't hold a tune to save her life, but that will never stop her.

She comes bouncing in my room, smiling from ear to ear, "Hey, you sexy bitch. I see you decided to rock the birthday suit today. Nice choice, although we might have some issues getting into the mall like that. I think there might be laws against this. But hey, more power to you!" She smacks my ass on the way over to park it on my bed.

"What the hell, Dee! Door. Closed. Knock!" I try to scowl at her the way Greg always does to us but end up laughing right along with her giggles.

She flops her flat stomach down onto my bed. "So, my sexy 'older' friend, what will be worn on your naked self today? I assume that is what you are doing digging around in that closet of yours."

"I don't know, Dee," I don't have to fake the scowl this time. "Do we have to do this today? Can't we just stay in today? I really don't think I am going to make good company at all." I'm pleading with her, and I am willing to bet I sound as desperate as I feel. I know I won't be pleasant to be around today. I planned on a repeat of last night. Shitfaced, falling down, rip-roaring drunk. Healthy? No, but it works. Why should I mess with a good thing?

"Iz, get your skinny ass ready now. We're going to drive down to the mall, get a new hot-as-fuck outfit for both of us, go see Sway at the salon, and have some serious pampering before Greg comes over to take us to dinner tonight. You aren't going to sit at home alone. I know that's your plan. Not again, Iz. Not this year."

Her eyebrows are puckering and she looks like she will drag me out of here naked if I don't agree. Jesus. There really is no sense in arguing with her when she gets this worked up. I'll just come up with some excuse later and ditch her and Greg for a night at home with Jack.

Now, that's a plan with some promise.

CHAPTER 2

W E'VE BEEN shopping for hours. Or at least it feels like hours to a person who does not enjoy shopping. Dee started dragging me around the second we walked through the doors. She is a woman on a mission.

We were in our second store—second store after the three different lingerie stores. I had more freaking panties than I would need in a lifetime. Apparently, step one of Dee's master plan was making sure I had new everything. I put my foot down the second I noticed her intent. No freaking way.

After a small fight, she finally agreed—one outfit, one complete outfit, and that's all.

And that brings us to now.

I have tried on what feels like the whole entire dress department. There is always something she finds wrong with each one. Finally, she thrust a bright candy-apple red scarf at me. I say scarf because there is no way there is enough material to call this a dress.

"Uh, Dee…where is the rest of it?" I question.

"That's it, Iz. I just know it. That is the dress!" She's bouncing—literally bouncing—up and down in place. Her curly hair is jumping right along with her. If I weren't so annoyed, I would think she is pretty damn cute right now.

"There is no way I am wearing that, Dee. Is there even a back on that thing? And…and my vagina is seriously going to be playing peekaboo all night. There is no way, no way at all."

I'm practically panting with anxiety. I've spent the last two years hiding my body. I lost all the weight I gained during my marriage, but I still see the fat girl I once was when I look in the mirror. Dee is constantly on my ass to stop wearing my 'ratty-ass jeans and man shirts,' which is what she affectionately calls my lack of style. I like my style. Jeans and tees—it's easy and perfect.

Shit.

Sighing, I look down at the scrap of beautiful red material, thinking to myself, *it's just one night. One night of wearing a scarf to keep that smile on Dee's face.* After everything she has done, parading around with my vagina smiling at the world is a small price to pay.

"All right, you pushy little shit. I'll see what it looks like on, but don't blame me if it doesn't work," I tell her with fake exasperation.

Turning from her smiling face, I step into the dressing room and remove my street clothes once again. Once I pull the miniscule piece of fashion over my hips, I bring the tiny strings that will hold this 'dress' on my body over my arms and set them in place on my shoulders. Reaching behind me for the zipper, I meet bare skin. *Called it,* I thought to myself. Placing my palm against my back, I confirm that there is, in fact, no back. I slowly turn around and face the mirror, sealing my fate. Unable to stop the small gasp that escapes my lips, I look myself up and down.

Is that me?

The dress fits perfectly, but then again, with Dee, I knew it would. The front of the dress fits snug across my chest, making my average-sized chest look a cup larger than my small C's. The straight neckline starts just under my collarbone, essentially covering everything. The small straps going over my shoulders make my frame look sleek and petite.

Not too bad.

Taking a deep breath, I turn around to check out the damage. Another small gasp escapes before I bite my lip and take in everything the back lacks. I can see the straps holding the dress up, hugging my shoulders as if they fear at any second they could snap. I follow the exposed line of my spine all the way down to the two dimples above my ass and the small piece of red fabric hugging my cheeks—barely.

How am I supposed to wear underwear with this dress?

Dee chooses this moment to start tapping on the dressing room door impatiently.

"Izzzzzy," she sings. "Izzy, I know what you're doing in there. Stop freaking your freak and let me see!"

I crack the door, giving her another one of Greg's mean looks. "I'm going to kill you for this."

She laughs as she pushes herself into the dressing room with me, taking me in from top to bottom and then back up again. The smile that comes over her face creeps me the hell out. I don't think I have ever seen *that* look before. She looks so... *Shit*...she is practically oozing joy.

"I knew it! I just knew it. Izzy, you have been hiding this banging body for way too long. No more. Maybe we should keep shopping." She looks down at her watch. "There's still time. I could have you outfitted in a few hours. The works—dresses, skirts, slacks, blouses..." She trails off; I don't even think she is speaking to me anymore. I am almost a hundred percent sure her eyes have just glossed over.

"Denise Anne Roberts, you calm yourself down right the hell now. I told you one outfit. ONE! I did not say we would spend the rest of eternity buying the whole damn mall. One, Dee. One dress. I already caved on the lingerie." I whisper sharply at her.

She gives me a hurt look before that creepy little grin comes back.

"Okay, okay... Damn, Iz. No more clothes for now. But one day you will let me do a complete makeover. We still need shoes, so let's go, birthday girl. Get naked and let me have that awesome dress while you put those ratty-ass jeans and ugly ass man shirt back on."

She's bouncing again, and damn it, even though I smile, I'm slightly worried about what I just got myself into.

Two hours later, we finally reach the salon and our favorite stylist in the world, Sway. Sway is a short, fat African-American man with long platinum-blond hair. When he isn't rocking his trademark heels, I can almost look him in the eye. Sway, whose real name is Dilbert Harrison III, is the funniest man I have ever met. How often in small-town Georgia does a small black man come up to you with four-inch heels, skinny jeans, and a tight-fitting shirt on, kiss both cheeks, and pronounce you looking "marvelous, darling"? Not very often, I promise you that.

Sway has been itching to get his hands on my thick, long mahogany hair. He was shocked the first time he styled it and I told him I didn't touch color products. I have always been blessed with perfect hair. It's dark brown with so many different shades of auburn that when the sun hits it you can almost see it set fire.

Exhausted from my shopping mission with Dee, I sit down and tell him to go for it, whatever he wants.

"Sweet baby Jesus in a manger… Sweet child, oh Lord have mercy, please tell Sway that I am not hearing things?" He turns his excited eyes on me with a look of elation, pure elation.

"Go for it, Sway. Just please don't make me regret this." Smiling at him through the mirror, I let myself drift off.

The first time I met Sway was when Dee and I arrived in town two years before. He was our second stop after unloading all of her stuff and my few boxes at our new house. Dee had explained to me on the drive that this was our new chapter in life. A chance to start from scratch and become new people. I knew what she was giving up to run with me. She had a very successful insurance company in Bakersville, North Carolina. Luckily, she was your typical trust fund baby, so it wasn't hard for her to up and leave. She'd left her second-in-command in charge with plans on expanding wherever we landed. We'd taken everything we owned and drove south. The one and only saving grace I'd had was an account Dee had helped me set up with the money my grandfather had left me when he passed away five years ago.

Her money had bought us the house, but mine insured I had time to heal before I needed to make any plans.

The one plan I did make immediately was to get rid of the Stepford wife look Brandon had pressed upon me. Sway tried but it took time, and finally my hair was long and lush again, falling almost to my ass in thick waves. I don't look a lot like that scared housewife anymore, thank Christ for that.

Sway is muttering off and on about the newest purses he just picked up at the Coach store, the earrings he planned on matching with each new purse, and which heels he would wear with what. I swear that this man was done a great injustice when he came out with a dick.

"Oh, honey, did I tell you about the new man who just bought up the space next door? Oh sweet love of all the gods above, he is huge, darling. Just huge. I bet he is huge everywhere, if you know what I mean?" He looks down at me with such seriousness that it takes me a minute to follow the flow from purses to man candy.

"What? Oh, right… Good-looking, huh?" I respond, hoping that I am following.

"Girl, you have no idea. What Sway wouldn't do to catch the eye of that walking wet dream. He was at least seven feet tall—at least! Huge—I am talking muscles on his muscles. I do *not* know how his shirt stayed together. It was stretched so tight against that sexy chest and those fine arms. Makes me want to just fall at his feet and pray he swings my way. But I tell you this, there is no way a man as man as him swings for the rainbow. No way. Shame for Sway, but girlfriend, as beautiful as you are, this is good news. Best news. We should set something up. You would love him. Thick black hair. Now, I would love to get my hands on that thick mop of lusciousness…yes I would." Did I mention that Sway could exaggerate slightly when he got excited?

I'm starting to get a little concerned about the orgasm Sway seems to be having about this man while he is holding scissors to my head. This could be bad.

I smile hesitantly up at Sway and his dreamy eyes. "Sway, babe? You know I love you, but I have no interest in you fixing me up. None. So get it out of your head right now."

"Oh girl, one of these days you will meet a man and he is going to knock you right on your ass! Mark my words, girlfriend. Knock you straight on that perfect little ass!" he replies with a naughty grin.

"Doubtful, Sway. I am done with the male gender. I might even take a page out of your book and start batting for my own team." I laugh and sit back, allowing myself to relax now that the scissor-wielding man has calmed down.

Dee and I finish up with Sway and his minions of beauty right around five with just enough time to rush home and get dressed before Greg comes to take us to dinner.

Pulling up to the house, I notice a package on the step. Calling out to Dee, I step out of the car and grab a few bags, stopping to pick up the package and unlock the door. Dropping the bags in my hand, I quickly disarm the security system and make my way into the kitchen. Dee comes in right when I drop the package on the island and turn for a knife.

"What's that?" she asks.

"Not sure. No return address. Probably something from a client for my birthday," I reply, distracted by my mission to cut away the tape.

Dee goes about her own business, walking down the hall to her room, surely to start her getting ready process.

Cutting the rest of the packaging tape away, I peel open the flaps and start moving around the packaging popcorn.

I move a folded piece of paper out of the way, placing it on the counter, and remove what appears to be a frame. Carefully turning it over, I gasp and drop the picture to the ground, shattering the glass all around my feet.

Dee comes running down the hall at my noise, trying to figure out what has me so spooked. She bends down and picks up the frame, turning it over to reveal the picture.

"That motherfucker," she says under her breath. "What a fucking *motherfucker!*" she screams.

Through the tears streaming down from my eyes, I look down at the photo of Brandon and me. He's taken something sharp and scraped away the belly part of my body. He is looking at me through the picture with that handsome, perfect smile on his face, his arm around my back holding me close to his body. I look sad but I'm still smiling. I think this was taken during our last Christmas together at one of his company parties. The arm not behind my back was resting on the portion of my stomach he so harshly scraped and dug off the picture.

Dee picks up the paper I laid out on the counter. Giving a quick peek, she slams it back down looking like she could spout steam at any second.

"Bastard! That bastard... I'm going to cut off his balls and feed them to him before I kill him with my bare hands. Fucker!" She starts looking around for her phone, momentarily forgetting she left the paper where I could see it.

I look down, and in his angry scrawl, I read, "Feeling empty today? How old would the bastard be this year? Happy birthday, dear wife."

Surprisingly, the sobs don't start right away. I stand there just looking down at the paper for the longest time, and when it hits, it hits hard.

Stumbling back a few steps until my back hits the wall, I slide down onto my ass, curling my legs up to my chest and wrapping an arm around myself protectively. My forehead hits my knees and everything I have been carefully storing in the 'do not open' box in my head comes pouring out. Giant, body-shaking sobs release, and I'm gasping for breaths between them. My whole frame is jerking violently with the force of my grief.

Dee comes rushing into the room. I can hear her on the phone, but she is so far away from my understanding right now. Her arms come around me and I feel her rocking me while still mumbling into the phone. The tears won't stop coming and the crying is getting louder.

I have no idea how long I stay ass to the floor in the kitchen, crying and rocking. I look up briefly when I feel strong arms wrap around me and hook under my legs, lifting me off the floor. Another sob catches my breath when I meet Greg's pained blue eyes. Resting my head on his chest, I let him take the lead. Walking over to the couch, he sits down and keeps me close to his body.

As grateful as I am for Dee, for everything she has done for me, it's moments like this when the only thing that can make me feel safe is being held tight in Greg's strong arms.

If anyone can understand where I am in my head right now, it's Greg.

Part of the reason that our bond is so strong is because of how much he can relate right now. About a month after I met Greg, he sat me down and explained that he had lost his sister when he was overseas. Her husband was a real prick and Greg always wondered, but never confirmed, if he was slapping her around. Unfortunately, he was never able to save his sister; she was beyond his protection when he was off fighting for everyone else's freedom. When he met me, he said that his first thought was how much I reminded him of her. That conversation wasn't an easy one for him, but it helped me understand why he'd gotten so murderous the day he saw me standing on the curb of my old house, beaten, bruised, and broken. Looking back now, I understand how he was able to recognize my fear, and instead of lashing out, he took it in and turned into my lifeline, my protector. He's been protecting me ever since.

"Baby girl? I know you're scared. Iz, mark my fucking words, he will not touch you. Do you hear me? He won't breathe your fucking air, I promise you that." His fierce voice rumbles in my ears. He means it; I don't doubt that. Greg would do anything to protect his family.

"I'll find him. I've got a friend who just moved to town—Reid. He's buying into Cage Investigation and Security. He's been more bodyguard and muscle, but he wants to expand into systems, installs, and investigations—my shit. So we got you, baby girl. He's been a big deal out West now for a few years. Ex-marine, badass motherfucker. I'll talk with Reid, explain the situation, and we will take this. I don't want you to even think about it, you got me, baby girl?"

How do you argue with that?

Easy....you don't. Not when it comes to Greg Cage in protection mode.

"Yeah, Greg, I got you."

With plans for the night squashed by one unexpected package, Greg settles down with Dee and me for movies, popcorn, and beer.

I'm out before Mike takes the stage for the first scene. I vaguely hear Greg's grumbles about watching "a fucking stripper movie" when the strippers have dicks.

CHAPTER 3

THE NEXT morning greets me much like yesterday, except I'm not hung over from Jack this time. My emotional hangover is much worse. My strength seems stripped from me in a way that makes it hard to remember that I am not that broken and weak woman anymore. I try to remember that I survived, there is no reason to fear life anymore, I'm free, and I am my own person. It's hard, God it's hard, to remember the positive in my life. I remind myself that I don't want to be this woman anymore; I am strong and I will overcome this.

Then I remember the picture.

The carving over my empty womb.

And then all that strength and drive to overcome flies right out the window.

Fuck strong, I just want to curl up and die.

Knock, knock...

"Uhh, Dee...come back later. I don't want to talk right now," I whine, turning my head into the pillow.

Maybe if I'm lucky I can just go to sleep and she'll go away.

"Not Dee, baby girl. Turn over so we can talk, yeah?" Greg's deep voice hits me, leaving no room for argument. Why ask the question? I know he won't leave until we talk.

But then I remember. Fuck that.

"Go away, G. Not interested in hashing out life lessons right now." My voice is muffled by the pillow. He'll get the point, and if he doesn't...fuck him.

"Iz, get the fuck up—now. Love you, baby girl, but I won't sit here while you self-destruct."

He's pissed, but not as pissed as me. Why can't they just let me stay in bed? Maybe bring me some more Jack, the asshole?

"Go away, Greg."

"So fucking help me God, Izzy, get the hell up now. Shower. Talk. Breakfast. That's all I am asking, which isn't fucking much."

"Not interested in helping you play Dr. Phil, Greg. I just want to go back to sleep." More of my muffled complaints fill the air, making it thick with bullshit.

"Goddammit, Iz," he grumbles, standing up off my bed, giving me a second to release the breath I didn't know I was holding. Thank God he's leaving, is the only thought I have before the sheets are whipped off and I'm flying through the air. "Not dealing with this shit, Iz. We have shit to discuss, and I do not have time to deal with you being depressed. I get it, baby girl. I understand where you are right now, but you need to wake up and do it now. You have people worried about you. Dee and I are not going to let you sit here and turn into yourself again. No fucking way." He is spitting each word out as he throws me over his shoulder and walks into the bathroom.

"GREG!" I scream. "Let me down now!"

"Not going to happen," is the only reply I get before he dumps me into the shower, twisting the water on and slamming the curtain shut in my stunned, cold, and wet face.

"I'm going to kick your ass, Greg Cage. Kick it fucking hard!" I scream out at him.

I swear I hear his laughter as he walks out of the bathroom.

I stay in the shower until the water runs cold, dreading leaving the solitude of my bathroom. Getting out, I dry off, brush my hair and teeth, and throw on my robe. I take a deep breath in and open the door.

There he is, the giant asshole, sitting on my bed with his elbows resting on his knees. He is looking right at me, trying to look serious while suppressing his laughter.

Asshole.

"All right, you wanted me out." I throw my arms wide. "Here I am. What is so important, huh?"

He smiles at me, letting a few gruff chuckles free. "Try and be a badass another day, Izzy. I'm fucking tired. Went to chat with Reid when I left last night. Told him a little about the situation, not everything. He knows there is a husband not wanting to become an ex and not being quiet about it. He doesn't know the significance behind the picture, but it's disturbing enough that he didn't question me too deep last night. I want you to be honest with him. It's important for him to do his job, Iz. He doesn't know a thing about shit other than this mess currently going on and the little he needed to know about your marriage to understand the threat. He's booked solid with shit for the next two weeks, but I told him I would keep my eyes open until we could put a plan of action into play. You meet with Reid, explain the whole situation, everything—and I mean everything—and then we deal. Understand?"

I take a second to process what Greg just said. It's a lot, and I know he means well, but I do not want someone else in my business.

"Greg," I start, "I really would feel better if it were just you dealing with this. I don't really know this guy, and—"

"Not negotiable, Iz. I'm good, but I am not as good as Reid."

Sighing, I look at Greg. Defeated, I reply, "Fine, G. You know best."

"That's right, baby girl. Don't worry. Reid's who you need. Him and the boys, between all of us, there is no fucking way that shit fuck is getting his hands on you, got me?"

"Yeah, G. I got you."

Greg left a little while ago, leaving me with a worried Dee. A worried Dee planning another 'forget the world' mission. I'm not sure I can handle another one of these. Her newest plan? Continue with birthday weekend. Since yesterday's plans went wonky, she calls up Greg to let him know the plan—drinks and dancing at Club Carnal.

Fabulous.

Just what I want.

My defeated mood continues throughout the day, and I just don't have the strength to fight Dee on this. I can handle one night out with Dee, Greg, drinks aplenty, and loud music to drown out the pain.

I spend my day vegging out on the couch and just hating life in general. Why can't he just leave me alone? The divorce has been sitting in limbo for six long months. I didn't want a thing—not the house, cars, or the money. Nothing that would tie me to Brandon. I'm beginning to think he won't ever just go away.

Dee joins me for lunch. She doesn't say anything about the previous day, but I can tell she wanted to. She is just working it out in her head, trying to figure out the best way to approach. No doubt she heard everything Greg said too. She knew I would crawl into myself and start going back to that dark place; no way in hell she was letting that happen.

I'm sitting on my bed, folding laundry, and avoiding the world when she walks in.

"Hey, have a second?" she asks, lacking the joy she normally greets me with.

"If you want to hash shit out, I just don't think I have it in me today, Dee. I love you, but I just don't know what you want to hear." I reply, setting the laundry aside and clearing her off a spot to sit.

"I just want to see where your head's at, make sure you're okay."

"I don't know. I really don't, Dee. I feel like there isn't anything I can do at this point. He knows where we are, even though I hoped we could stay invisible to him. It was stupid of me to even nurture that thought. I knew he had reach, I just honestly thought he wouldn't care. Why? I keep asking myself why he even *wants* to play this game?" I swallow the tears back down. I can't go there. Not again.

"Babe, we won't ever know what goes through that sick bastard's head. I think it's all about letting you know he could if he wanted to. He knows you are here, knows you want the divorce. Surely he knows you aren't that girl he controlled so easily. Iz, I don't know what his plan is, but I really think you need to speak to Greg's friend. I would be lying to you if I said I didn't have any fear that he might try something."

I know she's right. Hell, I lived with his evil for six years. I know more than anyone just what Brandon Hunter is capable of.

"I know, and I will. It's just hard. You understand that, right?"

She nods her head, compassion lighting her eyes. "I get that, I really do, but when it comes to your safety, your life…well, I won't take any chances, Iz. We have come so far. YOU have come so far. It just doesn't seem right that fate would be throwing him back up in your life."

Ha! Again with that bitch, fate. I should explain how much she hates me to Dee, but she wouldn't understand. Not with her hopeful optimism.

"I'll talk to him... Reid. I think that's what Greg said his name was. Two weeks. I have two weeks to prepare myself to open those wounds back up. God, Dee. I don't want to go there again, remembering it all, and Greg says I need to tell him everything. You don't think he means *everything,* do you? Surely anything from before Brandon isn't important?" I think that's panic in my voice. Surely not, but I can tell by Dee's watery eyes that it most certainly is.

"Izzy, babe, that picture. I think all the before Brandon stuff is kind of important. He knows what yesterday was for you, which means he won't stop pulling more of your pain into the open. It really is best you tell this guy everything. Greg and I will be there. We won't let you do this alone. Never again."

I look into Dee's big brown eyes and know that she is prepared to fight by my side, and I love her for it. Maybe it isn't right for me to depend on her so much for strength, but try as I might, I just can't find another way.

"All right, Dee. Together, when Greg sets something up, we can go talk to this guy, figure out what to do next."

With a small smile, watery eyes, and relief hidden in their depths, she gives me a hug and stands up. With a small clap, she has officially brushed herself off and decided that the heavy is done with for today.

"Well, now that we have had that talk, let's get ready. Greg is coming back after he grabs some stuff for the night from his apartment, stops by his office, and lets everyone know what's going on, all that stuff. That should give us plenty of time to start all our prep work for tonight." Huge smile. Yup, my Dee, the queen of joy and happiness, is back.

With a groan, I let her pull me out of bed and set off for the shower.

I have been thoroughly waxed, buffed, shaved, tweaked, and generally molested by beautifying products by the time we hear Greg's knock on the door. Just in time for him to sit back and enjoy the freak show.

I'm sitting on the living room floor painting my toes and Dee is sitting back on the couch finishing her fingers when I yell at him to come in. I hear the door click open and his heavy steps down the hallway. Looking up, I meet the fierce scowl he is famous for.

"The fuck? What the hell have I told you two about letting just anyone walk into the fucking house?" he growls—yes, growls—at us. If this were anyone other than Greg, I would be sitting in my own piss right now.

"Oh, come on, G. We knew it was you."

"Oh really? So you can see through fucking wood and steel now? I didn't realize you picked up fucking super powers. Remind me next fucking time to just have you beam me the hell over. Sure as hell will save on the gas."

Oops. Guess I didn't realize big bad protector Greg would be coming out to play.

"Iz, baby girl, I did not put this fancy-ass alarm system in for you to not only never set it when you are home but to leave the door unlocked and basically invite Tom, Dick, and Harry to come over. Do I really need to remind you of the dangers out there?"

If he was trying for the soft and tender route, he missed by a mile there. I instantly shut down, my gaze falling to the floor.

"Sorry," I mumble.

"Don't do that shit, Izzy. Brush it the fuck out of your pretty little head. Just promise me to start locking the door, use the alarm, and for shit's sake, check the damn door before letting someone in, yeah?"

"Got it. Alarm, lock, and check." I pick up all my nail products and head off to my room. I have some time to get ready. We aren't leaving until later tonight. I'll let Dee deal with keeping the bear happy. "I'm going to take a nap before we leave. Wake me up in a few, Dee," I call down the hall as I step in my room. I lock the door and shed my clothes before curling into my bed.

It takes me a while to finally fall asleep, but once I do, it is anything but restful. Nightmares of Brandon and dreams of a future lost invade my sleep. When Dee comes to knock on my door around eight o'clock asking me if I want to grab something to eat, it takes me a second to remember where I am and what we're doing.

"Yeah, let me get some clothes on and I'll be right down," I yell through the door, still shaking the dreams from my mind. I get out of bed and grab my robe, setting off to find Dee and Greg.

"Pizza. Sit…eat," Greg says around a mouthful of said pizza.

"Classy, Greg. I wonder why you're still single." I laugh over at him.

He levels me with a mocking hard glare that has me laughing harder.

We eat in comfortable silence, just enjoying each other's company. When it comes time to get dressed and do makeup and hair, we leave Greg in front of the TV with some sports shit to keep him happy.

Dee and I spend about two hours perfecting our hair and faces. Her shoulder-length brown locks are curled and perfectly in place, bouncing as normal. She curled my long hair and pinned it back to keep it off to one side, leaving it to fall down the front of my body, effectively keeping my back fully exposed. I have to admit, she may have missed her calling. Her makeup is done similar to mine, heavy and club worthy. She lined my big light green eyes with heavy liner and shaded my lids with a stunning combination of silver, black, gray, and white. My blush is perfect, but my lips are the focal point—lush and a bold fire-engine red.

Grabbing my new dress, I step into my room to put this piece of torture on. I may have realized she was right, and I do look good, but that doesn't mean I have to enjoy showing off basically every inch of skin. Baby steps would be nice, not taking off running.

I stand in front of my closet for the longest time, just taking it all in. Tight red dress, perfect hair, and flawless makeup.

If I weren't me, I would think this chick was stunning. But I'm me, and I'm currently picking out every single flaw. Breasts look too big, even with my height disadvantage I have way too much leg, way too fucking much back, heels too tall…I could keep this up for hours. Fortunately for Dee, she picks that moment to come walking in.

She looks stunning. Everything my dress lacks and doesn't cover, hers does. She has a simple black dress on. The hemline hits her about the same place my dress does—vagina level. Or at least it would be vagina level if she ever were to bend over, sit, or generally take a deep breath. It's form fitting, hugging her curves, and making her ass look fantastic. I have always been jealous of that girl's curves. She is slender with everything right where it should be. A great ass and a great rack. Where my dress lacks a complete back, hers is dangerously close to playing with nip-slip central. The front is cut right down the center, ending with a point at her breastbone.

"Holy shit, Dee... If you move wrong, your tits are going to come flying out." Gaping over at her, I'm sure I look ridiculous.

"Very funny, Izzy. Tape, honey. I have these girls so taped up there isn't anything falling out of here." She lifts her arms up and does some weird gyrating, hip-swirling move. I can't tell if she is dancing or trying to fly, but true to her words, her tits stay put.

Whatever. More important issues here. Like, how the hell am I supposed to walk in five-inch heels? I am a ballet-slipper, flip-flop-loving girl. I haven't worn heels like this ever. When I was married to Brandon, he wanted me to stay small. Heels weren't allowed because they would make me dangerously close to his height.

"Is there any way I can wear my flat sandals, Dee? I swear I will end up breaking my neck tonight in these things. How are you walking in yours?"

"All in the mind, girlfriend. And no. You will not ruin that dress with *flats*." She practically spits the words out.

Mumbling under my breath about the benefits of having health insurance for when I fall and break something important, I pick up my skyscraper heels from the bed and follow Dee out my door, down the hall, and into the living room.

Greg walks over with a smile on his face, looking pretty damn handsome himself. He is dressed in dark slacks and a light blue dress shirt with the sleeves rolled up, exposing his strong arms.

"Looking nice, ladies," he says, throwing a beefy arm over my shoulder and pausing mid-step into the kitchen.

It takes me a second to register that he stopped walking, so I end up a few steps ahead of him. I hear his sharp intake of breath and turn around. His face has lost the smile and a thunderous look has taken up residency.

"Iz, where the fuck is your dress?"

"You're looking at it, G, or lack of it. Dee's handy work. You know how she is. Last time I give her free range over my outfit, that's for damn sure," I reply with the exasperation clear in my tone.

He's looking at me like I have grown two heads and started speaking in tongues. Quickly, I look down to make sure all my girly bits are still tucked in their rightful places. Looking back up, I meet the still pissed glare of Greg.

Confused, I ask, "What?"

"What? Fucking hell. How am I supposed to protect you when you are walking around naked?" he booms.

"Seriously, this isn't that bad, I think. Plus, Dee was so happy. It's just a few hours of wearing this thing. It really is okay, as long as I don't bend over," I try to joke, but I can tell he still is not thrilled with my lack of dress.

What can I say? When he decided to adopt me as his little sister, he went all out. I don't have time for this big brother act at this point. As much as I appreciate it, he is keeping me from my alcohol and my ticket to Forgetville. I've managed to keep the claws of my past from taking root all day; I'm not going to let them take over now.

Turning around, I continue my walk to the kitchen, where Dee is giving me a knowing eye. Picking up the shot she just poured, I down it and then hold my arm out for a refill. Chuckling she pours me another before turning to address Greg.

"Well, big boy, you ready to have fun?"

"Yeah," grumbles Greg. Grumbles and rumbles... It sounds like someone isn't too happy with my lack of concern for his big brother worries.

"Are your friends still meeting us here?" she asks, peeking a look over at me to see if I caught this new development.

"What friends?" I ask both of them.

"My boys. Don't worry about it. They're meeting us at Carnal later. They got held up," he replies, his tone still sour and his eyes still glaring right at me.

Dee looks over with confusion, not understanding why he is so bent out of shape over an outfit.

"Seriously, G, you need to get fucking laid." I laugh at him, trying to lighten his mood.

He looks sharply at me, "Are you fucking kidding me, Iz? You two are practically fucking naked, and you expect me to be okay with that?" Pointing over at Dee, he says, "At least one of you decided to wear something."

I look over at Dee, with her short black dress and tits still breaking the laws of gravity and don't understand how he thinks she is less naked than I am. I look back at Greg, who has decided that pacing is a better method of dealing rather than sitting silently and fuming.

Whatever. I don't have the patience for this shit. Not tonight.

"Get over it, Greg, seriously. I do not need a fucking dad tonight. You know what I need? My best friends, alcohol and a good time. I don't want to deal with you being a little bitch because you have some misguided worry someone might find this look attractive. I don't care and don't have time for your shit."

I throw my heels down on the island, grab the bottle of tequila from Dee, and take a long pull from the neck, enjoying the burn it takes down the back of my throat. I look up and notice them both looking at me with unmasked sympathy. They know how hard this weekend is going to be, especially now with the added shit from Brandon. I'm sure they are coming from a good place with their worry; I just don't want any part of it. If anything, Brandon has effectively helped me get through the hardest hurdle by throwing it in my face yesterday. Literally. My birthday weekend, also known as the day I lost the last piece of love I had ever known.

"So, Greg," Dee starts, trying to steer our minds off the heavy shit, "who is meeting us there again?"

"My boys from my Marine days," he states, keeping his eyes lined with mine.

I pause for a moment, looking down at my shot. Still, after all this time, I can't help the shudder that passes through my body at the mention of the Marines.

God, I miss him.

Greg is watching me closely. He knows about my past, so he knows what that one little word does to me. We don't talk much about it, but he knows enough. I think he has just as big of a problem talking about those days. He never has told us why he was discharged. I know he was injured; I just don't know how. I figure he will talk if he wants to.

I glance over at Dee, who is giving me a knowing look, and she quickly changes the subject. We make small talk for about an hour before grabbing our stuff and heading off to Greg's truck. Both Dee and I have a nice healthy buzz going on.

We are all pretty silent during our thirty minute drive into Atlanta and Club Carnal. Living just outside of the city has its perks sometimes. I forgot how much I missed Georgia, having grown up an hour from where we settled in Hope Town. I still remember sitting at the rest stop and Dee pulling out a state map. She looked over with a huge smile and told me to pick, so I did. Hope Town is perfect, everything we hoped it would be for two friends starting over.

I haven't been back home to Dale since I left at seventeen. Too many memories I wasn't ready to revisit. Most of those memories are happy ones—my parents and our life before they were taken from me too early, leaving a scared and heartbroken teenager. When I left, at the time I didn't care what I was leaving behind. Now that my parents are gone, there is nothing left there. *He* already left, so what is the point now?

Shaking myself off, I quickly push the painful memories back into the box in my mind I marked 'do not fucking go there.' I have worked hard to beat the past, and at thirty years old, I finally feel the 'healthiest' I have ever been. I don't feel the fear daily. I surround myself with positive and generally happy people; negativity doesn't own a place of my soul anymore. The pain is still there, just not as sharp as it once was. I am happy, or at least I am on the road to getting there.

I see the street Carnal is on up ahead, and the line already out the door and down the sidewalk. *Well, Iz*, I think, *time to put that game face on and enjoy the night.*

CHAPTER 4

CLUB CARNAL is located just inside of Atlanta, in an old converted warehouse. It's been the club to go to since it opened four years ago, and Dee and I have enjoyed it a time or two since we moved to town. It's a classy club, dress code and all of that, valet standing at the curb, and a line that is never less than a hundred people.

Another benefit of coming with Greg? He knows people—everyone, it seems. He pulls up to the curb and tosses his keys to the young kid playing dress-up as a valet. After helping Dee and me out of the car, he saunters off to chat with the huge burly man standing guard at the door and shakes his hand. They do that weird man hug thing and exchange a few words, glancing back a few times at Dee and me. The bouncer nods once and lets us in. I swear, Greg can get anything he wants.

As we walk down the dark hallway leading into the main room, I can feel the music pulsing through the air. Lights are dim but bright enough for me to see the sea of bodies rolling with the beat. I ignore it all and head straight for the bar. It takes Dee and Greg a minute before they realize I have left their sides for my one-woman mission to become completely blitzed. When I leave here, I plan on being a blacked-out, stumbling drunk.

Signaling the bartender, I order three shots of tequila and tell him to keep them coming. Pointing over at Greg, I say, "He's paying."

Greg shakes his head but pulls out his wallet and hands his credit card over to the bartender to start a tab.

"Bottoms up, bitches," I say, quickly downing all three shots.

WE SPEND about an hour at the bar, just taking in the atmosphere and the general vibe of the place. Well, Dee and Greg might be taking it all in, but I'm too busy keeping my drinks flowing. Dee was keeping my pace, but she isn't on the same mission I am. Her goal is fun and mine is to become numb.

I steal the second Jack and Coke the bartender put down before she can drink it. I look at her, smirk and down it.

"Seriously, Iz…you can't even pretend to share?" She has a small frown on her face. She knows what I'm doing and she isn't happy about, it but being the friend she is means she will stand by my side and catch me when I fall.

I have just ordered us a round of Tight Snatches—vodka, peach schnapps, orange and cranberry juice—when I catch their eyes on me. At first, I think they are reacting to my decision to only order off-the-wall drinks, but when I look closer, I see it—the concern, the worry, and the uncertainty on how to proceed.

I pick up my drink and announce, "All right, let's fucking party! You're only thirty once. Whoooohoooo!" I'm screaming; why am I screaming again?

Giggling, I look up at Greg, catching his eye as he looks down at me with his stoic face. He shakes his head, accepting that his friend is well and truly sloshed. I can see his lip twitching from trying so hard to remain the untouchable bodyguard.

The hell with this.

Laughing even harder, I grab their hands and drag them out to the middle of the dance floor. Belatedly, I notice how much easier it is to walk on these sticks when you can't feel your legs. Lesson number one for hooch wear—be drunk. It might make dancing more of a challenge, but I'm not feeling a thing and it is beautiful.

The song changes to the familiar beats of Macklemore & Ryan Lewis's 'Can't Hold Us.' It fills my ears and pounds into my bones. Throwing my arms up, I turn around and look up at Greg, who is still trying his hardest not to laugh. I let the music take over my body, invade my muscles, and penetrate my soul with the pulsing rhythm.

I can feel Greg behind me now, unmoving—nothing different there. Dee is moving right along with me, just as enthralled with the music as I am. She looks over at me with a knowing smile. I give her the first real smile I have felt all day. She knows how to move. We used to be regulars in the club scene during college…before Brandon, that is.

With a wink to clue her in to my intentions, I turn around and wrap my arms around Greg's neck. Even with my heels, I have to come way up on the balls of my feet just to reach him. Smiling, I begin to move with his tall frame, which isn't an easy task. His hands finally grab ahold of my hips and dig in. Dee peeks around his from his back and gives me a smirk, and we start grinding together.

I can feel the rumbles of his voice against my chest when he whispers in my ear, "You're lucky I love you, baby girl." I laugh up at him, noticing that his expressionless face is finally smiling.

He hates dancing, but Dee and I have made it a mission, on the rare occasions we go out, to torture him as much as possible. He knew this was coming; it doesn't mean he has to like it. He puts up with this because he wouldn't dare leave our sides. He knows what kind of trouble the two of us could get into.

When the song ends, we head off laughing to the bar, once again, with the excuse to rehydrate. Maybe that's the case for them, but for me it's all about replenishing the alcohol I just burned off on the dance floor. I can feel my buzz slipping and we can't have that.

WE'VE BEEN at Carnal for a few hours now. The last time I even attempted to gain the time, the hands on the clock started dancing. I ask Greg, who says it's a little after 1:30 in the morning; sure, we can go with that.

Dee and I have been taking turns ordering the most outrageous drinks we can think of—with the help of our phones and Google, of course.

"Gimmie two Golden Showers, bartender!" I scream across the bar. When did someone take my last drink? What was that one? A blow job, I think. Yes, that was it. We spent a good fifteen minutes laughing our asses off after making Greg drink one.

He is currently giving us a look of extreme displeasure. He can act as mad as he wants, but yelling for Greg to deep throat his blow job was hilarious. Just ask the customers around us. They certainly laughed loud enough.

Even during times like this, when you know he could be doing something better with his time, he wouldn't dream of being anywhere else. He's been a constant presence in my life since that day he showed up with Dee. The big brother I never had, always there when I needed him the most. I can tell by the way he keeps looking around the crowd that he has slipped back into that protector mode; it's almost like he constantly thinks *something* is out to get him. Or me. I shiver. Brandon isn't ever far from my thoughts, especially not after the package. I can tell when Greg looks at me like he is afraid I might break at any moment that his thoughts are the same.

Dee's slurred voice interrupts my thoughts with a high-pitched screech. "YO, bitch, drink up! I got you one of those Pull-Down Pussy things. No...it was the Pussy Panty Pull-Down? Fuck." She spits the word out with so much frustration she almost falls off her stool. She looks over at me and I can see that she's trying to decide if she is more confused over the correct drink name or how she got to the club to begin with.

"That's not right, Dee! Greg! Greg, tell her the right pussy! You know pussy, right, Greg?" I laugh up at him, tilting my head to the side, wondering why his frown is wobbling.

"You two are driving me fucking crazy. Just because I know my pussy doesn't mean I know this shit. I eat it, and when drinking it down, I damn sure don't do that out of a fucking glass. For shit's sake, get some motherfucking water next time. Fuck me, the right pussy." He shakes his head at us both. "If you touch one more drink with fucking pussy in the title, we are gone, got me?"

Well. He thinks he runs this show, does he?

I look over at Dee, who is trying hard not to bark out a laugh.

Holding up my arm, I signal the bartender over. Again.

"What's next, my beauties?" comes his flirty question.

"Well, since pussy is off the allowed list, how about you surprise us? Either a Slow Comfortable Screw or a Screaming Orgasm. Bartender's choice." I hear Greg's annoyed curse even over the beating bass surrounding us.

I'm still laughing when Dee screams that our song is on. "Come on, Iz, it's our song! Get up! Let's go shake it."

"Every fucking song is your song, Dee," Greg deadpans.

Laughing, I spin around on my heels and run smack dab into a brick wall. *Fuck, that hurt.*

I put my hands up and try to orientate myself with my surroundings; I focus, or at least I try to. Wait a minute… Since when do brick walls have heartbeats? There is no way that is normal. What the hell kind of club is this?

I squeeze my hands against the wall. Hmm, heated walls. Nice touch, but kind of pointless in a night club, if you ask me. I take a small step back and focus the best I can. I look up and up and up a little more. Finally my eyes land on two laughing brown eyes. *Since when do walls have eyes?*

"Whoa there, sugar," the wall says.

"Huh?" I'm confused as hell.

"Beck, what's going on, brother?" Greg says from behind me. Grabbing my hips and bringing me to his side, he throws that familiar arm over my shoulder. "I see you met my girl, Iz. Izzy, this is Beck, one of the boys I was telling you about."

I can feel the smile in his words. Greg has talked about his "boys" often; I know he thinks of this group as more than friends. After all, when you fight alongside each other for so many years, trusting them with your lives, they become so much more than just people to you. A brotherhood with a bond so tight it is untouchable. I know he is over the moon to finally introduce these men to Dee and me.

I come out of my wall fog long enough to glance up at Beck. He really is one handsome giant. He is at least a few inches over six feet, close to Greg's height and build. He has such strong features—a nose that looks like he has broken it a time or ten and chocolate brown eyes that are twinkling with humor and have deep laugh lines crinkling the corners. He is obviously a man who smiles often. His brown hair is way overdue for a cut, but he makes it work. Really makes it work.

"John Beckett. Heard a lot about you, little lady. It's nice to finally meet you." He is holding out his big paw for me to shake. It feels strange shaking his hand after basically being plastered over his body. Awkward.

"Iz…um, Izzy West," I fumble out.

Dee must have just noticed our new arrival, because right in my ear, I hear, "Who in the hot hunk of sex are you?"

Leave it to Dee. She knows what she likes, and it looks like she likes Beck. Smiling, I turn to look at my friend, and oh yes, Dee is in lust heaven right now. I'm shocked she hasn't started panting and humping his leg.

Turning back to Greg, I notice that two new hunks have joined the party. Since Dee is now busy with Beck, I sit back down and enjoy my drunken happiness. Greg turns, noticing my sitting down, and grabs ahold of my hand.

"Baby girl, this is Zeke Cooper and Maddox Locke. Boys, this is Izzy." He introduces me with a huge smile.

I haven't seen Greg this happy in a long time. I know he has been waiting for this moment, introducing two sets of his 'family' to each other. I don't know much about these men outside the fact that they served with Greg in the Marines. It's my understanding that they work for the same security company in California, something they started up when they left the Marines. Greg couldn't wait to merge his company with theirs, turning Cage Investigation and Security into a large-scale operation.

"Hey, boys. Nice to look at cha," I tell them. Oh my God, did that just come out of my mouth? If their twin smirks are anything to go by, it most certainly did. Shit, does Greg only know hot guys? Both of these two easily top Greg's six foot three. They're giants to someone as vertically challenged as I am, and holy hell, they are nice to look at. Talk about easy on the eyes. Both men have bodies meant to be worshipped, long and hard.

Zeke has blond hair, clipped close to his scalp, eyes so blue that even in the club's dim lighting they look clear, and a blinding, full smile with twin dimples on each side. He reminds me of a model straight from Abercrombie. He is the perfect vision of the boy next door.

Maddox is his polar opposite. He has just as many muscles, but on him they look huge and imposing. His brown hair is longer than Zeke's, sporting that messy look like he was running his hands through it all day—sex hair. His face is hard but friendly in a weird combination that just seems to work. But it is his eyes that hold me captive; they are so dark they look black and bottomless.

I realize I have been sitting here eating them up with my eyes when I hear Greg clear his throat. Looking over at him, I see the biggest grin on his face. Thinking he is smiling at me, I give him one of my brightest smiles and start to turn around to properly introduce myself to his two friends. I am not exactly making the best first impression with these men. I open my mouth to speak when I hear Greg booming—yes, booming.

"Reid! Damn, is it good to see you again. Twice in one day. Must be my lucky day, you fucking bastard."

Jesus, there's another one of these men? Maybe this one will be short, fat, and balding. Ha, not looking like that's possible with this cast of man candy. Even their names are hot. Beck, Zeke, Maddox, and Reid.

I turn to my side, giving Dee a smile that I hope expresses how lucky we just became. She is still standing next to Beck, but her flirty smile is long gone. The look of shock and something else I can't name has taken over her face. What the fuck? She looks like she swallowed a damn fly and is looking right over my shoulder with her jaw on the floor.

Damn, this one must be even hotter than the others.

I make a mental note to discuss this with her later. I might be out of the game, but even I think that is a weird flirting technique.

I finish my rotation and end up looking at the biggest chest I have ever seen in my life. If the boys before this one made me feel small, this man makes me feel like a damn midget. *Well, I can understand her astonishment now. It isn't normal to be this large.* How is his shirt even staying stitched at the seams? His arms are so big and powerful that they are currently testing the strength of his black button-down shirt, which is stretched across his massive shoulders and tucked neatly into the tight black dress slacks, slacks that are doing nothing to disguise the healthy-sized bulge.

I shake myself off, mentally berating myself for going *there*. I just eye fucked this complete stranger without even saying hello. Maybe I shouldn't have had that last drink.

I look back up and meet the most stunning green eyes I have ever seen. Eyes I have seen before. Eyes I have spent hours gazing into. Loving and planning. Eyes I have been mourning for the last twelve years.

Feeling dizzy, I reach out to steady myself, catching the first thing I find, which I think might be Greg.

"What the fuck?" he mumbles under his breath.

This isn't happening.

This can't be happening.

He's gone. I know he is. If he wasn't, I wouldn't have just spent the last twelve years missing him so ferociously with every fiber of my being.

The last thing I think before I feel my world spinning and crashing down on me is that Axel isn't gone. He isn't dead. I didn't lose the last part of him when his baby bled out of my body on my eighteenth birthday.

And before I lose all touch with reality, I swear I hear, "Are you fucking kidding me? Isabelle is your goddamn Iz?"

I must be dreaming because MY Axel would never sneer my name with so much anger and hate.

CHAPTER 5

"**B**ABY," I hear his deep voice seductively rumble as he trails his fingertips up my spine.

God, I love how he wakes me up, always touching my skin like just the contact alone makes him feel whole. His hard body is pressed tightly to my own, keeping me snug and warm against his side.

"Baby girl," he croons in my ear, kissing the spot right behind it—the spot that never fails to make my body go from warm to boiling. Goose bumps instantly start to sprinkle against my skin.

No one has ever set me on fire like he has.

No one has ever loved me like he has.

Axel, my love, my heart, my everything.

I'm finally back in his strong arms.

How did I get here? My heart skips a beat and my breath stalls in my lungs.

It's all been a dream, it must have been. Just a terrible nightmare I never thought I would wake from.

My parents are still alive.

Ax isn't leaving me.

Our baby is still safe within my womb.

Everything is perfect.

The enormity of this moment hits me like a Mack truck. Big, body-heaving sobs rack my body.

He's here; my Axel is here. I am finally back in his arms.

"Baby girl," his voice says again, getting fainter like he is down a long hallway.

"Izzy? Baby girl, please wake up."

Why is Greg holding me? He shouldn't be here. This isn't right. Where is Axel? He was just right here. I don't want Greg, I want Ax!

My crying intensifies, and I can feel his body tensing, trying to figure out how to calm me down. I can hear myself; I must sound ridiculous with my hysterical babble. I'm begging Greg, begging and pleading for him to take me back to Axel. I know I don't make any sense but I just can't seem to figure out where reality is and where I left Axel in my fog.

I want that dream back. I can't lose him again... I won't survive it a second time around.

I eventually settle down to just a few shudders, my breath escaping my body. I try desperately to make sense of this situation. How did this happen?

Looking around, I notice for the first time that we are in an office of sorts and I am sitting on a large leather couch pushed off to one end. Maddox is standing next to the door like a guard. His face has lost the small touch of friendliness he had before and has now taken on a fierce look of pure rage. I look up at Greg with what I'm guessing is a face of pure confusion. He returns my look with a small, forced smile.

I can hear Dee now that I have finally stopped my grief-filled sobbing; she sounds like she is a million miles away. She is muffled enough that I can't understand her words, but the venomous tone to her voice is clearly reaching my ears. Greg is still holding me tightly in his arms, whispering reassuring words in my ear. At least I think they are reassuring. His tone is soft and slow, delicate. My mind can't catch them though; I am still searching for Axel.

"Move the fuck out of my way, woman. I will not tell you again." I hear the steel-like tone attached to the voice I haven't heard in so long. He sounds almost feral. *That* is not a tone I have ever heard his voice take. "I will get back there. Do you fucking hear me, Isabelle? I will be talking to you!" he continues to boom through the office door that Maddox is guarding.

At the sound of my full name, my body goes rigid. I can feel every muscle individually seize up. Each bone seems to have turned to stone, and tremors are starting to work their way through my body. My heart picks up speed and my breathing becomes shallow.

No one has called me that in two years; and no one would dare. That was the name, the only name, Brandon used with me, and it was almost always followed by his fist or foot. No one who knows me would use that name. The first time Dee called me that after I left Brandon, I had to be admitted to the hospital because I couldn't calm down.

God, I can't breathe. I look up into Greg's worried eyes. I know what he sees when he looks down into mine—absolute raw terror and fear. A fear that I am back in that place and terror that Brandon has finally found me.

Gasping to catch a small slice of oxygen down into my lungs, I start clawing at his arms, trying my hardest to get away. I have to run. I have to hide. If Brandon is here, he won't stop until he kills me this time.

"*Fuck,*" Greg spits out. "Mother FUCKING fuck!" He is pulling me closer to his body, trying with great desperation to calm me down. I try to soak up his warmth the best I can, attempting to almost crawl inside his body, but none of it is touching me. I feel like my body is being filled with ice, filling me completely to my soul with ice-cold fear. I can almost drown in the memory-induced terror; it is completely taking over my body and mind.

"Fuck," Greg rumbles again. He sounds so worried. I wish I had the words to reassure him that I'm okay, but what a laughable reassurance that would be.

We both know I am not okay; I am so far from okay I might as well be in another country. I haven't had an episode like this in a long time; not since the early months after leaving Brandon. I have been doing so well at beating back the panic and finally seeing the light of peace. In fact, yesterday's breakdown after the 'present from hell' was the first time I have felt the claws of fear take hold in months.

"Locke, come here, man. Hold her for a second so I can go bash that motherfucker in the goddamn head." Greg softly throws his request over to Maddox. I guess he has had enough of watching me come unglued. It can't be easy for him to watch the aftereffects of a beaten and broken woman. After he first witnessed one of my panic attacks, I remember he wouldn't leave for days. He kept his hawklike eyes trained on my every move, just waiting for me to crumble.

I feel my body being lifted and then set down within a new set of steel bands. Maddox hooks one arm around my shoulder and pulls me to his chest, taking my legs and pulling them up close to my body before wrapping his other arm in tight. I feel almost infantile in his arms as he starts to hum a slow tune. I never expected him and his hard exterior to be so understanding and nurturing.

Finally feeling some of the panic recede, I take what feels like my first gulp of air in hours, willing my heart to settle. Maybe it's his warmth or the way this big hard man curled me in tight and started to softly sing under his breath. Maybe it's just the fact that I don't want this new person to see how completely fucked up I am. But he finally calms me down enough to feel the stress and exhaustion of the situation start taking over. Looking up, I meet the concerned dark depths of Maddox's eyes.

"You okay, girl?

"No," I whisper back to him.

What an absurd question. If I could, I would belt out one hell of a laugh.

I don't think I will ever be okay again.

I tuck my head back down onto Maddox's chest and hope for a miracle.

Axel

YOU HAVE got to be fucking kidding me. What are the odds, after this long? Isabelle fucking West. I am still at a loss over this new intel. *My* goddamn Izzy is Greg's friend who needs help? No, that's not right. She isn't *mine* anymore. She stopped being mine when she couldn't wait for me, couldn't hold on for just a few months. She stopped being mine the day I finally found her—married to another fucking man.

Fuck! How is it possible that the Isabelle I knew all those years ago is the same woman Greg gave me the rundown on yesterday.

He described a scared, innocent, and very broken woman. The Izzy I knew would never let a person break her spirit. Hell, in the three years she was my girl, even I had a hard time keeping that spirit from overtaking me. She was so full of life and happiness. No fucking way this is the same girl.

When Greg called me yesterday to have a chat, he explained that his girl was in trouble. And not the kind of trouble a girl needs to be in. I didn't have the time yesterday to sit down and get the details, being in the middle of moving across the country and setting up shop with Greg; things are insane. I had finally handed over the West Coast operations of Corps Security just a few days ago, quickly jumping in my truck and heading east. I had bought my house quickly and we had just signed the lease on the new office space. Now all that is left is getting set up with Greg and becoming familiar with his case load. There is an endless backlog of people requesting consultations for investigative work. Luckily it hasn't taken much to convince Locke, Beck, and Coop to pick up and start over in Georgia with me.

During our quick meeting yesterday, he filled me in on the very hazy issue. He had a good friend escaping a bad marriage. How bad, I don't yet know. She has been living here for about two years and during the last six months has been having a back and forth battle for divorce. The bastard doesn't want to let go. Greg said that it hasn't been a big issue until yesterday when she got a fucked-up picture in the mail. He explained it to me. The ex sounds like one sick fuck and enough of a threat for me to tell him to set something up.

He didn't tell me her whole name; he called her Iz. I remember snorting humorlessly at the name yesterday. But yesterday, the last thing I thought was that Iz could possibly be one and the same, Isabelle West.

I've known Greg for close to a decade now. I still remember a few years ago when he called up, telling us he had to run to North Carolina and be some white fucking knight. I don't remember the details, even though I wish to fuck I did. I just remember him going radio silent for almost a month after.

He has always talked about his two girls here in Georgia. The guys and I have been giving him a hard time for a while now about handing over his nuts since he liked hanging with pussy so much.

He has always spoken about these two chicks like they are fucking queens, goddamn Mother fucking Teresas. I honestly don't think I have ever heard him say a negative thing about either one of them.

Such bullshit. This little scrap of female is blocking the club owner's office door like she would take out any threat that tried to get through her to try and reach Isabelle. Where the hell is the small sprite Greg said radiated glee like a fucking fairy?

"FUCK!" I roared. "Get out of my goddamn way, woman." How does this tiny, one-woman circus think she is going to fucking keep me from breaking that door into splinters? I look over at Coop and Beck; they seem just as confused as I am about this whole standoff. Jesus, I am getting in that damn office, even if I have to physically remove this woman from my path. I'm tired of playing nice. I might not have a mother, but even I know to respect women; this one though would try the patience of a fucking saint.

Just when I am about to pick her up and remove her from my way, the door opens and out steps a red-faced, spitting-mad, Greg Cage.

"You"—he points at my chest, getting right up in my fucking space—"get the fuck out of here. You might be bigger than I am, but when it comes to her, I will fucking kill you."

What. The. Fuck. The hell with that.

"Who the fuck do you think you are, *brother,* telling me that I can't speak to her?" I can feel the vibration of unshed violence rushing through my veins. Even with the small thought in the back of my head that I would do the same thing in his shoes, I still can't calm myself.

He takes a deep breath, looks me dead in the eyes, and spits out words that almost stop my heart.

"If you don't back the fuck off right fucking now, Iz will end up leaving here in the back of an ambulance…again."

The fuck? "What the hell are you talking about, Greg? Because it sure as fuck sounds like you're talking in code."

Sighing deeply, I can tell how much this little toe-to-toe is costing him. "Look, Reid. You know I respect the hell out of you. You have been my brother for a fucking long-ass time, but Iz… She is not in a good place right now. Yesterday was hard enough, but Dee and

I have managed to keep her chill. Fuck, even with the package from that sick fuck, she didn't go this deep. You need to back the fuck off for now. If you want to speak to her, fine, but it will be on her terms, not when she is fighting every demon that owns her soul. Not tonight. You hear me good, Reid. I will talk to her and set something up, but not until you tell me just how you know my fucking girl."

"What do you mean *your* girl, G?"

I must be acting like a fucking idiot, especially after all his long-winded bullshit. Greg is gaping at me like he is trying to find a solution for world peace or some shit like that. He holds my gaze for a long while, and I can practically see the gears turning at full steam.

Finally, with an eerily neutral tone, he says, "Reid, just how long have you known Iz?" He might sound neutral, but his eyes seem to be silently communicating that if he doesn't like my answer, there will be no talking with Izzy.

I look down at my boots and reach up to rub my neck, trying to ease some of the tension out of my body. What a loaded question.

"Why does it matter, G?"

"Humor me, brother. Just fucking humor me. How long have you known her?"

Straightening to my full six-foot-six height, trying to at least give myself that small advantage, I look down on him with a matching grim expression. What the hell is going on here? They are acting like Izzy is some wounded bird. No way in hell this is the same girl I knew.

"I've known Isabelle for going on sixteen years, and twelve years ago, when I left home, I left my heart in her fucking palm. I haven't seen or heard from her since," I respond with a calm I do not feel. Not in the least.

Greg's eyes fire instantly, and after a moment of silence, he grunts, "Do *not* call her Isabelle. Ever." Then he turns on his heel and leaves me standing in stunned silence with Beck's, Coop's, and Dee's burning eyes on my back. With the exception of Dee, they seem just as confused and shocked as I am.

What in the fuck?

Looking around, I back up and plop my ass down on the hard floor, preparing to wait this out as long as it takes.

I've been sitting out here in the hallway for what seems like hours. My ass is numb. Whether it's from sitting here or the music thumping through the floor beneath me, I have no clue. I look down at my watch to see that it's only been a half hour since Greg's cryptic comment. What the fuck is going on in there? I don't like this overwhelming feeling of helplessness; I haven't felt this way in a long-ass time. I have no idea what is really going on here. I feel like I have some big-ass puzzle with one missing piece. One piece some little shit took and won't give back.

What happened to the seventeen-year-old, stars-in-her-eyes girl I left behind twelve years ago? Sure, she was sad I was taking off for basic training, but she knew I was coming back for her. We had plans, dreams, and a future all mapped out and ready to roll. Why is *she* acting like the wounded party here? She wasn't the one who arrived home six months later, tired but elated to finally have his girl in his arms again only to find her gone. And she was gone, vanished into thin fucking air. There was not a single trail to lead me back to my girl.

I remember the day I rolled back into our hometown of Dale, Georgia. I was so excited to finally get my arms around my girl. Things with the Marines had been intense, but I was home for a little while. I had a new family now, a band of brothers with an unbreakable bond. I couldn't wait to bring Izzy into that fold, making my family complete.

Basic training was nothing like I'd expected it to be. I'd known I would be the perfect candidate for the Marines when I signed up; I'd just never imagined excelling at such a rapid rate. Arriving one day, then the next being pulled into a conference room and being handed one hell of a life changer. I was good, damn fucking good, and they wanted me. Only problem was, like with most everything deep within the government, I wasn't to tell a soul. Top secret to the highest degree. I received my first letter from Izzy the same day, reminding me how hard it was going to be to go dark on my girl; she knew me though, and she knew what this gig meant to me. I wrote her one hell of a hearts-and-flowers letter and mailed it off the same day I left for special training, knowing it would have to see her through until I was home. When I finally got a call home, I had been gone for three long, hard months. I can still feel the shock I felt when the operator informed me that her number had been disconnected. With no one to ask, I just had to pray that my girl knew me and knew our love enough to be there when I came back to her. I couldn't worry; I had to have my head about me. So with all the hope of a naïve teenage dreamer, I believed everything would be fine.

Izzy and I, we were what some would call a fairytale, if you believed in that shit. I met her the first day of my sophomore year. She had been a scared little freshman, a fish completely out of the water and terrified out of her mind. But did she let it show? No, not my Izzy. She marched right into Dale High with her shoulders back and her head high. Her pale green eyes were trained right ahead, ready to take on the world. And I had taken one look and knew she would be mine. From that moment on, she was mine and I was hers.

She came from a great family. Her parents were the kind a kid dreams of, accepting everyone and anyone, regardless of where they came from. They didn't mind that their only child, their only daughter, had fallen in love with a foster kid from the wrong side of the tracks; she loved me, so they did too. I was shocked when I learned about their deaths. Adam and Holly West were amazing people, and I knew Izzy had to be feeling that deep.

In my love-soaked mind, I still believed she was waiting; now I just wondered where that was. I knew she had some extended family, but no one seemed to know where they lived. And trust me, I asked. All of her friends just said that she had been devastated; when they had spoken to her at the service for her parents, she'd been silent. They said that she had turned completely into herself, like a zombie. She'd just sat there and looked off into space. That killed me more than anything, knowing she had been hurting and alone.

I became frantic in my search. I had just a little time before I had to return to training. The only thing I was able to find out was that she was in North Carolina, or South Carolina, living with her mom's parents. Only problem was, no one knew her mother's maiden name. With no more answers and my time back home gone, I headed back to base, confused but still determined to find her.

I didn't catch a break for four long years. I had pulled every string I had, and every penny I didn't, to find her. When I got the news, I felt like I had been shot straight through the fucking heart.

Married.

My girl was married.

Isabelle West-Hunter had been married just four months earlier. My info was light, but I was assured that she looked happy and healthy.

From that point on, my heart was completely closed to anyone. Locked in a fireproof safe and sunk to the deepest depths in my body. I wouldn't make that mistake again. No one would be making me a fool for caring, especially not a bitch like Isabelle West.

CHAPTER 6

A T SOME point I must have fallen asleep against Maddox; his arms haven't let up their strong hold. I woke up about ten minutes ago when Greg came storming back in the office; he hasn't stopped pacing since. What is going on now?

I know we are still at Carnal. I can hear a faint thump of the bass coming up from the floor below us. The buzz I was enjoying is long gone, packed off and headed to Mexico with a one-way ticket.

Maddox is a quiet man. He keeps his soothing humming and vise grip, but the quiet is what I need. He isn't forcing me to talk, even though I know he must have questions. He has to think I am certifiable. One second I am smiling and the next fainting at his feet. As far as first impressions go, I think that one will be lasting.

Greg finally stops his pacing and muttering and looks over at me. I can see the anger bleed off of his face; instantly, calm and understanding finally dawn.

"Come here, baby girl."

A new sob bubbles up as I quickly climb off of Maddox and rush forward into Greg's protective arms. I can't even count how many times this man has been my rock, my strength and support, picking up my pieces and not stopping until he has successfully glued each piece back together.

Axel

I HEAR the door click and immediately straighten from my folded position on the floor. The look of pure wrath in Locke's eyes has me pausing before completing my way up from my seat. He is not a man who shows emotion—ever. Fuck, I can't even remember the last time I was able to tell what he was thinking, let alone what he was feeling. There is no question right now though. He is throwing fire right into my eyes. It didn't take much of a leap to reason that he was pissed at me.

Yeah, well get in line motherfucker.

I just marginally calmed myself down over the last forty-five minutes or so. For the most part, I'm over my initial anger. I feel reasonably sure that I'm calm enough to be in the same room with the only girl I have ever loved and try to hear her out. My mind demands answers. I want to know why. Why she didn't wait... Why she had married another.

No, my calm isn't going to come back completely. I'm still worked up for another reason altogether and it has nothing to do with anger. I can't get over seeing her stunning face, the face that has consumed my dreams and haunted my memories for way too fucking long. Even with my rage at seeing her openly touching the men I consider brothers, I still couldn't stop my dick from trying to break out of my pants. All it took was one look at her tight, sexy-as-sin body wearing next to nothing and I found myself having to immediately adjust myself. So hard my dick was aching in a way I haven't felt in many years. I didn't even know who she was then and the attraction was that strong, just like it always had been.

When I walked up to the bar, coming up on that firm ass encased in skin-tight red fabric, I turned feral. I was like a raging bull being set free with one target in sight. My eyes traced her spine, each delicate little bump on her exposed skin, and my only thought was getting her to a bed and following that line with my tongue until I was buried deep between her creamy thighs.

And then she turned around and I froze in my tracks. Lust left in a snap, and instead of rushing this hot piece of ass off to the nearest empty room, I wanted to throw her over my shoulder, drag her off, and demand answers. I have been waiting for this moment for twelve long fucking years. The last thing I'd expected her to do if I ever saw her again was faint to the floor.

"What the fuck are you glaring at, Locke?" I spit out at him. I don't feel like dealing with more of this bullshit. I'm just itching for a fight now.

"I'm looking right at you, motherfucker. It shouldn't take a big leap of 'clue the fuck in' for you to realize I'm looking right at your dumb fucking ass," he snarls at me with such ferocity that I'm momentarily rendered speechless.

"What the hell? Is there a reason you seem to think I pissed all over your shit?"

He looks right at me, cocking his head to the side, and I find myself shocked on my ass once again tonight when he opens his mouth. "I just sat in there and held some chick I do not know, a chick who not even an hour ago looked like she was on the top of the fucking world, happy with life, and spending time with her friends. Her smile died. Do you understand that, Reid? One look into your eyes and that big bright smile just died. The life went completely out of her eyes and her body gave out. Do you fucking get *that*? I just sat there and let her basically crawl into my fucking body with nothing but fear oozing out of her. Fear YOU seem to have put there. That happy woman from earlier is long fucking gone and I would love to know how you are the reason."

Shock holds me silent. Shock and confusion.

Sniffling to my left distracts me and I glance over at Dee. She is looking at me with part confusion, part anger, and a whole lot of hurt.

Shaking my head, I look back over at Locke. "I couldn't fucking tell you since I haven't seen nor heard from her in twelve years. Bitch up and disappeared, so if you want answers, you are asking the wrong fucking person."

"Excuse me? This is the chick who left you? The same one you claim is a cold, heartless bitch? Because I have to say, Reid, the woman who just broke the fuck down in my arms is not a cold, heartless bitch. That woman is feeling the weight of the world on her shoulders."

"What the fuck are you talking about? This is the same shit with Greg, talking yourselves in goddamn circles. Maybe if you want me to buy a fucking vowel, you could give me a fucking hint," I roar right back at him.

"All right, you want to know what the fuck I'm talking about? There is a woman in there who looks like her world just ended. She looked like she had seen a ghost. Lost and scared. So scared she is shaking. She was trembling so violently she would have fallen to the ground had I let her go. So I will ask you one more fucking time, you sure that is the chick who left *you*?"

I hear another gasp off to my side. Swear to Christ, this bitch needs to calm her tits.

"What the hell does it matter now, huh? It's been twelve fucking years. I don't think two fucking minutes of her time is too much to ask. I'm sure her husband wouldn't mind." I know I'm shooting low, but I am so livid I can't even see without red closing in my vision.

Another gasp at my side.

I look over at Dee. "Are you fucking okay?"

Her jaw is opening and closing repeatedly. She looks like a damn fish out of the water struggling to breathe. I do not have time for this shit.

"Seriously, do you need something? Water, a chair, a fucking Midol?"

Her mouth snaps shut and a thin line forms before she marches right into my space, coming up on her toes in attempt to meet me eye to eye. "Listen here, you…you big bully, you will not sit here and be a little shit. You have no clue what is going on, but I promise you this. It is bigger than your need to 'chat.' Do you understand me?" She follows that burst with a few pokes to my chest.

"No, little girl, I do not fucking understand you, not one little bit. So maybe your ass can clue a bastard in?" I feel like the walls around us could have fallen with that burst of anger from me. Any second my head is going to explode. I can feel it now.

Sighing softly, washing the frustration and anger off her face and looking up at me with sympathy, she says, "I can't, Axel. This isn't my story to tell."

Wait a minute. "How do you know my name? I haven't gone by Axel in a long fucking time, sweetheart, so if anyone knows what's going on, my guess would be you."

"Of course I know what's happening, but like I said, this isn't my story to tell." She points over at the closed door. "It's hers. It always has been. I just never thought I would see the day it would need to be told."

Again with that cryptic shit. I feel like I just walked into the Twilight Zone.

Shaking my head in exasperation, even with my confusion, I can't stop the rage that bubbles up every time I think about just who we are fighting over. "All right, fine. Don't fucking tell me, but let me ask you this. Does her fucking husband know she is out dressed like that, flirting with anything that speaks to her?" I can't stop the shit that is slinging from my mouth at this point and I'm past the point of caring what I'm saying. The only thing I'm seeing at this moment is that report I read eight years ago that told me my girl hadn't waited.

"You son of a bitch..." she sneers at me.

Before I can even register what is about to happen, I catch a small hand right over my cheek. Damn, that bitch is strong for such a little thing. Before righting my head, I spit the little bit of blood her slap created onto the floor.

I look over at her shocked face. "What the fuck was that for?" I rumble. Looking past her, I see Beck and Locke with shocked eyes and fucking smirks on their faces. Coop lets out a loud laugh before quickly stifling it. It looks like she isn't the only one thinking I deserved that for some unknown reason.

"Oh shit, shit... I am not sorry for that, get that straight right now, but you need to watch your mouth and what you say about Iz. Until you know what's going on, you have no room to say anything. Not one damn thing."

I am at a complete loss right now. Obviously I will not be getting anywhere with this crew tonight. They seem to have decided to band together to protect the little coward hiding behind locked doors. Reaching behind me and pulling out my wallet, I take out one of my cards and hold it out to Iz's protector. "Here. Give her this and have her call me."

"I'll tell her but I won't make any promises to you. If you understood what you are asking of me, well…you would just understand where I'm coming from."

I open my mouth to rip her a new one when I hear the office door click again. The first thing I see is a pair of the sexiest fuck-me shoes I have ever laid eyes on followed by the hottest fucking legs ever to wrap around my hips and Greg motherfucking Cage holding the body that belongs to them. Nestled tightly to his body, covered in his jacket, is a sleeping Izzy. His jacket covers every inch from her chin to her thighs, but I know what's under there. Sex…pure sex. I can tell she's been crying. The tear streaks covering her cheeks are a dead giveaway. Her eyes are swollen and rimmed red. Even with all that, she is still the most beautiful girl in the world to me.

My arms itch to snatch her away from him, to claim what is mine. Even with all my anger, I still want her. I stand there completely knocked immobile, just looking at her. Taking her all in.

Greg completely ignores me like I'm not even standing there in front of him. He looks down at Dee and softly says, "She finally calmed down about ten minutes ago. Let's get her home, yeah?"

"Sure, G. Let me go get the bouncer to open the side door. They already have your truck parked back there so we don't have to take her through the front," she weakly responds, looking completely trampled.

It seems like everyone knows what is going on right now—everyone except me. No one thought to clue the poor sap in to what exactly caused this scene. The biggest question floating around my skull is not where she has been and why she left. No, I want to know what happened to my Izzy, the girl who wouldn't let a fucking thing knock her down.

I see Beck and Coop off to the side walking off with Dee to find the magical bouncer with the keys, leaving me standing with Locke, Greg…and Izzy. Both of them are looking at me like I am the bad guy here. I just wish I knew what I'd done to earn those looks of contempt.

Izzy

I OPEN my eyes when I feel someone lay me down, opening them long enough to see Greg looking down at me with his brow creased, noting how exhausted he looks. It takes me a second, but then I remember and quickly sit up.

I'm home, in my room. Glancing over at my clock, I see that it's closing in on four in the morning.

"How did I get home, G? Where is Dee?" Pausing, I gasp up at him, "Oh my God, was he really there? Axel?"

Cursing softly under his breath, he looks away. I can tell he is trying to school his response, weigh his words. He always seems to worry that I'm going to slip back into that dark place I was in when he found me. I won't lie, sometimes I do too, but I can't have him treating me with kid gloves all the time.

"Greg, please...please just be honest with me," I beg of him.

"Iz...baby girl, I just don't know what to say. If I'd any idea that the Axel you told me about was Reid..." He trails off, looking back off into space. I have no idea what is going through his head, but if I know Greg, he is riding the guilt train hard.

"What? You would have made him come to me? Little too late for that, G. He had his chance to come to me YEARS ago! Years! It's not like I didn't let him know how to find me. I left my grandparents' address with his foster mother. I was waiting. I waited for years and I would have waited forever. But where was he? Huh? Where was he when I needed him? All those times I needed him. That's right. Gone." I can feel the tightness of anger forming in my gut. "I thought he was dead this whole time. You know this, Greg. I've thought for twelve long years that the boy I loved was gone forever. Twelve years of feeling empty, lost, and so unbelievably alone." I'm crying again, and I just can't seem to stop. The weight of Axel's return is so heavy; I needed him so badly. "You know I went back to see June, his foster mother, about a year ago. I just wanted to make sure, as stupid as that is. You know what she told me? She told me he was in a better place without me. How was I supposed to take that?"

AXEL

Greg gets back up and starts his pacing again. I have no idea what's going through his mind right now, but I can tell he is struggling with it. He knows all about my past with the infamous Axel. I remember one very bad night for me, about six months after I left Brandon. We were watching movies. I have no idea which movie; it was something stupid and cheesy. I remember watching the actors promise to love each other forever, that nothing would ever tear them apart. And then I lost it. I threw my wine glass at the TV, screeching and screaming about how everyone leaves and nothing is forever. Greg had to forcefully hold me down until I was able to calm myself. He sat there holding me still for almost two hours. When I finally stopped thrashing around; he sat me down and demanded I talk.

I told him everything from the day I met Axel at fourteen to the day he left when I was seventeen. I told him about every single wonderful memory we had shared within those three years. Then I told him about my parents, the baby, and then the parties. He knew about the deep devastation I'd felt when I had lost and lost and lost some more. He knew how and when I'd met Brandon—rich, successful, and handsome, Brandon. He knew how vulnerable I had been when he walked into my life and scooped me up; unbeknownst to me, that he was the devil in disguise.

Greg knew everything there was to know about me, but with everything I had shared…not once had I told him Axel's last name. I'm guessing this little bombshell was quite a hit for him. Being ex-military, he always sympathized with the Axel I had told him about. He would always tell me that Axel wouldn't want me to be in pain over him and what a strong and heroic person he must have been.

Lies. All fucking lies.

Axel didn't die a hero; he lived a betrayer.

All the dreams that we had, promises we had made, they all seemed like the biggest slap in the face now.

I have mourned the loss of him and the loss of us for so long.

He was the only reason I survived at the hands of Brandon. I would just close myself off and think of him and the times we had together. He was my salvation in the darkest of dark.

"You know what? It doesn't matter. How can he possibly explain this, G? I can't go there anymore. I can't go back there. Not with him.

Nothing he can say will heal the wounds he inflicted." Defeat and overwhelming melancholy have taken root.

"Iz, I don't know what his reasons are. I don't feel like this was intentional, baby girl. I really don't. I talked to him, I saw his face, and he seemed completely clueless. I don't even think he has put together that you are the person I talked to him about yesterday. There is something missing. I just can't figure out what it is."

"Clueless, Greg? Are you kidding me right now?"

"No, baby girl. And as much as it pains me to say this, I really think you two need to sit down and talk."

"What? No way, Greg. No. I have nothing to say to him. Not one thing. Did you see how mad he was? I didn't even see his face but I could hear it. I could feel it. He is acting like I did something horrid. What is so horrible about loving someone?"

"I don't know, Iz. I just think there is something to be said about closure…for both of you."

Closure? I laugh to myself as I lie back against the headboard. This man has lost his fucking marbles if he thinks I can, or want, to have a sit-down with Axel. I can't. I just can't. This must be some cruel joke from above. I knew I was onto something when I stopped praying. No one who throws so much shit at someone should be trusted. Haven't I been through enough? I just started to feel 'normal' again. Hell, I just stopped seeing my therapist a month ago!

"Just go, G. Please, just go."

I turn over, pull the sheets over my head, and cry softly into my pillow. I hear the door shut and heavy-booted feet stomping down the hall, followed by soft murmurings.

Just when I'm about to fall asleep, I feel slender arms wrap around me, holding me tight.

"Love you, Iz. We will get through this."

Dee's reassuring words are the last thing I hear before I fall into a restless sleep, hoping for some peace to be found.

CHAPTER 7

"**G**OD, IZZY, *you feel so fucking good wrapped around my cock. So…fucking…tight," he rasps as he slowly thrusts his long, thick length into my waiting body. "Never felt anything as good as you."*

His hands tighten on my hips as his pumping picks up speed. His powerful rocking is rubbing my erect nipples in the most delightful way against his sheets. I dig my fingers into the sheets, trying, but not succeeding, in keeping my moaning down. All I want to do is scream out in pleasure with every single thrust and every single roll of his hips. He gives a good push in, the tip of his generous cock hitting my cervix. Each thrust now has tightening up and lightning bolts of sheer pleasure shooting from my pussy to every part of my body. My fingers tingle; my toes curl; my breasts feel like they are throbbing. Every single inch of my skin is on fire for this boy.

"Fuck me…" he rumbles, his breathing coming in fast bursts against my back. "Like you were made for me, baby."

I'm afraid to open my mouth, to respond with any kind of sound that will let him know he has me feeling the exact same way. I know the second I unclench my lips, screams of pure ecstasy will come bolting out. God, I love him. He's right; we fit together like we are meant to be. Both our bodies align perfectly, our movements are in perfect sync with each other, and our thoughts communicate wordlessly.

His hand reaches between my thighs and he starts to roll his thumb in deliciously circles, making my body's pleasure reach even higher than before.

"Come with me, Princess. Come fucking with me."

Right when my pleasure reaches insurmountable levels and the claws of the most powerful orgasm start taking hold…

I wake up.

Sitting straight up with a giant jolt, I hear a thump to my right and look over to see Dee sticking her tired head up over the side of the bed. Unhappiness with a twinge of confusion mars her pretty face. Her hair is sticking up in every direction possible, and her flawless makeup from the night before is smudged under her eyes and lips. If I weren't still feeling the effects of that dream, I might laugh. She looks absolutely ridiculous.

"Jesus Christ, Iz. A simple wake up would have sufficed, too."

"Sorry," I snort, earning me a new glare.

I take my eyes from the tiny ball of unhappiness on the floor and slowly look around my room, trying to figure out what feels so different. Well, besides waking up with Dee in my bed, freaking weirdo. A knock at my door has me frowning even deeper. For the life of me, I can't seem to figure out what feels so off.

The door opens a crack and Greg pokes his head in. "Hey," he says hesitantly, "Okay if I come in?"

And that is all it takes for it all to come rushing back in crystal clear HD Technicolor. My birthday, the package, Club Carnal, and Axel.

Dee pulls herself off the floor, rubbing her ass as she pushes past Greg on her way out the door and mumbling heated words under her breath.

"Someone woke up happy," Greg says, walking over to the edge of my bed, taking a seat. He looks over at me, digging in for what seems to be a nice little visit. "Mornin', baby girl. Sleep okay?"

He looks so awkward in my girly room. His brown hair is tousled in a just-woke up way, giving him an almost boyish look to his normal hard face. He's wearing sweats and a tight white undershirt, showing off his thick, muscled arms. He screams masculinity in my frilly room.

"Slept decent, I guess. Or at least I think I did." I pick at some imaginary lint on my comforter, not looking up into his knowing eyes. I feel him shift, turning to his side so he is facing me. Still, I don't look up.

"Look at me, baby girl. I need to see that you're okay."

64

I take in a big pull of air, hold it, and look up. His sleepy look is long gone and his hard controlled stare is firmly in place. A stare of which I am not used to being on the receiving end. I've seen him give it a million times before. It's his look that always means business, business no matter what—a look that you do not want to cross.

Guess this means it's game on; I was really hoping he would have just let this go. There wasn't anything left to hash out.

"Look, G, I know you mean well, but this shit… This shit isn't something I want to deal with. Not now, not later. I'm not even sure I want to ever deal with it again. What's left to say at this point, huh? That road? It is not one I want to go down again. It's been blocked off with detour signs for a long time now, huge fucking warning signs telling me to walk the other direction. I would be setting myself up for more pain and heartbreak and that is not something I want to do. Is it too much to ask for me to just be allowed a little happiness, some of this dark cloud to dissipate?" I don't even give him a chance to get a word out, cutting him off before he can try and plow right over me. "We know…now, that you and… You and him are friends. Let's just leave it. You can be friends with him and you can be friends with me. I don't see why the two ever have to intermix. Ever."

I can tell he is trying to talk his temper down, or maybe he is just having some convoluted one-sided argument with himself. Who knows. I don't care at this point; there is no way I am doing this. Not when it is still cutting so fresh into my skin. I feel like I have a movie rolling in my head, over and over with the same images. Images of a past forgotten and a future lost.

"Izzy, this isn't going to just go away. Sooner or later it will have to be dealt with." I know he's right, I really do, but that doesn't mean I have to agree with him. Denial is a perfectly acceptable place to pack up and move to. "He is going to be my partner now. He lives here and is staying, Iz. He isn't going to just disappear."

I don't have the energy for this fight, and I know it will end up being a heavy one, a fight I will need all my wits for; going into battle with Greg is never easy.

"I get that *this* might not be going away, but that doesn't mean I have to deal with it right fucking now." I feel like punching something. Why can't we just pretend that last night never happened? I'm the queen of fucking brushing it under the rug. That's a game I can play with the best of them. Out of sight, out of mind.

"Baby girl, this pains me. I feel guilty as shit right now. You might be able to forget, or try to, but I can't. I know what last night has cost you and I can't sit back knowing you are in pain." He shakes his head, his blue eyes losing that bright shine. "I should have known, but…fuck, Iz, I didn't ever know him as Axel." He pauses again. Whether he is going for dramatic flair or just trying to figure out the best way to piss me off, I don't know, but right when I get ready to freak the fuck out on him, he continues. "I have only ever known him as Reid. When we met at basic, he was H. Reid, and from then on, we only ever called him Reid, Axel… Fuck, baby girl, but he was never Axel. When we first got out and he started up his security gig, that was the only other time I have ever heard him refer to himself as anything other than Reid, and I promise you this—it was not Axel."

Why is this so important? If I didn't care so much about my friendship with Greg, I would fucking kill him. Go all crazy white girl on his ass. "Holt, right?" I laugh without humor. "He always hated that name. Said it reminded him of his old man," I mumble, back to picking at the invisible lint. "Greg, can we please, please not do this right now?"

He looks at me, assessing for a while, taking me in, and once again trying to figure out how to weigh his words. "Iz, we are fucking doing this. I won't let you sit here and fester in your hurt. Not when I can fix it. Not when I have the power to do something this time." Hard and spitting. No argument. His tone leaves no room for wiggling. He's settled in and ready to go at it.

Stubborn fucking ass. We really are too much alike sometimes.

"I'm fine, really. I just need to process," I lie. He knows I'm lying; I can see it in his face. He might have come in ready to play, but he didn't have this hardness about his eyes at first. My lying just confirmed his thoughts that I'm not handling this well.

"You aren't fine, baby girl. Far from it, and if you expect me to sit here and buy that plate of shit you are insisting on dishing up, you're out of your fucking mind. You forget I know you. That play won't work with me."

"Greg, seriously?" I screech. "Are you fucking serious right now? I am not trying to serve you some shit. I just don't want to go there. It really is just as simple as that. I have no hidden motive here. Just give me a goddamn break. You know… You fucking know what he meant to me. Could you just give me a minute to, I don't know, process this shit? Dead, G. He has been dead for twelve years and all of a sudden he isn't. That isn't something I can just wake up and deal with." I can tell I struck a nerve and I might feel bad if I wasn't so pissed off. He isn't letting me figure this out. He isn't letting me think. I just want a second, just a fucking second to wrap my head around this colossal mindfuck.

He looks a little more understanding after my outburst—not by much—but I can see that he is trying hard to see this from my shoes. "I'll give you today, Izzy, but hear me this. We will be talking about this. No pushing it away, no locking this in tight. The can has been opened, and try as you might, there is no way you're getting those worms back in." He squeezes my leg and stands, leveling me with one more serious look before he turns to stomp heavily out of my room, firmly snapping the door shut behind him.

Well, that went well.

I know he is right. I do. I have to deal with this. I might not want to, and it isn't going to be pretty, but I have to face this. With everything else going on, it isn't something I even want on my radar, but it's there. I'll deal with it, but on my terms, and it will not be today.

I lie back down and roll onto my side facing the big picture window, looking up into the bright, cloudless Georgia sky. What a fucked-up mess. I still have to deal with Brandon, the divorce—or actually the lack of one—and his continued reminders that he is in my life and knows how to reach me…how to hurt me. Now I have to deal with Axel and a past I have been struggling to forget and move on from for almost half of my life. Oh how cruel fate is.

IT REALLY is funny sometimes how everything comes full circle. Just when you think your life is headed in one clear-cut direction, the light turns red and the turn signal comes on. There isn't a day that goes by that I don't wish my parents were still here, happily residing a few counties over in our old small three-bedroom ranch. If I hadn't lost them, I never would have had Dee come into my life, and even though it doesn't take away the pain of their loss, I have to consider myself lucky on some counts. Even through the dark times of my marriage, when our contact was few and far between, I always knew she was there and always would be.

Through Dee came Greg, another thing I wouldn't have in my life if my parents had survived that wreck. He is another person Dee roped in with her overwhelming personality. She met him when she was dating his cousin, and even though the cousin didn't last, her friendship with Greg did. She can't help it. She just has something about her that people want to be around. She has that permanent outlook that everything is right in the world. And lucky for me, he just happened to be close the night she came to save me, even though I don't remember him showing up with her. By the time she made it to me, I had completely blacked out. The first time I saw him, my initial reaction had been fear; Greg mad is not someone you want to be around. When he saw me step out of the van that day, his reaction scared the shit out of me. Huge, raging mad, and ready to kill. No one was more shocked than I was when the feral giant turned human shield. He was ready to protect me from anything, and that has never changed.

I know I am lucky with the friendships I have with Dee and Greg. They are the only two people I have left in the world. The only two people I know would die before they hurt me. They are my family now—family I sometimes want to hurt, but family nonetheless. It is hard sometimes to deal with all my fuckedupness. I know it isn't easy for them. When I have a setback, they both have to deal with it right alongside of me. I go and crawl into myself, Dee goes into worried mother mode, and Greg goes into his protective grizzly alpha persona.

Dee and I are close, and we will always be, but Greg and I share a bond of loss and heartache no one else will ever touch. I still remember the look he had in his eye when he told me about his sister. That was the only time I have ever seen his hard self shed a tear. I broke down, clinging to him, mourning his sister, but also feeling the pain the last six years of my life had imbedded in me with the stark, cold knowledge that I could have had a very different ending. That was the day he promised me he wouldn't let my husband touch me, the day he promised to do everything he could to keep the pain at bay.

I roll back over and stare up at the ceiling, following the fan's rotations with my eyes, letting the memories of the past come rolling back over me.

I remember when I was as constantly happy as Dee, always looking at the world with rose-colored goggles. I wasn't the most popular girl in school, but I had a good number of close friends. My childhood was so full of laughter and love; my parents were the things dreams are made of. They were always happy, always smiling, and always full of love. Love for me and love for life. For a parent-child relationship, ours wasn't the most conventional. I could go to them with anything and they never cast judgment or scorn. Not a day went by that I didn't feel the joy I had brought into their lives.

I was lucky enough to meet the love of my life young. We had a relationship that reminded me of my parents'. Always happy, always smiling, and always full of love. I had three of the best young and dumb years in my life with that boy.

I thought I was untouchable, and I thought that our love was unbreakable. Together we could overcome anything that life threw at us. By his side, I was complete.

Axel left for boot camp three days after he graduated from high school, and that, unfortunately, meant he was leaving me behind in the process. I understood this. Hell, I had even rallied behind him. I wanted what would make him happy, and I knew he was setting his own path, proving to the world that he was nothing like his parents, who had cared more about their next big fix than their own son. Axel had been living in and out of foster homes for the better part of his eighteen years, and knowing he had nothing to offer me for a solid future, he did the only thing that made sense to him; he enlisted in the Marines.

Together, with my parents by my side, we dropped him off at the bus station with a promise to reunite and live out all of our dreams when I graduated the next year. That day was the first hard day of my life.

I let a bitter laugh escape my lips when I think back to all those stupid dreams. They are funny things, the dreams of an innocent teen. You never know when you're planning them that you are planning nightmares instead.

I wasn't too broken by him leaving. Sure, I was upset, but I knew that he would be back; he would return to me. My parents planned a few trips that summer to keep my mind off missing Axel, at least until I could hear from him again. I was so excited for that day, even knowing it might just be a letter. I couldn't wait to hear about all the changes he was encountering and how he was dealing with them and without me.

But that day never came. Two weeks after I waved goodbye to my love, my parents were killed in a car accident. I was devastated and heartbroken. Looking back now, I can say that was the start of my downward spiral. I didn't deal with their deaths well, especially without Axel there to ground me. My parents had both been only children, and my father's parents had been long gone before I was even born. With no other family left to take over my care, I was shipped off to live with my mom's parents in North Carolina. Even through all my grief, I still held on to the hope that Axel would be back in my arms again and that he would take all that pain away. I loved my grandparents. Don't get me wrong. But they were older and just didn't know how to deal with my pain on top of their own.

I had left their address in the care of Axel's foster mother, June. I knew she hated me, but I had hoped that if I couldn't contact him, this would be the next best thing.

The fog from my parents' death had finally left me when I found out I was almost two months pregnant. It had been almost a month since I'd lost them and not a day had gone by that I hadn't felt the stabbing grief, but this pregnancy gave me something to focus on. Something to look forward to. It was Independence Day when I found out, ironic enough. I remember sitting in the bathroom of my grandparents' house, thinking I had the next best thing to having Axel with me—a piece of him and our love. I was still scared; what seventeen-year-old wouldn't be? I was basically alone and pregnant. I loved that baby from the second I saw the positive test strip. I just knew that any baby created with our love would be beautiful.

With a new lease on life, I started to move on and plan for our new future. I couldn't wait to share the news with him. Every day I wrote to him, sending the letters off to his old foster home. Not knowing where he'd settled, I thought that was the next best thing. It worried me that I hadn't heard from him, but I knew he would find me. He would always find me.

I was around ten weeks pregnant when I got a letter in the mail from June. She told me to stop sending my letters to her house, because Axel wasn't coming back and he had told her to let me know to leave him alone. I was confused and heartbroken. My Axel wouldn't have said that. He loved me; we had a future together.

I tried to write him at the base he'd originally arrived at, but my letter was returned, saying that there was no one there by that name. I didn't know what to do. I knew June had told me that he wanted me to leave him alone, but I felt he deserved to at least know about the baby. So with no other options, I tried to contact June again. I wrote her a letter detailing the importance of having Axel contact me. The letter I got in return shocked me to the core.

I opened the letter and immediately the smell of smoke wafted around my head. Unfolding the single piece of paper, I read the words that stopped my world from spinning.

Two words.

He's dead.

I couldn't believe it. I just couldn't. June had to be lying. I tried to write him at the base again, but my letter was returned, saying that they were sorry but no solider by that name was listed in active duty. When that letter came back, it was then that I believed June and I shattered.

It was two weeks later that I lost our baby.

That was the day I lost all touch of reality and sank into a deep depression filled black hole. I pushed everyone away when I lost that last piece of Ax I had left. I turned to alcohol and spent as much of my hours awake as possible drinking anything my underage hands could find. My grandparents were still dealing with the loss of my mom, and either they turned a blind eye to my behavior or they just didn't notice. Either way, I was completely alone again, with no hope of Axel saving me this time.

Almost eight months later, Dee burst into my world and slowly brought me back to life. The rest is, as they say…history.

History I didn't think I would have to deal with again.

I don't know how much time I spend lying in bed, looking off at nothing, remembering those early days. By the time my stomach starts reminding me I need to eat, lunch has long since passed. I pull myself up, mentally dusting myself off, and start off for the shower. I don't want to be weak again, and I am determined to be strong, to deal with this new fuck you from fate. It is time to dump the old Izzy and start finding the girl I used to be.

Fifteen minutes later, I'm making the trek down to the kitchen, hoping to grab a quick bite to eat alone before I dive into my work. I have a few new clients I need to email back, proposals to be approved, and some sites that need routine maintenance work done. It is all pretty basic, but it will keep my mind busy and off everything else swirling around me.

I have been working for a few hours when I hear the garage door open. "Damn," I mutter. So much for having a nice peaceful afternoon. Someone coming in means that I won't be able to completely ignore life around me, which is just smashing. With an overdramatic sigh, I save and close out of the programs I have been working on, shut my laptop, and straighten up all the paperwork I have scattered on the kitchen table.

Dee walks in, throwing me a sad smile right as I am pushing everything away. "Hey, you. How are you feeling?" Ah, I was expecting her to at least attempt throwing her cheer at me. Guess even she understands how big last night was. Hesitation and this cloud of timid do not suit my friend.

"Better than last night, or at least I'm getting there." I attempt a smile, but it feels forced. I'm sure it looks even worse because she gives a small flinch before sitting down next to me.

"I know you don't want to talk about it, and I respect that. Really, I do. We can figure this out later, and you know I won't judge you at all if this is the way you want to play this. But just let me say this and it will be the end of it until you're ready, okay?" She doesn't wait for me to answer. She knows what I would say if she did. "Here. He gave me this last night and... Well, even though I'm not going to push, I think you should have this." She reaches into her jacket pocket and pulls out a small white card, sliding it over in front of my seat. She stands, giving me a small hug, and whispers in my ear, "I won't push, Iz, but I think you need to do something with that." A small smile later, and she walks out of the room, leaving me scooting back from the small card like it holds the plague.

After a nice inner smackdown, I finally reach out and flip the card over. It shouldn't come as a shock, I knew what I would probably find when I did, but nevertheless I still spit out a rapid burst of air.

Holt Reid
Corps Security
770.555.6839

If anyone were watching me, they would think I have completely lost it. Every screw is loose and I am not only off my damn rocker, but I am running far from it. Hysterical laughter bubbles up before I can suppress it. Wiping the tears from my eyes, trying to calm down, I finally focus back on that stupid, stupid card.

Holt. He will never be *Holt* to me. I sit there for I don't know how long...hours, minutes—hell, it could have been seconds—just looking at his name in the elegant script, trying to figure out exactly who Holt Axel Reid is today. Is he married? My heart skips a beat at the next thought that filters through my mind... Does he have children? It's a logical question; we aren't those blind-by-love teenagers anymore. It makes sense that he might have moved on. I did...even if it was a laughable move I made. Why does he even want to talk to me? He obviously decided a long time ago that he was done with me. Fate is being a huge fucking bitch by throwing us back in each other's paths.

I stuff the card into the front pocket of my hoodie and pull my work out for the second time today. What can I say? Denial and I are going to become best of buds.

Dee comes back a few hours later and asks if I want to order some takeout for dinner. I couldn't really care less, but I tell her sure and to order whatever looks good. I know if I don't at least act normal—or as normal as possible—she would start fretting and force me to talk. I am not ready.

Four hours and two bottles of wine consumed between the two of us later, I find myself sitting back in my girly room, looking down at that small white card again. *Holt. Holt Reid.* I'm sure the giggle that comes out this time sounds just as wonky as it did earlier, but I just can't help it. How fucked up is this whole thing? *Holt...*

It may be the stupidest decision that I have made in a long time, but I pick my phone up off the nightstand and slide my finger across the unlock screen. I add his stupid new name to my contacts and store his information. Opening up a new text screen and thinking, *What the hell? Might as well.* At least this way I don't have to look into those brilliant green eyes.

Me: So we go by Holt now, huh?
Axel 'Holt': Izzy?
Me: Ah, bingo…anyone else out there not know you as 'Holt'?
Axel 'Holt': Plenty, Princess.
Me: No, I am not your Princess.
Axel 'Holt': Okay, so we are going to act like we're still fucking kids? You texted me, IZZY, so you tell me what's going?
Me: I am not acting like a child. I just don't understand why you even bothered to ask me to contact you. I think we can both agree the past needs to just stay there…in the past.
Axel 'Holt': No, I don't agree with that. Not at all. Where are you? I'll come to you. We are not doing this over a fucking text.
Me: No, no. I don't think that's a good idea. If you're dead set on dredging this back up, then fine, but we do this on my terms. I need to process this. I can't just sift through all this in less than a day. You want to talk, fine…but not now.
Axel 'Holt': Process? What the hell is there to process? Where are you, Izzy? Not asking you again, and I am not fucking doing this text message shit like a goddamn prepubescent little shit.

I really should have known better. Sighing, I set my phone down. There really is no point in continuing to argue with him. I did what I wanted to do and I asked him to let me have my time. If he can't respect that, then fuck him and closure be damned.

Ten minutes later, my phones chimes. Then a minute after that, I hear the reminder beep, followed shortly by another chime.

Damn.

Axel 'Holt': We will be talking about this Izzy. I know you, don't you fucking forget that. I won't let you just forget me like you did before.

Axel 'Holt': Understand me this, if you think you can just ignore me and ignore this, then you are up for a big wake up call. You want fucking time, fine. One week, that is all I'm willing to give. Next Saturday, I don't care if I have to knock on every goddamn door in Georgia. I will find you and we will be having this talk. Got that?

Well, shit.

Me: One week, 'Holt.' Guess that's going to have to be enough, isn't it? I'll let you know on Friday if I'm ready. Goodnight.

Axel 'Holt': If you call me Holt one more fucking time I'm bending you over my knees, yeah? I am not Holt to you, and you damn well fucking know it.

With a gasp of surprise at his audacity, I quickly turn my phone off and throw it across the room like it's on fire. I definitely can't deal with *that*.

CHAPTER 8

THE NEXT morning comes way too quickly, but I wake with a new resolve that it will be a good day. I have to deal with Axel, but I won't be doing that today. Sundays are usually the day that Dee and I lounge around the house, catching up on our DVR backlog, and spend some time just the two of us. Since our normal 'Sunday Funday' was interrupted with the new drama in my life, we rescheduled for today. Dee called into work and we started planning our 'Monday Funday.' This time together is important to us, especially with yesterday, so I'm happy to have this time today. We might live together but we stay pretty busy during the week—or at least she does. My work is a more 'at your own pace' thing, so I often find myself working at odd hours here and there.

Working from home has its benefits. Well…one benefit: solitude.

I feel better by myself, being alone and not worrying about checking my surroundings every two seconds.

I feel safer.

I might have come a long way since Brandon, but a lot of that has to do with my not leaving the house much. And when I do, I never leave alone. I stopped looking over my shoulders and fearing the shadows; I stopped living a life destined for death. I feel like I'm healing.

The first step to my healing was starting this new life. It took a while, but I am finally happy. Happy-ish. My business is growing and my friends are great—both of my friends. I don't need a million friends to feel like I have accomplished something with my life. I am perfectly content with Dee and Greg. I don't trust easily—or at all—so this is progress and it works for me.

The first year and a half after Brandon was spent in therapy and getting our life set up, buying the townhome, helping Dee get her new business up and running, and finally starting my own. There really hasn't been much time for me to just be me. It was a healthy—or maybe a not so healthy—distraction phase. It took me a while to decide that I was okay enough to start living again, and I won't let Axel's change that.

So it is time to do what Izzy West does best: distract.

Dee and I spend all day Monday lying around the house and watching old '80s movies. We turn all the phones off, close the blinds, and just enjoy spending the day together without the world stomping all over us. If Greg tried to call, we didn't know, and that is just fine with me. I am not ready to deal with his intrusive questions right now.

Tuesday is spent catching up on my work and fielding calls from Greg. I fake work issues and I am able to put him off. I know this won't work, but once again, I am not ready for him. I don't completely lie to him; I do have plenty of work I need to get a good head start on. Word is spreading quickly, and I have finally picked up some rather large businesses out of Atlanta. Dee is gone longer than normal on Tuesday. I know she is in the middle of some issues with her branch back in North Carolina. So by the time she gets home, she is too tired to push much from me. Again, that works perfectly for me.

Wednesday is spent running errands around town, cleaning out my closet, and organizing the pantry. I even scrub all three toilets in the house.

By the time Thursday rolls around, I am running out of excuses to beg off Greg and things to keep me distracted. Worse yet, Saturday is looming even closer and closer. Greg seems to be busy enough trying to get the new and improved Corps Security up and running. For once, the timing is working out in my benefit. He calls twice, but when I send them both to voicemail, he must have give up. I should be worried about him going silent on me, but I am too busy trying to keep my panic about Saturday down.

Friday is spent hand mopping the floors and dusting every surface in the whole damn townhome. Dee is working from home today and I am sure she is starting to think I have lost it. I am just sitting down in front of our massive DVD collection to re-alphabetize it—

again—when I hear my phone start ringing. I jump up and run off to my room to see if I can ignore Greg's call again. When I pick up my phone and see "Axel 'Holt'" calling, I scream and drop it. I run back into the living room and pick my stupid mind-numbing task back up. I hear my phone ring three more times before I'm done. Deciding I need to bring out the big guns in my mission to distract, I set off to find Dee.

This is going to be easy enough, even if it is painful for me. All it will take is one mention of her finally getting that makeover she's been after and I've been dreading for her to forget everything else and focus only on shopping. It might be a dirty trick, but it is the only one I have at the moment.

I will have to spend a day with Dee, allowing her to take over and drag me all over the state shopping, but it will work. Not only will I successfully not be thinking about anything besides how much money she is costing me, but I will be away from the house and Axel won't be able to find me. I hate shopping, but if this works, the payoff might be worth it.

Me and Dee against the world. She might not know it, but she is about to become my hero.

MY EARS have finally stopped ringing from Dee's insane screeching when I announced I am finally ready to shed my 'ratty-ass jeans' and tees and let her work her magic. Just as I thought, she immediately went into crazy mode and forgot about the world around her. Sometimes I love how easy it is to basically bribe her.

It's Saturday morning and we have been at the mall for a few hours when my phone rings. Looking at the display, I can't help but smile when I see "Greg Calling" across the screen. I have successfully kept him away all week, and now that I am away from the house and out of Axel's reach, I am finally going to pick this call up.

"Hey, you," I smile into the phone.

"Baby girl, you speaking to me today?" His deep baritone rumbles through the line.

"Depends on you. What do you want to speak about?"

"All right, I guess that's a no. What are you doing? I drove by the house but no one was there."

"Shopping!" My voice must be dripping with sarcasm. "Dee and I are over at Lenox Mall. I've decided it's time for a new wardrobe. Going all out. You should meet us over here…carry all the bags or something productive like that. It will be just so much fun." Yup, sarcasm is hanging thick in the air. Dee is completely oblivious to my conversation. Either that or she is just so in her element that she decides to ignore it.

"Carry your bags, huh? You must be out of your damn mind if you think I will be joining you on that estrogen field trip. I like my balls right where they are." He laughs back at me, finally losing that hard tone he seems to have adopted with me. I don't like being at the receiving end of his anger.

"Pussy," I joke. "Big old pussy is afraid to come and walk around the mall with your best friends. I think you might have already lost those balls you're so fond of, G." I throw my head back and let out a loud laugh, earning a few nasty looks from the rich bitches out shopping for shit they do not need. Kind of like me, minus the rich part.

I can hear him trying not to laugh. This right here is the Greg I love so much, this banter between us.

"Come on. All joking aside, I think we will be stopping for lunch soon. Or at least I hope my master will let me eat."

I look over at Dee, who has been vibrating with excitement since we started this grand makeover day, to confirm a plan for food at least somewhere in the near future. She isn't looking anywhere near me. Instead, she is focusing on another store. I might as well just hand her my credit card and tell her to meet me back home. I haven't had a single input on a single purchase since we started, and if the seven bags hanging from my arms aren't enough, I might just run. What the hell was I thinking?

Oh, that's right…a distraction, being away from the house and away from Axel, who has already called three times since the day began.

Clearing my throat, I speak into the phone again. Even if Dee doesn't agree, we will be eating soon. "So, what have ya? Want to meet us over here or what?"

"Sure, Iz. If that is how we are going to play today, I'll meet you there. I'll call you when I get there and find out how to track you down."

"Perfect. Just give me a ring and you can save me!" I look over at Dee to make sure she at least has some understanding of this new plan. She looks disappointed that we have to stop, but Christ, woman, I can only shop for so long without food.

"See ya then, baby girl." He disconnects and I pocket my phone, turning with a bright smile to Dee. She has the most ridiculous pout on her face.

"Stop that right now, Dee. I have been a good little girl and followed you around like a little bitch while you racked up thousands of dollars of shit on my card. I don't think feeding me is too much to ask, huh?" I try for stern but end up laughing in her face when she has the nerve to wobble her chin like she might cry.

"Okay, okay...but if we have to stop soon, we're going to Neiman's first. Shoes, Iz. I can hear them calling our names from here."

Freaking weirdo.

Almost an hour later, I am finally able to drag Dee away. Greg has been calling for the last fifteen minutes, asking why the hell we haven't popped out of this 'stupid fucking girly store' yet. I can just picture him pacing the entrance to Neiman's now. He would die before he stepped one badass foot in here. We walk out with six more bags. Six fucking bags. I swear I will end up selling a kidney to pay off my next credit card statement.

Greg is, as predicted, pacing in a tight line. When he finally spots us, he stops and crosses his arms over his bulky chest, throwing that scowl back in place. It wouldn't kill him to at least look happy to be here, but even grumpy, I'm glad he's here.

"Holy shit. Now that is definitely worth stopping our shopping for."

I'm a little taken aback by Dee's husky whisper. I was so focused on uncomfortable Greg that I hadn't noticed the good-looking man next to him. Joe? No, that's not right. I vaguely remember him from the club the last week. A friend of Greg's, his boy, which means he is a friend of Axel's too. Lovely. I really hope this isn't some ploy from Greg to get me to open up. I don't know how much these other men know about my past with Axel, but I won't be opening up to him today.

Sauntering up to the men, Dee and I both take turns giving Greg warm hugs. He might annoy the shit out of me at times, but he means well. Right now, though, it's hard to remember that he is coming from a good place with his caring and protectiveness.

I start thrusting bags into his arms, not even giving him a chance to reject them, looking over at Dee to see her practically drooling over the man standing next to Greg. She doesn't even seem to notice her fingers turning blue from her heavy burdens. I look over at Greg with a twitch of my head at Dee and a smirk. He laughs but still looks pissed that I'm making him carry my bags.

"Dee, quit," I whisper quietly at her. She shakes her head and looks over at me with rosy cheeks and lust-filled eyes. Oh-kay… Looks like Dee won't be pissed about stopping this trip anymore.

Greg finally has all my bags in order, huffing his attitude. "You two remember Beck?" He jerks his head over at his friend. Beck! That's right—John Beckett.

I mumble a hello but notice that he isn't focusing on me. He and Dee are practically past foreplay and moving into some serious hot sex with their eyes. Interesting development here. Dee has her fun, but I can't remember the last time she took interest in a man like this. She's focused on her career, and for the last few years, her focus has been me. I feel guilty about possibly having kept her from finding love, but she insists that she wouldn't have it any other way.

I look back at Greg to see if he has noticed the sparks flying between Dee and Beck and notice his shock matching my own.

I clear my throat, hoping to stop this eye fuck before they both have some weird orgasm in the middle of the mall. "So…"

Greg laughs when they both jerk like they got caught stealing. "You two want to stop this shopping shit and head over to Heavy's for some BBQ?" he suggests, knowing that Heavy's is my favorite place in town. Dirty trick…. Looks like he's bringing out the big dogs today.

"Beck, did you know that sex is biochemically no different than eating large quantities of chocolate?" I can't help but laugh at that one. Or maybe it's his face alone that's hilarious. Dee and I have spent the last hour sitting here spouting off useless sex facts. It's hilarious to watch these two big men squirm. Greg is used to this, but Beck seems to be having an issue with our topic of choice, probably because he is still back at the mall having creepy eye sex with my best friend.

"It's true, you know," she pipes up. "I can get just enough pleasure from a bag of Kisses than I can from any man." I look over at Dee and laugh so hard I have to hold my sides.

"You are not wrong, my friend. Kisses are so much more pleasurable than any of my battery operated boyfriends. Just as satisfying but no work necessary." I think we are on our second—no, make that our fourth—pitcher of beer now, and my laughs are coming so frequently that I'm worried I might piss on myself at any moment.

"Iz, you're nuts… Anything is better than a fucking dildo. I'm talking real men here, but throw me some chocolate and I'm golden."

My laughter is coming even louder now when I see the shock of what she just said register on her face.

"Sugar," Beck interrupts my ruckus with a wink, "if chocolate is more fulfilling than sex, then someone isn't doing their job right." He smiles back over at me but quickly turns his eyes back on Dee. A Dee who, I noticed, has gone silent again.

I'm sitting between Greg and Dee at the round high top we claimed when we arrived at Heavy's. Greg keeps pushing more food in front of me. He must think he can somehow slow down my drunk by keeping me full of shit.

Whatever.

"I don't know what her reason is, but that's just it for me. It's better because 'the someone' doesn't exist anymore. I get my kicks where I can." I punctuate my seriousness with a stab towards them with the fry I'm munching on. "I've got chocolate and chocolate-induced satisfaction. I love chocolate. Might get messy sometimes, but there is no drama."

Dee is nodding her head enthusiastically now. "It's true, and you should see our chocolate stash. We're good for at least a solid year of orgasms. Who needs a boy when you have Hershey's!"

Greg smiles over at us, laughing right along with Beck now. "You two are fucking nuts, you know that?"

I open my mouth to respond when Dee yells, "Hey, is it true that you guys think about sex seven times a day?" She is looking directly at Beck. I might laugh if I didn't decide there was a serious need in this knowledge.

I stop long enough to ponder that one. I've never really given that much thought. Case in point, I am not having sex, therefore why do I need to think about it? "Yeah, is it something like, because you have a giant dick bobbing around down there, you are constantly reminded to think about using it? Like you have some sex beacon?" I am completely serious right now.

Beck and Greg look at each other and then back at us. Then they throw their heads back and laugh so deep and so loud they draw the attention of almost the whole place.

I don't think they understand how serious I am right now. "This isn't funny," I pout.

Greg stops laughing and starts to answer with humor twinkling in his eyes, but his phone interrupts him. Glancing down at the display with a small frown, he excuses himself from the table.

Okay, whatever. I look over at Beck and throw my question back at him. "So? Do you? Do you think about sex that much?"

"Sugar," he starts before turning his attention back over to Dee, "I have thought about sex—hard, fucking dirty sex—about a hundred times since we sat down to eat." Looking back over at me, he says, "Does that clear it up for you?"

Oh, my.

"Ah, well...okay. I think we need more beer!" I grab the empty pitcher and take off to find the waitress for more. I glance back at the table on my way to the bar and notice that Dee is still locking eyes with Beck, a look of complete rapture on her face.

I take my time returning, giving those two dirty perverts a second to do whatever it is they seem to be doing before I make my way back over.

"So what's next on the schedule for today? Or I guess tonight now," I ask, trying my hardest not to snicker at my two tablemates. If this gets any more heated, I might feel like I was an unwilling three-some participant.

Dee clears her throat and looks over at me, lust still clouding her brown eyes. "Um. I know! Let's go get some tattoos! You keep talking about how much you want one."

"I don't think that's such a good idea, Dee. I think they frown on people being a mile over the legal drinking limit."

Dee and I are debating on the benefits of getting tattoos when you are far from sober when Greg returns. The laughter and lightness that had taken over his face is gone and his scowl is back. It looks like grumpy Greg is back.

"G, Dee wants to go get some ink. Personally, I think it might not be the best idea... You know, numerous pitchers of beer and all. What do you think?"

He seems shocked by my question. Maybe he was expecting me to push him on his mood, or it could be the fact that I have suddenly decided branding myself with something permanent might be a good idea.

"I don't think that's a good idea, baby girl. Not something you do when you aren't thinking straight, and damn sure not something you do when your head isn't in the right place." He's looking right at me when he says that. There is no denying that he is only speaking to me. No joking to be found in his tone now. Seriousness is painted heavily all over that reply. No fucking way. I knew he wouldn't be able to leave it be for long, and that comment just pisses me the hell off. My head is fine just where it is, and I do not want him psychoanalyzing me.

I look over at Dee, who seems to be just as shocked at his answer as I am, which just further pisses me off. Damn infuriating man. "Dee, where's that place you told me about the other day? You know, the one your assistant was telling you about?"

She looks at me, trying to judge if I'm serious or not, and I practically bug my eyes out of their sockets to communicate that I am very fucking serious.

"Right, you mean Smudge, the new parlor over on Grove. She said the big guy who does her work is the best, but I couldn't tell you his name."

"Perfect. Just perfect. Finish up, people. Places to go." I clap my hands together and look at Greg with all the seriousness I have in me. He will not stop me. No way in hell, he would have to lock me up now.

"Head not in the right place." Fucking asshole. He's pissed, I know he is. I down another two beers, locking eyes with Dee. She has a look about her that says she's down for whatever but clearly confused by my agreement to visit Smudge. She brought it up, so she better be ready.

Greg leans over and says something to Beck before getting up and marching out the door again. I watch him throw the door open and storm out and then look over at Beck. "What the hell is his problem now?"

"Don't know, sugar. He just said he needed to do something and he would meet us there."

Okay, I might have overreacted slightly. But you know what? I am sick of being treated with kid gloves like some breakable porcelain doll that might shatter with the smallest touch. My path to find the old Izzy starts right now, and I'm not going to let Greg and his shit-fit mess this up.

"You two almost ready to go? I'm going to go track down our ticket so we can get out of here. Think about what you want to get, you little bitch. Remember this was your idea."

I stand up and walk off, once again leaving them at the table, but I doubt they are drenched in their lust cloud anymore. Beck is probably trying to figure out what brand of fucked up he has stumbled on and Dee is probably back to worrying. At least this time she isn't worried about my mental stability—or at least I hope she isn't. She is probably worried about this big-ass boulder that seems to have popped up between Greg and me.

CHAPTER 9

DEE IS pretty silent when we first get in the cab after leaving Heavy's. She is probably still playing back my refusal to ride with the boys. We left her car at Heavy's and jumped in the first cab I saw, leaving a fuming Greg and a confused Beck standing at his truck. Greg was waiting outside of Heavy's when we walked out. So much for his having something to take care of. I knew that if we let Greg drive he would control the destination, and I was seeing this through.

For the first five minutes, she sits silently gazing out her window. Soft country music plays through the speakers, not loud but enough that the silence isn't awkward. She finally has enough and turns to me.

"All right, tell me what this really is about, Iz. This is more than a few drinks and sex jokes. What's really going on up there?" She reaches over and taps my head.

"Nothing is going on up there, Dee. I'm sick of everyone looking at me like I am some unfixable toy. Some toy that, no matter how many times you slather Elmer's on, keeps falling apart. I'm sick of being that girl, Dee. Greg just pushed my buttons when he said I wasn't right in the head. I'm *fine*. Just because I don't want to talk about…Axel, that does not mean I'm not right in the head. It doesn't."

"Who exactly are you trying to convince, Izzy?" she asks softly.

"I don't need to convince anyone. I just need you to have my back and trust me to handle this on my own terms." I let out a frustrated huff and turn my head to watch the city zoom past. I'm so tired from this week of dodging Greg and running from Axel. I just want it to be over, this bad dream that I am beyond ready to wake up from.

"Okay, Iz. I understand. Or at least I'm trying to. I just don't like seeing you hurting, and I don't like seeing you and Greg fight. You know he's got to be hurting too. He would do anything to take your pain away. You know that. Don't think he is being pushy to be a dick. He really does care."

I don't reply. What's the point? I don't know what to think about Greg. I know he cares, but now that his loyalty is torn, I can honestly say that I don't know which way he is going with his need to chat with me. He wants me happy, I know that much, but at what cost?

We pull up in front of Smudge a few minutes later; the cabby lets us out right at the front door. I quickly pay him and rush for the door. When I see Greg's truck roaring up the street, I take off for the inside of the building. He won't cause a scene, not in a public place like this. He might look at me with his displeasure and judgment, but he won't say anything. No, I will get that later.

We walk into the brightly lit building. The walls are painted a deep red; the ceiling and the tile are black. They have the room set up with little cubicles against the sidewalls, each one with a wall about four feet tall. There are some rooms against the back wall, but all three have blacked-out windows. Not sure I want to know what happens back there. I walk over to the huge U-shaped display case set up in the middle of the room. There is a young, heavily tattooed woman standing behind it. Her short pixie hair is sticking out in random directions and dyed electric blue. Her face is classically beautiful and would look odd against her body art and hair of choice, but she has the most elaborate makeup on. Her eye shadow is as bright and as blue as her hair, thick black lines outline her almost violet eyes, and her lips are painted red.

"What's up, ladies? I'm Trix. Welcome to Smudge. We've got a few clients ahead of you, but I think we can fit you in. Which one of you plans on getting some ink tonight?" she asks with a cheerful smile.

Dee looks over at me, clearly starting to second-guess opening her big mouth back at Heavy's, but no way am I letting her off the hook. "Both of us," I shoot over at Trix, giving her a smirk of my own.

I hear the bell over the door clank. I don't need to turn around to know who just came in the door. Even if I didn't know it was Greg, the look Trix is shooting over my shoulder says it all. Greg might be like a brother to me, but even I can admit how hot he is. Next to Beck, I'm sure the boys are quite an eyeful.

"Right, so where do we need to wait?" She can lust after them when she gets this show on the road.

She looks back at me, a slight blush spotting her white cheeks, "Sorry. Okay, I just need a copy of your license and for you both to fill out these forms. Have a seat over on those couches and have a look at the photo books on the table if you need to get an idea of what you want. I'll go see who is almost finished and can pick y'all up next." She turns to look over at Greg and Beck one more time before walking down the rows of cubicles. I have just enough time to register her hot pink tutu as she disappears into one of the back rooms. Hmm, maybe next time I need to ask *her* to take me shopping. Tutus look pretty freaking awesome.

I grab Dee's arm and pull her over to the couch, thrusting the clipboard with the forms on them in her arms. "Fill them out and then look," I say, pointing over to the binders. I make quick work of filling out the sheets, pull my license out of my wallet, and walk back over to Trix. Handing everything over for her to do her thing with, I walk back over and sit down next to Dee. She is slow enough with her papers that I know she is trying to find a way to back out. No fucking way.

"This was your idea, remember?"

She looks over at me. There might be some fear in her eyes, but she is mostly curious about just how far I plan on taking this.

"I know. Don't worry I'm not backing out. Just promise me we can talk about this soon?" God, I love her.

"Sure, Dee. Sometime." I reach over and pluck one of the books off the table, opening the cover and taking in a very up close and personal dick with a metal barbell attached to the head. Okay, clearly they don't just tattoo here. I turn a few more pages and come to some female piercings. Now those don't look quiet as traumatizing as the decorated dicks. They almost make this chick's tits look…beautiful.

I must have been looking at them for a while. I can't imagine how weird this looks, my zoning on someone else's tits. Dee looks over and gives a soft snort. "Seriously, Iz? Nip rings?"

"Maybe," I mumble, going over in my head the pros of a piercing over a tattoo.

I'll admit that when I had my fit over Greg's words I didn't completely think this through. Sure, I have wanted a tattoo for a while, but it should be something I think and plan, not something I decide in anger. A piercing though, well...I can take that out whenever I get sick of them. Permanence isn't even an issue there. It's just something pretty to look at for a while.

Dee is flicking through one of the tattoo books. She is not really looking at anything, just flipping and stealing looks over at Beck. Greg is rod straight and clearly very pissed, his eyes burning holes right into me. I stand and walk back over to Trix, leaning over the display case to whisper my request in her ear. When I stand back, she has a huge grin on her face. She gives me a small nod and walks back to one of the black window rooms.

"Izzy," Greg starts, "what the fuck are you doing?"

I turn and give him a smart smile, not even bothering to hide my simmering pissed vibes. "Why nothing, Gregory. I'm just enjoying my head being all fucked up."

I walk back over to Dee, who is looking at me, and even with her worried eyes, she is trying hard not to laugh. We are clearly a dysfunctional family.

"You pick anything yet?" I ask her.

"Yeah, nothing big, but I got it."

"Perfect, but if this isn't something you want, don't feel like you have to do this just because I'm set on proving a point to the big idiot."

She has her happy smile back on her face. She might not have meant to actually show up here, but I can tell she doesn't mind now.

"It's all good, Iz. I wouldn't be here if I didn't want to be. You seriously going to get some rings hanging off your tits?" She snickers.

"I might be pissed, but I'm not stupid. I need time to figure out the perfect tat, and some stupid fight with Greg isn't going to make me jump the gun. Plus, I think my tits will look fucking hot with some bling."

We are both laughing hard when a good-looking guy walks up

and asks which one of us is Izzy. For some reason, I expected the person doing my piercings to be a female. Don't I specifically drive a town over because I don't want to see a male gynecologist? Now, the person who will be shoving a needle through my fun bags is going to be this hunk? Shit. Didn't see that coming.

"Izzy would be me," I say, standing up and holding out my hand. I can see Greg out of the corner of my eye. If anything, he looks like he is going to explode soon. He looks carved from stone, and I know he is just gearing up to shut this down. I bring my focus back to the man in front of me.

"Tyler. Nice to meet you. Ready?"

"Sure thing, Tyler."

We set off for the black window rooms; I can hear Greg speaking harshly behind me. I don't turn around to see who he is talking to. He isn't stopping this.

We walk into the room and I'm shocked to see how bright it is in here. Something about the windows had me expecting some gloom and doom back here. The walls, ceiling, and floor match the décor outside the door. There is a single dentist-looking chair in the middle of the room and a long table against the back wall. He's already set up the things he will need on the little tray next to the chair.

"First piercings?" Tyler asks while motioning me to jump up on the chair.

"Yup, other than my ears."

"Ah, perfect. I love poppin' cherries." He smiles over at me.

He really is very nice to look at. This might be more fun than I thought it would be. He has light brown hair, which is a little on the long side and curling under his ears and behind the back of the cap he is wearing. His eyes are light blue and bright with mischief. He must be assuming that this is some kind of kink I have. His face is model perfect. If it weren't for the huge gages through his ears, a lip ring, two eyebrow rings, and the colorful art running up both arms, I might think he was in the wrong place.

"Ha, I'm sure you do. So what do you need me to do?"

"Strip down, sweetheart. Shirt, bra, and you can take the pants off too if that's what works for you. Get comfortable and recline on back. I need to mark you first to make sure I get these bars in perfectly. I wouldn't want to mess up those perfect tits."

Choosing to ignore his blatant flirting, I reach down for the hem of my tee and pull it over my head. I flick my bra off, throwing them both on the chair in the corner. Putting my back flat on the chair, I reach up and pull my thick hair into a messy knot on the top of my head; all the while, I'm watching the lustful look take over his face.

Tyler reaches over and helps me to lean forward so he can mark my nipples. His gloved hands are cold at first, but he makes quick work with the marker. He gives me a quick squeeze before releasing the swells of my breast. I'm sure that was more for his benefit than the alignment of my holes. At this point, I don't even care. It's been a long time since anyone other than myself has touched my tits, so even though it's awkward, his touch isn't exactly a turn-off.

"You ready?" he asks. I can feel the soft bite of the needle against my left nipple. It isn't an unpleasant pain, bordering the line between pain and pleasure for sure. Surely, it isn't natural to be this turned on right now.

"Yup. Do your thing." I close my eyes tight, and wait for it.

He gives me a sharp pinch before I feel him push the needle through. I let out the breath I was holding... Not bad. The pain is already receding and a weird burning numbness is taking over. If this is what every body piercing feels like, I can understand why Tyler here has so many now.

"Not bad, huh?" he asks while walking around the chair to the other side. He seems to have lost his playful flirting and turned into the perfect professional. He looks up and gives me a small wink. Okay, so maybe not all the flirting has left his system.

"No," I laugh, "definitely not bad."

"All right, ready for the next?"

"Go for it."

I close my eyes tight again, and the process is repeated, but right when I feel him finishing up with the tightening of the ball at the end of my new piercing, there is a loud thump at the door and suddenly it's jerked wide open. He jumps to stand in front of me, trying to protect my modesty. From my spot hidden behind Tyler the piercer, I can see one very long jean-covered leg and a big-booted foot. I don't know those boots. The only other thing I can see past Tyler is one giant fist flexing and pulsing by the leg's side.

Then I hear the softly spoken command, the command laced with so much fury only a fool would ignore it. I squeeze my eyes shut again, praying that I'm wrong about who is standing in front of Tyler.

"Move. Move *the fuck* out of my way. Right fucking now."

Shit. Shit, shit, shit!

Tyler looks over his shoulder at me, trying to figure out if I know who this is or if he needs to have him removed. Laughable, really—there is no way he would be able to move this man. It might take every person in this whole building to remove this pissed-off brute. He reaches off behind his back and pulls out a towel he had hanging off the back of his belt. Might not be the cleanest thing in the world right now, but at least it would hide my body. Or some of my body.

"Thanks," I softly say to Tyler. "It's okay. I'll be right out to pay."

"Okay. You sure?" he asks, and at my nod, he quickly gives me a rundown on after care and tells me he will leave a sheet with the instructions with Trix up front.

I look down and make sure the towel is covering me enough before I look up and meet the blazing green, very pissed depths of Axel's eyes. This isn't going to be fun. Not only am I sitting in front of him naked from the waist up, but seeing his face again is still a punch straight to the gut. It physically hurts to breathe. He looks so different than the boyish face I remember in my dreams. He is still Axel, but he looks harder. Age has done wonderful things to this man. He was always tall, but never this tall. When he left at eighteen, he had a boy's body, but there is nothing boy about him now. He looks to have doubled in size, and his muscles were pulsing on his arms, flexing with pent-up energy. Angry energy. His black tee is stretched tight, not only hugging his heavily tattooed arms but his flat stomach as well. I can even see the rippling of his abs through the material. His legs are long and thick, covered in denim. I can feel the vibes coming from him, and they aren't happy ones. I have a feeling he isn't just unhappy about me blowing him off today. He did say *every door* when he threatened to track me down. How the hell did he know where to find me?

He takes a menacing step forward and closes the door behind him, shutting us in the room and standing between my clothes and me.

"What did I fucking say, Izzy? I would find you. You aren't fucking hiding from this talk, you hear me? Now, want to fucking tell me what the hell you're doing with your fucking shirt off back here?" No need to look at his face to judge his mood. He's well passed pissed.

"Can you please pass me my clothes?" That's what I go with. Seems like the safest bet at this point. Maybe I can avoid him long enough to escape. "Please, Axel."

He bends, snatching my bra and tee off the chair behind him, not even bothering to look away. Fine. It isn't like he hasn't seen them before; he just hasn't ever seen them like this. Suddenly my act of rebellion isn't looking so hot. I pick up my bra and let the towel drop. His sharp intake has me snapping my eyes up to meet his. His eyes are focused directly on my chest and their new jewelry. I can see his chest moving rapidly, his nose is flaring, and his hands are back to flexing in and out of a tight fists.

"What the fuck? You let some stranger put his hands on your fucking tits?" He doesn't even mention the barbells. How can he miss them? They are standing out in all their silver glory against my pink nipples.

"Not your business, Axel. It hasn't been your business in a long damn time." My voice sounds funny. My earlier confidence is gone, and I sound almost dead. The fight has left me, and I know it's futile to even try to run from him. Like it or not, this talk is about to happen. I just have to figure out what and how much to tell him. And just how I will get through it?

"Not my fucking business? We'll see about that, Izzy. Get your fucking clothes on before someone else sees you."

I make quick work of redressing, careful with my sensitive and sore nipples. When I am completely covered and standing in front of him, I look up and just take him in. I can't believe he is really right in front of me, very much alive and pissed off. I can't tell what's working behind his eyes. The anger is dominating him right now, but it almost looks like relief.

He reaches out. I don't even know what his goal is, but I immediately shrink back, closing my eyes tight and turning my head away from his hand.

"What the fuck is this shit, Izzy?" I don't answer him; I can't. I'm still turned to the side, waiting on impact. "Turn around. Now." he roars. He curses under his breath when I flinch even further, turning completely away from him.

At this point, I can't help the tears that silently run down my cheeks. I know deep down that Axel wouldn't harm me, but this has been my reality for so long that the instinct to protect myself is just too strong.

"Izzy, please, Princess. Turn around," he says after a long pause. I can still feel his anger but his tone is soft and reassuring. I slowly turn, bracing myself for any reaction, but I am completely shocked by the pain in his eyes. "Let's go. We're talking and we're talking now. Izzy, hear me this right fucking now. You do not fear me. Ever. Even as mad as you have me, I wouldn't ever put my hands on you. Do you hear me? I would never harm a single fucking hair on your head, Princess."

I flinch but it has nothing to do with fearing him. Hearing him call me Princess again is almost as painful as seeing him before me. I never thought I would hear that word coming from those lips again. I nod once, giving him that before following him out the door.

I trail behind him, eyes to the floor, walking past the cubicles and around the display case. I look up and meet Trix's eyes. Surprisingly, she isn't enamored by Axel, but she looks at me with uncensored concern. I give her a small, very wobbly smile and ask her how much.

"Already paid. Here are the instructions from Ty. I wrote the shop number on there in case you have any questions." She looks at me and I can see her communicating something. I just can't figure it out right now. My mind is focused on one thing and one thing only.

I thank her and then look around the front for Dee. I find her silently crying next to Beck, who has his arm thrown tightly around her shoulders, hugging her close. I can't even fake a smile for her. She knows me too well, so it would be completely pointless. I walk out the front door and stand there, waiting for the rest of this fucked-up entourage to join me on the sidewalk. Axel is out first. He takes his post behind me, boxing me in and making any thought of running impossible.

Dee comes up and gives me an awkward hug. "It will be okay,

Iz," she whispers into my ear before pulling away and standing back with Beck. He gives me a sympathetic smile but doesn't say anything, and really, what can be said? Then I meet the blue eyes of Greg.

"Games, baby girl. I won't sit back and watch you self-destruct with these fucked-up games. You can be mad, and I get that you will be, but you will not play these fucked-up games. I'll call you tomorrow and maybe by then you will understand why this was the only move you left me. I love you, baby girl, but that shit stops now."

My eyes widen in shock. I hear Dee gasp behind him, and I feel Axel's deep rumble behind my back. I can imagine that Dee is just as shocked as I am that Greg just admitted to letting Axel know where I was; I have no clue what the hell Axel's deal is. I am crushed. How could he do this to me? The tears start streaming down again, even heavier than before. I can see Greg, and he looks visibly shaken up by my tears.

Everything I had been building up—the fight, the drive to be strong—is gone in an instant. I am completely flattened with his betrayal. I let out a mighty breath before addressing Greg. "Do not even bother, Greg. Don't. As far as I'm concerned, you can lose my number. I'm dead to you, you hear me? I do not exist to you." I look right into his eyes, with tears flowing quickly; I don't even bother to mask the pure pain.

He looks stunned at first, and then a look that I'm sure comes close to the pain across my face takes hold of his features. I don't even give it a second thought. I turn and look up to Axel's blazing eyes.

"I didn't drive, took a cab here. So if you want to talk, you either do it here or you meet me somewhere." I don't even recognize my voice; it's flat and expressionless.

His eyes flare and he slowly brings his hand forward, grabbing my hand. I don't flinch at his touch, but the bolts shooting up my arm from this exchange has me widening my eyes at him. If his quick intake of air is any indication, he feels it too.

"Not leaving my fucking sight, understand that right now. Say goodbye to your friends. We are going to have this chat and we're doing it right now before you decide to run. Again." There is no room for arguing; he means it and I don't even care. Greg's deception is hard enough to take in, but knowing I am about to rip open old wounds better left alone is gutting me.

I have no idea how I am going to make it through this.

CHAPTER 10

I GIVE DEE another look; she seems to understand and gives me a small nod. I completely ignore Greg, turn, and prepare to follow Axel to parts unknown. I know what is coming, and I might not be ready, but something is telling me that I have no choice. Axel wants answers, he warned me, and I knew he would be determined.

He might think he can bully himself back into my life like he hasn't just been gone for the last twelve years, but he has another thing coming if he thinks I am just going to roll over and play dead. My fight might be gone, but I am far from out.

We start walking down the sidewalk. He's leading and I'm following silently behind him. When we reach his mammoth truck, I stop and look at it. How the hell am I supposed to get in that thing. I am eye level with the footboard thing. Isn't the purpose of that thing to help people get into vehicles? Typical man, making these damn things impossible. Axel is standing next to me holding the door, waiting for me to climb in. I look from him to the truck a few times. He can't be for real right now.

"Get in now. I don't have the patience for your shit." His voice still sounds lethal. I have no idea what would had made him so mad. He has me and it technically is still Saturday…even if there are only a few hours left. So I didn't exactly do anything wrong. The deadline is up and I'm here, right?

"Hate to point out the obvious, *Holt*"—I can't seem to help myself from sneering his name, his new name—"but how exactly do you expect me to get in *now*, as you have so kindly demanded?"

His eyes flash and fill even more with blinding rage. His face takes on an even harsher hard… stone-cold look. "What. The fuck. Did I tell you about calling me Holt?" he throws at me.

His face is almost nose to nose with mine. His rapid breaths are hitting my own mouth in warm bursts. I can taste him on my tongue, and I gasp in shock. My eyes go wide at his close proximity. Even in my current mood, I can't help but remember all the times I looked into these eyes before. All the times they didn't hold anger, but untainted love.

"One more time, and I swear to God. Get in the fucking truck," he bites out, pushing each word towards me with great force.

"You idiot, what do you think I am doing? Standing here for shits and fucking giggles? No, definitely not. I *can't* get into your stupid truck. If you would take a second to actually look, you would see this. Your little Napoleon complex is cute. Really, it is. But it is also keeping me from *getting in the fucking truck!*" I scream the last part in his face so loud that even my ears are ringing. I instantly slam my hand over my mouth, regretting my outburst and fearing his reaction.

He shocks me when, instead of lashing out, he starts to shake with silent laughter "Napoleon complex, hmm? Do I really need to remind you just how untrue that statement is, Izzy? Take a look at me. My height isn't the only thing that fucking grew since you ran off." After he throws that unexpected remark out, I am once again stunned.

Ran off? I would have thought he was talking about this past week if it hadn't been for the offhand comment about him changing. What is he talking about? I didn't run off. He did. As my confusion grows, I am even more convinced that I do not want to have this conversation with him.

Finally, having lost his last thread of control, he grabs my hips and lifts, unceremoniously dumping me into the seat. He harshly mutters for me to buckle my 'fucking belt', before he slams the door and disappears around the hood. My jaw is still hanging when he opens his door and slings his giant frame into the seat, turning the key and bringing this beast to a roaring start. He slams it into gear and shoots away from his spot.

Coming out of my stunned silence, I look over at his harsh face. "Where are you taking me? My house is the other way," I meekly ask.

"I know where your house is. I also know that you have been there all week, even while ignoring me. I'm not taking you there, where you can have the protection of your little pit bull roommate.

We're talking and we will be doing it with no fucking interruptions and no one to help you cower behind a locked door. Hear me that, right fucking now."

"I don't think that's a good idea. Maybe we can just go to the Starbucks around the corner?" Maybe if I had little more conviction, he would have taken me seriously. The last place I want to be is in his space, alone with him.

"Forget that right now. What I have to say to you will not be said around others. Get ready, Princess, because I am done playing games. I don't care if it takes an eternity. You will fucking talk."

I snap my mouth shut and turn to watch the city fly past him, trying frantically to think of a way out of this, a way to escape. I'm not ready, and I am even more convinced that I might not ever be.

Axel

MY HEART feels like it might burst from my chest at any second, just blow up, right out of my body. The pounding of my heart, even booming in my ears as loudly as it is, is doing nothing to disguise the soft sniffling coming from the other side of my truck. As much as I wish I could keep my heart hardened from her, the sound of her crying is tearing me up. I shouldn't have any compassion left for her; it should have died a long time ago.

I know from my reaction to seeing her again last Saturday that this chat won't be easy. There are still feelings—feelings I thought were long gone and lost forever—trapped in that box with my heart. This girl ripped my heart to fucking shreds and I never knew why. It would have been quicker if she had stuck around and shot me in the fucking chest. At least I would have died instantly instead of bleeding out slowly for the last twelve years.

Jesus, I can't get the image of her slender body holding that small excuse for a towel against her chest out of my head. When she let it drop from her tight hold, I thought I was going to swallow my tongue.

Her tits had always been fucking perfect but, to see them like that, with her nipples erect and sporting two hot barbells, I might have shot off in my pants. As much as I wanted to drop to my knees and suck her pert, pink nipples into my mouth, I couldn't help my first thought: that motherfucker had his hands on her. He'd held her tits in his hands. There was no reasoning with my brain that she wasn't mine; I saw red.

Those are my fucking tits and she is my fucking girl. It doesn't matter to my mind that it has been well over a decade since I have been able to enjoy them; someone else touched what was mine. If I hadn't thought she would take off and run again, I would have killed that little shit.

All week I have thought about her. She has been a constant stress that I don't need when I am trying to get everything in my life in order. Greg and I have been busy enough with all the legal paper-work and issues that keep popping up with the new company. Plus meetings and moving into the office space, briefings with him and the boys, and consultations with new clients. I don't have time to be strolling down memory lane.

It wasn't until Wednesday evening that I remembered Greg coming to talk to me about his friend. Iz, with the threat and husband who did not want to let go. Livid—that would be the first thing I felt. I remember thinking, very briefly, when I first saw her about the connection but it instantly fled when all hell followed our collision. I need more information and I need it yesterday. I don't know what kind of threat she is under and I don't even really know much about her marriage. I assumed for so many years that she was happy. I was crushed and pissed because I couldn't bring myself to barge into her life if she was happy.

Even now, craving answers as fiercely as I do, my main focus is figuring out what is happening with this douchebag. The time to get my answers will come, but first we will be talking about this husband of hers.

I waited for her call yesterday, anticipating some bullshit reason why she wouldn't be able to meet today. I hadn't expected her to pull some vanishing act and hide all day. I should have. When lunch rolled around today and I still hadn't heard from her, I set off for her house.

When I got there to find it locked tight and no one home, I was pissed.

I called Greg to see if maybe I could gain one fucking supporter in this fight. He said, "Not getting in this. She knows how I feel and she will talk when she's ready. I don't agree with this, but I will support her because she's my girl." He was not happy when I blew up in his ear. She is not his goddamn girl. It didn't matter how many times I asked or straight-up demanded—he wasn't telling me where they were.

Imagine my shock when I got a call not even an hour later from Greg, spitting fire and giving up her location. When I arrived and walked into a tattoo parlor of all places, my rage joined his.

Fuck, those tits looked fucking hot though.

After another five-minute drive and sporadic soft sniffles from Izzy, I pull up to the security gate of my house. After entering the code, I pull the truck up my driveway. I feel like I'm looking at the house from a new set of eyes, trying to see how she will view my success. I might be a thirty-one-year-old man, but even that doesn't stop me from hoping she sees how far I've come, how I have finally taken myself from orphaned and penniless to this. Part of the plans we once made together, only this isn't the one-bedroom apartment we had our eyes set on. As much of a douche as it might make me, an even smaller part of me hopes she feels just an ounce of jealousy for how good my life is and see how much I was able to accomplish without her in my life.

How laughable that thought is. I would have gladly given every single penny to my name away if it meant I would have had my Izzy with me all these years. But this Izzy? No. I don't even know this Izzy.

The house I bought was over the top, I know this, but fuck if I would ever live cramped for space again. I'm sure there are plenty of shrinks who would love to get into my head; there's plenty of jacked-up shit in there. I know why I bought this place and I don't need anyone to tell me that I am making up for my childhood haunts.

We clear the last of the Bradford pears that line my half-a-mile drive and the house is coming into view. Large and imposing. The deep red bricks almost look black against the night sky. The light next to the red double front doors beams bright and cheerful, almost inviting. Again, laughable. The colonial-style house is made to be a home, not this farce I have going. The huge front porch looks cozy with the rocking chairs positioned between the large four columns, and the flowers look domestic; it is just some huge juxtapose of my life. The outside doesn't match the inside. The house is just as vacant as I feel right now and I don't like it at all.

Time to get this over with.

Time to figure out whatever the issue is with her husband and find out what the fuck happened to *her.*

Izzy is still just gazing out her window, but since we are sitting in my dark garage, my guess is this is her attempt at avoiding me. How the hell she plans on doing that when she is in my damn house and unable to leave without me taking her is beyond me.

I can feel my temper rising. I'm fighting myself for control—control against my own frustrations, control over the pain that has no place in my heart anymore, and control against my raging hard-on that seems to be pointing right at Izzy. I have never had this many issues with controlling the situations around me.

She must feel my eyes on her because she finally turns to me.

"What now?" It's barely a whisper, and if I hadn't been looking at her, I might have missed it.

"Get out of the truck. We talk. Simple as that. It only becomes this giant mess of immature games when you become difficult. So work with me, because I'm sick of fucking playing games." I think that is nice enough until the tears start rolling down her velvety cheeks.

Goddammit.

I climb down from the cab and start making my way around the hood to her side, fully expecting to have to pull her out and throw her over my shoulder. Surprisingly, she is waiting next to the door, and is clearly pissed about her long climb down.

"This way." The welcome is just rolling off my words. I'm sure she can feel the vibes choking her. It's hard to miss when someone would rather be anywhere than with the person they are with. Hard to tell if I would even be going through all this shit if it hadn't been for Greg and his request to help his friend. My gut tells me that I should just leave her alone, forget about her and the answers I crave. My gut is screaming at me to let it die, pass it over to Locke or Coop, and pretend I never looked back into those pale green eyes again.

Fat chance of that.

I open the door to the mudroom off the garage and motion for her to enter. The house is dark, so she pauses next to the door. Coming in behind her, I enter the alarm code and snap on the light to the kitchen. There are chrome appliances, dark wood cabinets, granite counter-tops, and a whole lot of nothing else. No table, just two barstools next to the island. It screams welcome home.

I point over to the stool and bark off one word. "Sit."

She is looking at her feet, doesn't even attempt to fight me, and sits. I give her a second. She knows why we are here, so hopefully she will just tell me what I need to know without making this a big deal. Ten minutes go by with me looking at her and her wringing her hands together in her lap.

"Talk," I bark, the sound vibrating off the naked walls.

If I hadn't been observing her for the last eternity, I might have missed the small jump she takes at my tone. It's hard to tell if I scared her or if something else is working behind her eyes when she snaps her head up.

"I don't know what you want me to say." More whispers. Seems like I might need hearing aids for this conversation.

"Well, let's see. I didn't drag you down here to give you a tour, I don't need to catch up on the latest town gossip, and I sure as fuck didn't bring you here for the company, so that just leaves one thing. First, you explain, in detail, what is going on with your husband." I spit the word out, the bitterness on my tongue loud and clear. "Then you can explain to me what that fucked-up package meant. Details, Izzy. This isn't a game, and I tell you this, if it hadn't been for Greg basically begging me to help you, I would not be doing this."

It takes her a second; I can see my words working around her mind. She opens her mouth a few times, but words never come out. Right when I start to lose any thread of patience I have left, she finally speaks.

"Can't someone else do this? Do you have to be the one?" I want to throttle her. Fucking bullshit. Greg will owe me big for this.

"End the high school bullshit. He didn't ask me personally to take your shit for the hell of it. I'm good at what I do, Izzy. Locke and Coop? Sure, they could do it, but I can do it better. Now, what the fuck?"

She closes her eyes for a few minutes before inhaling deeply. "Brandon, my ex…well, almost ex. We had a…challenging marriage. I left a little over two years ago and moved here. He's been fighting the divorce." Didn't take much of a deduction to guess she was leaving something out—a whole lot of somethings.

"Let me ask you something, Izzy. How do you expect me to look into this, into him, without anything other than your telling me your perfect marriage didn't work? What, did he cheat on you or something? Finally get enough of living the perfect little life? Tell me, because I just don't get it. The little I was able to dig up this week makes it look like you had everything your little heart desired. And what I really don't get—what I really don't understand—is why he won't just let you go." Even to my own ears, that comes out harsher than I intended it to.

A little light on this situation would have been nice, because when she bursts into tears and runs off into the darken halls of my house, I am completely thrown. Shocked. What in the fucking hell? Grumbling like a fool, I take off to find her.

Almost thirty minutes later, I finally narrow the search. Really, it shouldn't have been this much of a challenge since I have more empty rooms than furniture. This is what I get for buying a six-fuck-ing-bedroom house I do not need. I look in every room on the main floor—nothing. I jog up the stairs and look in every room—nothing. I finally catch a break when I pass the bedroom next to the stairs—soft crying. I already checked this room and she wasn't there. I use this room to store all my old case files. Being that all the other rooms except the one I sleep in are empty, she couldn't have picked a better hiding spot.

I finally find her wedged between two big stacks of boxes. She has completely moused her way between them and turned into herself, legs pulled close to her chest and arms wrapped tightly around her body. She is rocking, fucking rocking, back and forth.

"Izzy, come out." I try.

Nothing but soft cries.

"Come on now. Get out of there." And try.

Silence.

"Really, Izzy, I'm too fucking big to crawl in there for you. Out." And try.

I keep going for ten long-ass, frustrating minutes with no luck.

Enough of this shit. I start picking up the boxes around her, moving one at a time away from her small ball-like body. Once I have enough cleared that I can touch her, I reach my hand out to pull her up and out. I don't expect her to throw herself back away from my outstretched hand. She has holed herself up so well that there isn't much room between her head and the wall. She makes contract with a sick thud.

"Fuck," I hiss out before scooping her up and carrying her down to my room. Flicking the lights on with my elbow, I walk over to the bed and place her gently down against the mattress before running my fingers through her hair.

Nice lump, stupid girl.

"All right, Izzy. Enough of this. Now we can add explaining what the hell that was to the list."

My patience is shot, blown to fucking dust. My mood is deteriorating with every second, and she just looks at me with empty eyes. It's like she isn't even here with me. She just keeps roaming her eyes over my face. As pissed as I am right now, I can't help but become sucked into her all over again. She looks so scared, but it's the longing I see all over her face that has me transfixed. It's like someone just kicked her puppy, killed her cat, and told her she wouldn't get a pony for Christmas.

"Please, talk."

She jumps at my hushed pleading. It takes her a minute and more of that heavy analyzing gaze before she speaks again. Her tone is dead; she sounds so small and defeated. Chills break out all over my body with her next words.

"It was so hard, Ax. So hard." She looks away, focusing off into space instead of on me. "The first year was okay. He worked a lot but it wasn't bad. He didn't want me to work, said the only thing I needed to do was care for him, the house, and any…kids. What did I know?

Stupid, broken Iz, what did I know? Huh?"

She finally looks back at me; she looks like some spirit has returned but not much. I know this won't be good before she even says a word. I have to fight the urge to punch something, reminding myself that I asked for this.

"The second year was when he started to change a little. We didn't go visit my grandparents as much. He was always asking me to stay home and not meet Dee for lunch or dinner. Little things that I didn't notice at first...until they became big things." She gives a bitter snort before taking another big intake of air. "I hadn't seen Dee in a few weeks. I think it was a Wednesday... I don't know. He was going to be late that day, and the only thing I could think was, *Finally... finally I can see Dee*. A half-hour coffee date with Dee turned into a split lip. I didn't even think he was out of line, you know. I thought I deserved it. I think Dee always knew things were off in the Hunter house. About a month after that, I ran into her again. She begged me to open up to her, but I told her I was fine. Fine. What a joke that was."

If I couldn't feel my blood rushing through my body right now, I would be convinced I have turned to stone. Words were beyond me, and my earlier taunts were smacking me all in the face.

I will kill this motherfucker.

"Princess," I reach down for her hand but she pulls it close to her body. "Was that the only time he put his hands on you?" I try for soft, but the lethal fury in my voice can't be missed.

"For a while. They didn't start getting bad for another few months. He acted like he was sorry and it was an accident. They didn't get bad until around our third anniversary."

"What exactly is defined as bad? Because I can't find any good way for a man to touch a woman like that."

When her eyes come back to me and that single fat tear slips from her eye, I know. I just know.

"Don't you feel pity for me. This wasn't your mess. You didn't make him do it. I should have left, been strong enough to leave. I didn't have anyone, Axel, so don't think I didn't think about it. He was smart. He cut me off from everyone. I didn't even get to go to my grandmother's funeral, and Pop... He wasn't doing well either. I didn't want Dee to know how bad it was. I was stuck... Stuck with no one."

This heavy pain shoots through my left side at her words. I should have been there, and as ridiculous the thought is, I can't shake the thought that I let this girl down somehow. I have spent years hating her, thinking she had just forgotten us and moved on. To know she suffered is not sitting well.

"You know about Mom and Dad, right?" She looks up at me, all sad and broken, for confirmation. With my weak nod, she continues. "Dee was all I had left. She finally caught me alone one day. I was picking up some groceries. That was one of the only things I was allowed to do alone. She pulled me into the bathroom and begged me to talk, begged me to leave. I brushed her off again. She bought me a prepaid phone and told me to call her, day or night, if I needed her. We were able to sneak a few calls and secret meetings but not many. She didn't live far, close enough to come when I could get away." She stops for a while, and I just sit there, struck dumb, waiting on her to continue, all the while struggling not to go find this fucker.

"Are you sure we need to go over this? It isn't pretty, Axel."

I want to scream, *No. No I don't want to hear this. Anything but this.* "Yeah, Izzy, keep going."

"Okay..." Pause. "Well..." Pause. Inhale. Exhale. "A few years back, I went to meet Dee. Nothing big, just wanted to see her. We had it all planned. I called her the day before from the phone she gave me, told her I missed her and just wanted to spend some time together. I set dinner in the slow cooker, ran my errands, and snuck in a Dee visit. It would have been fine and he never would have been the wiser but I was running late. He got home right after me, and even though I thought I had made it...he knew." She stops and levels her eyes with mine. Her eyes almost look gray. Her eyes always used to change with her moods...and gray was always the one I hated the most. "That was the night I finally used that phone for her to save me."

I don't realize I'm not breathing until my chest starts hurting. I can't even move, can't even allow myself to move. My God...

"I got lucky. When I passed out, the game wasn't fun anymore, and for the first time, he left after he finished with me. Dee got there and got me out quick. I haven't seen him since the day I picked up my stuff. The divorce has been in limbo for the last six or so months."

I can't stand to hear this story. I wish to God this were just a tale, not the life she was living when I thought she was happy. Not touching her is becoming unbearable. I reach over and grab her hand before she is able to pull it away, rubbing my thumb over her soft skin and looking into her eyes. As hard as it is for me to hear, it can't be easy to retell.

"I don't even know what to say right now, Princess. I…I just don't know. It kills me to know you had to live with any abuse for a second, but years… Izzy, I have never wished harder that I would have been there." Before I even finish speaking, she wrenches her hand away and scoots to the other side of my bed.

"No…you do not call me that, Axel. And we are not going there. I've explained my marriage, but I will not go there with you. Leave it in the past, please." Her raw desperation is the only thing that keeps me from fighting her on this. We will be talking about that, but I'm smart enough to know she will shut down if I force her now.

"All right, Izzy, I got you. Explain the package to me. Greg told me what it was, but I don't get how it matches the story you told me. Did you have…kids?" The cost my control takes to get that out with a neutral tone is high. The thought of another man touching her is enough, but to think of another man planting his seed in her body—unimaginable.

She was mine.

She is mine.

She will always fucking be mine.

I can see the walls coming up instantly; she is blocking me out and masking her emotions perfectly. I have no idea what made her shut down this time. I could stick a metal rod up her ass and she still wouldn't be as stiff as she is right now.

"We couldn't have children," she says quickly and quietly. "That's all that was—a reminder that I couldn't give him children."

Done. That statement is said in such a way that I know there will be no talking about that in detail. I'll give her that play. I don't know many women who aren't a little upset about not being able to have children, and deep down, I can admit the world without a chance of more Izzy in it is a dull place.

"That was the first time he contacted you?" I ask in an attempt to change the subject, making a mental note to ask Greg for more detail later.

"Not at first. I think he had a hard time finding me. I just recently started working, so he would have had to look for Dee to find me. There have been some calls, but nothing bad. Not until the package."

There's something I'm missing. I can't ignore the feeling that there is a big part of this picture missing. This asshole has been pretty silent and distant for so long. With the exception of the divorce hold-up, he hasn't been making waves. Something is off, but I can tell she isn't going to open up much more. I check the time and see that it is creeping up on dawn, just cementing the fact that we are done for the night.

"We need to sit down with Greg and the boys. I need to check out the system in your house and then you need to tell me how you want this to go. But that can all wait for tomorrow. It's late and I'm sure your earlier brush with adventure isn't exactly keeping you wide awake. I'll grab some clothes. You can use the bathroom then sleep. We can call the guys over in the morning."

Her eyes are wide—wide and shocked. "I'm not sleeping here. You can take me home or I can have someone come get me. You wanted to talk and we talked. Now I want to leave."

Throwing my head back and laughing was probably not the wisest move, but she must be out of her fucking mind if she thinks I am going to let her out of my sight before I can nail down a solid plan. She doesn't know it yet, but we are about to become the best of friends.

"Not fighting about this shit. It's late and I'm sure anyone you would call has already gone to bed. One night isn't going to fucking kill you, babe. This bed might as well have the Gulf in the middle of it. I'll stay on my side. Tomorrow we will figure this out and get this mess straightened out. Don't piss me off. Take the clothes. Go get fucking cleaned up and sleep." I walk over to the dresser and yank out a tee and some briefs, tossing them over to her, hitting her right in her stunned face. That seems to knock her out of whatever has her all tied up. With a huff and a whole lot of sass, she stomps over to my bathroom and slams the door.

I feel the strings of the years of hating her slowly start to loosen.

I can't ignore the desire to make her mine. It is still there, but I can't forget that she left and forgot about me pretty damn easily. I will take care of this problem and then—then—we will take care of us. We have enough to deal with right now; figuring out everything else can wait. I just can't decide if I want to figure us out for closure or to bring us back together. Only time will tell; one thing at a time.

I step out of the room, pull my phone out of my pocket, and dial up Greg. One ring and that fucker answers like he has been waiting. I'm not sure what to take from their relationship, but I am not happy with how close they seem.

"Is she okay?" he asks, and fuck me, he sounds wrecked.

No, not wrecked. He sounds destroyed.

"She will be. Told me about the ex. You did not tell me he fucking hurt her. You did not tell me a fucking thing about how bad it was, Greg. Problem husband not wanting a divorce—that is what you said. Can you imagine my shock when I find out he slapped her around?"

"Act like a bitch later, Reid. How is she?"

"That shit isn't finished with me and you, hear me that. She's changing. Keeping her here for tonight. Family meeting, motherfucker—my house, tomorrow morning." I should be glad she has someone determined to be her support but that is getting locked down. I am back and Greg isn't taking that job from me.

"She's sleeping there? You have one bed, Reid. I can be there in ten to take her home. I'll stay there until tomorrow when we can get together. Then we can reassess."

"No. End it, Greg. I will fight you and fight you hard on this one."

His harsh exhale comes over the line. "I don't like this, not one fucking bit. If you fuck her up, swear to fucking Christ, I will kill you."

I pull the phone away from my ear; surely I did not just hear him right.

"No time, Greg. We will talk, but right now, I have more important things to deal with. If you take anything from me right now, know this and remember...never would I harm a fucking hair on her head. Never."

"If you believe that, Reid, then you're more delusional than I thought. I guarantee you, just being there is hurting her enough to last a lifetime."

With that, I hear him hang up, leaving me more confused than I was earlier tonight.

CHAPTER 11
Izzy

IF I could stay inside this lush bathroom all night, I would. My heart feels like it's been torn from my body and trampled on. Gutted, completely gutted. It was hard enough to live through those years with Brandon, but I did and I have worked so hard to move on. Rehashing that with the one person who has always held my heart, the one person I thought was gone forever? The pain is unfathomable. Never in my wildest dreams did I believe Axel would be back in my life.

The severe torment of just knowing he has always been very much alive is what is weighing on me the hardest right now. I keep running through my head all the things I needed him by my side for. All the things I was forced to deal with alone.

When he asked me about the picture, my heart stopped. Right there in the middle of his room, it just stopped. I'm not under the delusion that Axel is back and mine. Oh, that ship has sailed. I held on to the smallest hope that he was out there somewhere, but I can't ignore the fact that he left me. He left me, and when he did that, he left his baby—the baby that I wasn't able to protect. Of course Brandon would know how hard that was for me. Not that he ever was willing to share me with any child we would have created, but he knew why I had so readily agreed never to have children. My baby is gone, just like its father, and that is something I will never share with him. He doesn't deserve to know, and if I'm honest with myself, I doubt he will care. After all, if he could so easily leave the person he professed to love so deeply, a child wouldn't change anything.

I make quick use of his bathroom. I take a brief shower, wincing when the hot water rolls over my sore nipples. I dry off quickly and pull on the soft tee that smells like Axel; it hits me all the way to my knees. Jesus, he wasn't this large when we were kids. He was tall but never so...solid. I don't even bother with the briefs. What's the point when I am already swimming in his tee? Running my fingers through my hair, I do a quick scan of his counter, look in some drawers, and hope for an extra toothbrush. Negative. Isn't that just wonderful. *Fuck it.* That asshole wants me here, might as well use his shit. After I finish brushing and giving myself one hell of a 'stay strong' mental lecture, out I walk.

Shit...shit, fuck.

There he is. Walking back into the room, all large and mouthwatering. I want to leave, run, and never look back.

"Which side?" The slight wobble in my voice is hardly noticeable, and I am mentally cheering myself for keeping such a brave face.

"Don't care. A bed's a bed." And with that, he walks into the bathroom and shuts the door.

Well—I guess that's that then.

Walking over to the side farthest away from the bathroom door, I make quick work snapping the lights off, and diving into the sheets, and burrowing down. Naturally, my luck would be to pick the side he must sleep on. I feel like I have dived into an Axel-scented cloud.

With just the hint of his scent, I can feel the memories slamming back, fast and fierce. Biting my lip as hard as I can without drawing blood, I squeeze my eyes shut, running through every single mental exercise I know to try and jump this massive hurdle.

The past can't touch me.

I am stronger than this.

I am a survivor.

Fuck you, fate... Fuck you hard.

After a few minutes of listening to the shower and my inner chants, the stress of the week and the events of the day finally drag me under. Not long after that, the bed dips, and in my dreams, I smile, because I hear a soft whisper. "Missed you...so fucking much, Princess." Sometimes, dreams don't let you down because that is the only thing I have been waiting to hear since the day he left me forever. In my dreams, all my problems melt away, because I am safe. Safe and back in Axel's arms.

Axel

I WALK out of the bathroom—after spending a fucking stupid amount of time in the shower taking care of the problem Izzy has stirred up—and just stand there, water still dripping down my chest, disappearing when it reaches the towel tightly knotted around my waist.

Izzy is back in my bed. *Fuck me.* A weight that has been sitting solid on my shoulders for way too long lightens up. Not by much but damn, anything is a relief. I should have known if she ever walked back into my life that I wouldn't be able to hold on to all of my anger.

I walk around my side of the bed to get a closer look at the tiny ball under my sheets. And there it is—that face that can bring me to my knees. She looks so peaceful in her sleep, her hands folded under her cheek and her hair fanned out against my pillow. Like an angel, my Princess.

We have missed so much, wasted so much time. Even though I know how much we still have to work out, including the small detail of reminding her she is mine, I still can't fight the instantaneous contentment that washes over me.

I feel whole again.

I know better than to hope but I can't help the thought that I would stop anything from taking her from me again.

Walking back over to the other side, I drop the towel and climb in. She makes a small whimper in her sleep that has me throwing caution to the wind and shifting to wrap her in my arms.

"Missed you...so fucking much, Princess."

And with Izzy back in my arms, pressed tight with no gap between our bodies, I finally find sleep.

Izzy

THE FIRST thing I notice when I start to wake up the next morning is how unbelievably warm I am. Finally, Dee is listening to me when I tell her we can't keep bumping the AC down to artic temps. I nestle in, wiggling and trying to find that perfect spot that will take me back to the blissful sleep I was just in. That wiggle is all it takes for me to become wide awake and all that warmth to wash away, leaving me frozen solid.

There is a large hand covering my very tender breast and soft breathing tickling my neck. That warmth I was loving a second ago is kicking my ass, almost quite literally. I can feel the solid, very naked wall of muscle and strength against my back, fitting like a glove tight against my body. I try to pull my legs up but they are tangled with larger hairy ones. The biggest—and I mean biggest—issue I seem to have right now is the large erection poking me, settled right against my pussy. And all that wiggling, all that searching I was doing for the warmth in my sleep? All that did was cause me to drip with desire.

Cracking one eye open, I take in the room. My trip around the large master starts with one tall dresser and ends with a pile of laundry on the floor next to it. Other than that, empty. Looking down at the offending arm that holds me tight to its owner's body, I try to think of a way out of this hold. He has his arm snaked up my shirt, cupping my breast tightly like it's his anchor. Shifting, I try to dislodge him naturally but all I get is a tightening of his hand and arm and pressure pulling me even snugger against his body.

Blast my stupid hormones. His rock-hard erection just jutted even deeper between my legs, hitting my clit with a sharp jab.

I suck in a sharp breath of pure pleasure.

Oh my God. I need to get him away from me.

I slam my elbow back, earning a grunt and more tightening.

Shit! Just my luck. My body is telling me to start humping, my heart is telling me to run, and my mind is sitting there enjoying a cigarette as his hips start to move against me.

"Axel Reid, you wake up right now!" I yell. "Get your paws off my tit and call your dick off its search for my pussy. He found it, asshole. Now back off."

"Urmmpf…"

That's all I get. Nothing. He pulls me back again. Only this time, I have the added bonus of some whiskers against my neck and some humming. If he has a wet dream against my body, I might kill him.

"AXEL!"

"Shut up, Izzy. I'm trying to enjoy this." Wide awake. That jackass is wide awake, not even a small sliver of sleep left in his voice.

I move to pull away, grinding my hips against his dick again, not even able to keep the moan silent. Finally, after a small struggle to detangle my legs and push his arm away, I am free. I scoot all the way over to the edge and jump off the bed. I turn, ready to ream him a new one, but stop dead. Mouth drops and I am drooling, I'm sure of it.

Perfection. He's lying against his stark white sheets, all large and solid. He has one thick arm thrown over his eyes and one resting against his perfectly sculpted abdomen. Both of his arms are sporting some thick tribal tattoo that wrap around both shoulders and around the front of his chest. He has a large angel against his side with her hands brought forward in prayer and her wings wrapping around to his back. I can't see her face clearly, but from here I can tell it is a beautiful piece. My eyes travel down and see some more ink disappearing under the sheet riding low on his hips. The thin sheet is doing nothing to hide the tenting from his erection. Long, solid, strong, and very aroused.

He moves his arms and his bright emerald eyes meet my startled ones. I do one more sweep of his body before looking back and meeting his questioning look.

"Holy shit, what happened to you?" I praise. At least it should have sounded like a praise, but it came out more like a weak whimper.

He gives a soft laugh, which just makes all those lickable muscles clench. *I want to lick them so badly.* "You talking about the ink or the body? Hit a growth spell, grew a little. Work out hard. My body is my protection so I can't slack. Nothing much has changed."

He has got to be joking, "Nothing much has changed?" I echo him. "You look like you gained fifty or more pounds of solid muscle, maybe a few inches, because I do not remember you looking like *that.*

And yeah, well…the tattoos are definitely new."

"Things change when you go from a kid to a man, Izzy. I'm still me."

"I don't know about that. And you're right. Things change. You might be you, but I am damn sure not the me I was." I dig deep to collect my thoughts—and my brain off the floor. "I don't have anything to wear and I would like to get ready to go home now." There, that should close the conversation up real quick.

"Yeah, avoid. Got it. Dresser—grab some sweats and a new tee. I'll meet you downstairs." He is so quick that I don't have a second to turn as he whips the sheet off, displaying his body completely and rendering me even more speechless.

Not much changed, my ass. Looks like his few inches weren't just in his height. With heavy steps and a tense body, he walks into his closet and slams the door. I run to the dresser and then enter the bathroom to get dressed.

Thirty minutes later, I make my way down the long hall and stairs, searching for the kitchen. It shouldn't be too difficult, but this house is huge, and judging by the smells, breakfast is cooking. I make a few wrong turns and only find more empty space. He must have just moved in last weekend; there is absolutely nothing here.

Rounding the corner, I finally walk into the kitchen. Axel is standing next to the island stove flipping some bacon. The eggs are already dished off to the side and some orange juice fills in a cup next to the stool.

"Sit and eat. Greg and the gang should be here within the hour." He leaves no room for argument, just gives me a cold stare and throws some bacon on my plate before fixing himself some food, and leaning his hip against the island, and digging in.

We sit like that, in silence, while we finish up. He doesn't even look at me. Not one time does he even glance my way. I should be comforted by this but I would be lying if I said it doesn't bother me that he is able to turn everything off. Try as I might, having him this close to me again is messing with my mind. I just want to run into his arms and let everything just wash away, forget the world.

Clearing my throat, I break the silence. "So, what happens now?

I would really like to go home."

"Told you last night, we would discuss where to go with every-one else. You will go home when we figure out what happens next. Don't take this lightly, Iz. We might not know why he sent that, but it was for a reason. My job is to find out why and what kind of threat, if any, it holds on you."

"Hmph…" I'm beyond frustrated. All I want to do is go home and hide from my problems—and from Axel. The last thing I want is for him to be a permanent fixture in my life. I just have to hope Greg and Dee can keep quiet about everything else they know that Axel doesn't.

I am still silently stressing over what would happen if Axel finds out everything else when a door slams and heavy steps echo through-out the house. If Axel's relaxed body language hadn't stayed the same, I might be concerned. This must be the cavalry arriving.

"Yo, Reid. Where you at?" voice one booms through the house.

"I'm fucking starved, Coop. Reid better have some food this time," voice two says.

"Too early for this shit. My head is still swimming from being up all night buried balls deep in Jasmine. Or was it Jane? Judy?" voice three grumbles.

"Shut up, asshole." Greg—I'd know that voice anywhere. I look up when Axel slams his plate into the sink and gives a hard look to the open doorway.

It is the soft giggling after Greg's voice that has me snapping my head up and staring right along with him. *Dee?* What is she doing here?

Dee pushes through first and immediately rushes over to wrap her slim arms around me. "You okay?"

"I will be. I just want to leave."

"Soon, Iz. You have to trust these guys. I know that won't be easy but they know what they're doing," she whispers in my ear.

"How are you even here? Didn't Greg take you home last night?"

She pulls back and looks away, but not before I catch the blush that dances across her skin. What the hell is that about?

"You two done with your female shit? We need to talk."

I look up to Axel's stormy green eyes and frown. "Remember this little tea party was your idea. Don't get a stick up your ass because you got your demands answered."

The group behind me lets out a few manly grunts, either in humor or shock that I would snap at the bear. I look over at this testosterone-driven group, avoiding Greg's face but not missing the small upturn of his lips. Coop and Beck are doing their best to not laugh while Locke looks like he has better things to do, but I don't miss the mirth dancing in his dark eyes.

"Shut up, Izzy. This isn't a fucking game. Locke, you find out where the ex is?"

"Yeah, California, business convention or some shit. The chippie secretary told me he left out Wednesday afternoon with his new girlfriend. Doesn't seem to have a care in the world."

"What?" I ask, "Really, he can't sign the divorce papers but he can keep his bed warm?" No one answers me, but then again, an answer isn't really needed.

"Coop, background check back?" Axel continues.

"Clean. Few parking tickets but nothing serious. Looks like he had some issues with fighting in high school but wasn't anything past college. Credit card debt sitting at a nice 65K." He looks over at me with sympathy before continuing. "Escorts, there was some small gambling, but most of it is racked up in escorts and some local strip joints."

That throws me for a loop. As much of an asshole Brandon was, he was always there and always controlling. How did I not even know about this side of him?

"Beck, anything?" Axel asks, his tone harsher than before.

"Not much. Talked to a few people who will do more digging for me locally. If it's there, I will find it."

What? "What are you talking about?" I direct my question to Beck, figuring my luck for an answer would be better with him.

"Nothing, sugar. Nothing for you to worry about." He has a smile on his face, but it isn't masking the seriousness in his posture.

"Ah, no. This is my life and I don't want to be kept in the dark. Do not expect me to be okay with you just brushing me off." My temper is starting to rise, and even though I know these men mean well, I can't stand not knowing and not having just a little control.

"Izzy, look at me," Axel says. "Trust me to take care of this and not burden you with the unnecessary issues. I promise not to keep important information from you."

"NO, Axel. You want me to just let you play this white knight role with no issues? What the fuck ever. Too late for that shit. The only reason I'm here right now is because YOU wouldn't take me home last night. I'm not stupid, and I recognize that you are the best to figure out this situation, but I won't go at it blind. Every damn step, I want to know everything or I will go at it alone." I'm right up in his space, jamming my finger in his chest with as much strength as I can throw into that small jab.

Rubbing his chest and stepping away, he says, "Jesus Christ, you are a pain in my ass. Beck is checking with some local cops to see what they know about Brandon. Nothing for you to worry about. Pulling a few favors and asking some locals to keep an eye on his goings."

"And what are you expecting to find?" I ask, not sure I like where this is going.

"Not sure yet. With the money and the women, my guess would be drugs or at least something like that. I want every play I have in my hands before I go chat with this fucker."

"What the hell are you talking about? Why would you go talk to him?"

Dee reaches over and grabs my hand. For the first time since this conversation started, I remember she is there.

"You want a divorce and you want him to leave you alone, right?" he asks.

"I think that would be pretty obvious."

"Well, I talk and get you your divorce and also ensure he leaves you alone. Pretty simple."

"I don't think so. I go through my lawyers for that, not you." The last thing I want is for Brandon and Axel to be around each other. I had a few pictures of Axel when Brandon and I first started dating. He might look different now, but it wouldn't take Brandon much to realize who he was, and that would not end well.

"We'll see, Izzy. Leave it alone for now." He gives me another hard look before brushing me off and looking back over to the group standing in the kitchen. "Greg, tell me about the set-up at her house."

"Full system with every upgrade. There is no getting into her house without her wanting you there...when she sets the damn thing." The last part is said with its usual frustration over me never remembering to set the alarm when I am home.

"Damn it, look at me, Izzy." I look back into his eyes. "I'm going to let that slide, for now, and only because this shit just started, but from now on, you set it. When you leave, when you come, when you are there, it is fully armed. No questions."

"Whatever..." I mumble. I know he's right. Doesn't mean I have to be nice about it.

The conversation continues around me. Axel dishes out more duties and they talk about the next step in getting Brandon out of my life. It seems to be agreed upon that I need to push stronger on the divorce and see if that can't end the connection. I have been pushing as strongly as I can, so that gets tossed out quickly. Finally, Axel says that someone needs to personally go talk to Brandon about signing.

"No, not happening," I say, cutting off Beck, who is about to reply to Axel. "Let the lawyers handle this. I'm not asking for anything. The only thing I need is for him to sign."

"Baby girl, he hasn't signed in six months. What makes you think he will just automatically wake up in the morning and sign?" Greg asks.

"Shut up, Greg," I spit back at him.

He flinches but recovers quickly.

"I'm serious, Axel. You are not going to talk to him." I hold his eyes until he breaks contact and looks over at Maddox.

"Fine," he spits out before looking over at Maddox. "Book a flight and go visit this asshole. Get the fucking signature. Whatever you need to do, and take Coop with you." He looks back at me and, with an arrogant tone, asks, "Is that okay with you, Princess?"

"I hate you," I spit back at him, earning me a laugh.

God, this is going to be a nightmare.

I look over at Dee and motion her over. Time to find out why she is here.

"Well...spill," I whisper in her ear.

"Nothing to spill," she says with a bright blush sparkling her cheeks. "Beck and I had some fun last night. No big deal."

I knew it! "Oh, we will be talking about this later. I can't believe you, Dee! Do you even know anything about him?"

"Come on, Iz. It was just some fun—not going to happen again. He is one of those anti-relationship men. Fine by me. I was just looking to let out some stress anyway. And you need to let up on these guys. They aren't the enemy, Izzy. Please let them do their jobs." She lets out a huff of exasperation before walking back over to the group and throwing in some suggestions.

What in the hell is going on?

CHAPTER 12

I T'S BEEN a little over two months since Axel barged in on me at the tattoo parlor. Two months of his constant hovering and throwing his demanding bullshit in my face. I am sick of it; he's been annoying me every single day. Nothing else has happened with Brandon, and the biggest shock of all was getting a call Friday morning telling me that he signed. I am officially a divorced woman.

Finally.

Maddox and Zeke, or 'Locke and Coop' if you ask the men, went back to visit Brandon Monday. They came back and said that they had no issues and Brandon seemed nice enough, agreeing he needed to sign the papers. Agreeing? What a joke. I don't know what they did to push this along, but I am thrilled it is over.

Maddox and Beck have become pretty permanent fixtures at Dee's and my house. Beck is there for obvious reasons, and they all start and end with Dee. Little hussy. Maddox and I have struck up an odd friendship. I can tell he doesn't let people in often, but for some reason he chose to let me past his stoic exterior. For whatever reason, he seems to need the friendship as much as I do. I am starting to learn all his moods, and he can tell right when I need a good calm-down. Bottom line, he is a good friend and a wonderful distraction. Plus, having him around as the 'protector' is the perfect excuse for why I don't need Axel around.

Greg and I haven't spoken much since his role in the 'Axel abduction.' I miss him but I can't seem to be in the same room without flipping my shit all over him. He, out of everyone, knew why I was avoiding Axel but decided to take matters into his own hands. Deep down I know he meant well, but I'm not ready to forget how easy he turned on me. Having Maddox around has another plus when it comes to Greg; Maddox doesn't play well with others, even his 'brothers.' If I get upset, Maddox turns into a grizzly. I have been so used to only having Dee and Greg that it is almost refreshing to have another person I can trust in my life.

It is Saturday morning, and November is in full Georgia force, and we have a nice cold, rainy day on our hands. I call Maddox to see if he wants to come over and watch some football, drink some beer, and celebrate my newfound singlehood. Dee has already been to the store and bought a cake, streamers, and freaking balloons. I think she might be more excited than I am. I haven't heard from Axel since earlier in the week when he called to let me know he was going to be out of town and to let him know if anything happened. No chance in that.

Maddox shows up early in the afternoon with one of his rare smiles in place. Dee lets him in and he wastes no time coming to congratulate me.

"Hey, girl. Happy?" Leave it to him. All it takes is those three words for me to let the water works flow.

"Oh. My. God." I get out between broken sobs. "It's over, Mad. Can you believe it? The last eight years of my life are done with just one signature. Freedom. Do you know how long I prayed to be free from Brandon?"

"Yeah, I get you, girl. No more worries." He wraps his strong arms around me and just lets me let it out. Tears of relief, joy, and maybe a whole lot of shock.

I don't know how long we just sit there. Words aren't necessary because he just gets it. He knows I need to let this out in order to move on and completely let the pain of my marriage die. After I am done using his shoulder as a tissue, I look up and meet his normal blank face, expecting to find annoyance but instead get a smirk before he throws his head back and laughs. That is another Maddox moment that doesn't happen often.

"Girl, you look like a drowned raccoon. All that black shit you chicks use is all over your face. Go clean up before I'm forced to call animal control to come take your ass."

I throw a pillow off the couch in his face before leaving the living room and going to clean myself up. I hear him click the TV on and the game day broadcast takes over the silence. Walking into the hallway, I almost jump out of my skin when I nearly collide with a damp-faced Dee.

"He really is a big softy under that 'don't touch me' vibe, isn't he?" she asks.

"Don't let him hear you say that, but yeah. He's been great these last few weeks."

"I'm so happy this is over. I know I haven't been around much, but you know I'm here if you need me." She looks so guilty, and even thought I know she means well, it breaks my heart.

"Dee, don't you dare feel bad about having a life. I'm good, really. I feel good and I haven't been alone. Mad's been around and Coop comes sometimes. Plus you're here...even if it's holed up in your room shaking the walls with Beck." I walk away leaving her red faced but laughing.

"Love you, you stupid bitch!" she yells after me.

The alarm has beeped a few times while I was in the bathroom getting cleaned up, signaling that someone has opened and shut the front door a few times. Assuming that it is either Beck or Coop, I just brush it off and continue to get ready. I throw off my yoga pants and tank, switching them out for some worn jeans and my favorite University of Georgia tee—game day gear, a must for any Georgia fan. My face is clear of all black tracks under my eyes and down my cheeks from my crying fit earlier. I am just pulling up my long hair in a ponytail when a deep voice clears his throat behind me, causing me to jump about a mile out of my body.

"Baby girl, can we please talk?"

"Not if you plan on dragging me down, Greg. Today is not the day to do this. We're celebrating."

"Izzy, you know how much it hurt to hear the asshole finally signed from Locke? He's known you a few months and you tell him first? Every step of the way, Izzy, I've been here for everything and you didn't even call me."

"Okay, you want to do this? Fine. I am pissed, Greg. You went behind my back and called him. You not only called him but you might as well have thrown a fucking bat signal into the air and beamed his ass right into the shop. How could you? How fucking could you?"

He bows his head and lets out a long sigh. "Do you know what it's like to sit back and watch someone you love turn into themself? You were headed back to that fucked-up hole you always push yourself in. Don't think I did that lightly, Izzy. Not for one second. You avoided talking about shit to me and Dee and ran around God's green earth to stay busy enough so you didn't have to deal with the shit in your life. We were worried. Worried about that shit Brandon was pulling, but mostly worried about how you were handling Axel showing back up. Don't think I didn't know the real reason you ran. And you know as well as I do, if I hadn't forced your hand, you would still be running today."

"It wasn't your decision to make, G. It was mine, and by forcing my hand, you took my control, the one thing I have fought to regain in my life. If that wasn't enough, you forced him on me. I just don't know if I can forget that so easily. I can forgive you because, even pissed as hell, I know you wouldn't hurt me, but you knew—you fucking *knew*—how hard that was going to be on me. I wanted that meeting on my terms when I was ready." It's hard to keep eye contact with him because he has started pacing around my room. Surefire sign that Greg is frustrated and worried.

"I'm sorry. I'm fucking sorry. I don't know what to say other than that. You're my family, and given the chance, I would do it all over again if it were the best move to help you. Axel aside, that shit with Brandon was fucked up and you needed all the power behind you that you could get if he tried something else. The only thing I regret was upsetting you."

I hate fighting with Greg. This is by far the worst, and to be honest, not having him around is hard. He is my rock. Maddox is becoming just as important, but no one can replace what Greg means to me.

"I get it, I do. It hurts, but I can see where you were coming from." I get up and walk into his open arms. "No more fighting, okay? But don't pull that shit again."

"Alright, baby girl. No more fighting."

"Come on. Kickoff should be soon and if you make me miss that you're watching the game somewhere else."

Laughing, he follows me out of the room, almost knocking me to the ground when I reach the living room and stop dead in my tracks.

"What the hell are you doing here?" I ask the man relaxing on my couch, feet propped up on the coffee table with a beer in hand.

"Well, hello to you too, Princess. Coop called, said he would be over here watching the game with Locke. Joined along. Didn't think you would mind." Cocky, arrogant asshole. He is just daring me to throw a fit and kick him out.

"You're a dick, you know that, Axel Reid? Shut up and get your feet off my table." I kick his feet off the table when I walk past, only earning me a deep laugh before he props them right back up. "Get them down, asshole," I grumble under my breath as I continue my way into the kitchen to grab the food and a beer.

Coop and Maddox are standing around the island when I walk in. I get a small smirk from Maddox before walking over to Coop and smacking him on the side of the head. "Ass. You do not invite him here."

Maddox gives a boom of laughter before grabbing the tray of taco dip and walking back into the living room. "Girl, he probably didn't even feel that with his hard head."

"Shut up, Mad." I smile at his retreating back before throwing another scowl at Coop. "Jerk."

I grab the chips and a few beers before walking back in, just in time for kickoff. Dee and Beck are cozied up on the loveseat against the far wall. Greg and Coop have taken the recliners, leaving Maddox and Axel sitting on the couch with one empty spot between the two of them.

"You have got to be kidding me. Sit on the floor, asshat." I try to give Axel the mean, hard look Maddox is always sporting, but apparently I lack the conviction.

"You look like you need to take a shit, Princess. I won't bite... unless you want me to." His evil, arrogant smirk and that cocky twinkle light his emerald eyes up.

I can play this game. I can act like being in the same room with his handsome self isn't ripping me apart. Easy, right?

"Don't you know? I prefer it hard and rough now, Axel. But you keep your teeth and everything else to yourself."

That wipes his face clear. No more look of male giant ego and arrogant pride. Nope, he wasn't going to get the upper hand on me.

Dee and Beck are too into each other to notice the tension in the room. Greg looks concerned, Coop looks like he might laugh at any moment, and Maddox is just looking at the TV but I can tell he wants to speak up. I just plop down as close as I can to Maddox without sitting in his lap and ignore Axel as long as I can.

The third quarter is just wrapping up when the doorbell rings. I wave off Dee and head off to the door, noticing a little too late how lightheaded I am. I have been throwing back beer after beer for the last hour, not eating much because I am still holding on to my snit about Axel being in the house. Walking around the corner of the living room and down the short entryway, I can hear the loud cheers and male grunting signaling another touchdown as I reach the door. This better be good.

As I swing open the door, it takes my beer-filled mind a second to register who is standing on my porch. When I do, my first reaction is to shut the door. Serves me right not checking the peephole. But when I go to shut it, I'm met with the resistance of his foot.

Before I can even get a shout or scream past my terrified lips, he reaches in and pulls me outside, closes the door, and pushes me back. My back meets the frame of the door hard, causing me to let out a small grunt of pain. He closes his hand around my neck and squeezes, cutting off my air supply and keeping my cries for help from escaping.

"Hello, Isabelle. You think you can get rid of me that easily? Look at what your boyfriend did to my face!"

His nose has a bandage over the bridge, clearly holding the broken bone together. His eyes are both bruised and blackened and his lip has a small cut in the corner. If I weren't so scared, I would smile. Finally Brandon has had a taste of his own medicine.

"Don't think I don't know who he is either, Isabelle. You talked about him enough for me to know exactly who he was when I opened the door. You think you can threaten me? Tell my father and the board about my little extracurricular activities? I don't think so, Isabelle. And if you know what's good for you, you will call off the trashy animals sniffing around in my business. You got your papers signed, but hear me, you will always be mine. Call them off. Now." He looks raging mad, so close to my face that the spit from his whispered words hits my face. I have no idea what he is talking about. "Answer me, bitch. You will be telling them to leave me alone, you understand?" he forces out, again spraying me with his spit.

I claw at his hand, trying to get him to loosen up his hold; I can feel my lungs burning, demanding oxygen. My nails are clawing his hands and wrist, trying desperately to get some air. My lack of being able to breathe must have missed the mark with Brandon, his rage blinding him from his actions. My vision is getting black around the edges, but not before I see him pull his arm back and bring his fist racing forward, meeting my right eye with unbearable pain. My head hits the doorframe, sending another wave of stomach-rolling pain shooting through my head. He releases my neck and throws me down onto the porch, standing over my body with his feet on either side of my stomach. He leans down and whispers in my ear, "I will be in touch, Isabelle, but you tell those motherfuckers to stop fucking coming around and asking questions. I did what your *boyfriend* said and signed those papers, but I don't need those fucking *papers* to prove who you belong to. You fucking hear me, bitch? You are mine. I will fucking kill him if he touches you. Got that? I'll be keeping an eye on you, Isabelle." He gets off another punch to my right eye, finally releasing the scream that was trapped moments ago. Then he's gone. The amount of pain my body feels is the only think keeping me from thinking I just dreamt this whole thing.

I can feel them from my position on the porch floor running inside the house. The front door is pulled open and strong hands lift me up. I wince in pain when my back meets a solid arm.

"What the fuck!" Greg, I think, says from somewhere behind me.

"Oh my God, Izzy! She's bleeding, oh my God!" Dee screeches from the same direction.

My vision is blurry. I can only make out that the person holding me is male. If it weren't for the deep scent of leather and cinnamon, I wouldn't have known it is Axel who is holding me so tenderly.

"Coop, Locke, go fucking find that motherfucker before he gets away," he grates out, his tone lethal. "Someone call the god damn police. Now! Princess, are you hurt anywhere else other than your head?"

"Neck." Gasp. "Back." Wheeze. "It was... Brandon...was here." I can't make out his expression, my right eye is throbbing and swollen shut. I can't even open my left eye because the movement causes more excruciating pain to blast through my skull like lightning. Belatedly, I feel what must be warm blood running down the back of my neck.

The arms holding me go rock hard at the mention of Brandon. Not what he was expecting to hear. But then again, he wasn't exactly planning on football Saturday turning into this mess.

"Here, hold this," Greg says, placing something over the back of my head.

Axel adjusts his hold on me and stands from his crouched position on the porch. I can feel him walking through the house to the living room. I can hear the sounds of people moving around the room. Axel sits down on the couch but doesn't release me.

"Sit up, Princess. Let's take a look at your back, yeah?"

He helps me lean forward, making my stomach lurch, and I feel warm hands moving up my shirt.

"Fuck!" Greg yells. "How the fuck did this happen? You've got welts all the way up your spine, Iz!"

I don't answer, because really, what's the point? I think it's pretty obvious how I got like this.

I can hear the sirens approaching, making me snuggle closer to the safety Axel's strong arms are providing. Just when I think I am finally free... What a joke that was. I'm beginning to think I won't ever be free of Brandon's reach.

Dee is directing the police officers and the paramedics into the living room. I can hear Greg off to the side somewhere talking in low tones with Maddox answering back. I can't tell where anyone else is, and I'm in no hurry to open my eyes and check.

"Ma'am." A new voice joins the group. "Ma'am can you open your eyes?" Axel shifts and moves me away from his warmth, placing my body in a way that allows this person to start touching my face. Immediately, I draw back into his body.

"Shhh, Izzy, let them look at you." His warm breath tickles my ear and his arm tightens around my shoulders, reminding me that he is here and I'm safe. His head turns from my ear and he addresses the new voice. "I don't think she can open her eyes without pain. She tried a second after I reached her but they snapped shut quickly. Hasn't opened since. Her breathing sounds raspy and her voice seemed hoarse when she was able to talk. Hasn't spoken since. Her back has what looks like a welt-like bruise from tailbone to shoulder blades. I haven't been able to take a good look at it. Neck injury, and the source of the blood is from the back of her head. Again, I haven't taken a good look." He must be speaking to the paramedic, because when he finishes, I feel soft gloved hands start pressing into my face, around my neck, and up my throat.

"Ma'am, I need to lean you forward a bit so that I can look over your back and head slowly, and let me know if you feel like you're—" He doesn't get a chance to finish before I empty the contents of my stomach all over the floor.

"Okay, that's okay. Do you feel nauseated?"

"Y-yes," I answer back, again not recognizing my own voice. I sound like I've spent the last few hours screaming.

"Did you hit your head?"

"No...yes," I whisper my reply, "I don't remember. I was pushed into the doorframe before he grabbed my neck. I don't remember much after that."

"That's okay. Let's check you out right now, okay?"

His soft hands spend a few minutes taking my blood pressure before they continue to press and poke around my tender skin, earning a few hisses of pain from me and growls from Axel. They have me lean forward again, moving my hair around to check out the source of the bleeding, and then he checks my back. I can feel the torn skin on my back stretching and pulling tight with every small movement of my body.

"Sir, I can't be sure without taking her to the hospital, but I'm willing to bet on a concussion. The head wound definitely needs stitches. Her back is troubling, but again, I can't guarantee the damage done is only on the surface. That isn't even counting her facial injuries. I would strongly advise a trip to the hospital."

"That's fine, but I'll be driving her. I'm not letting her out of my sight."

Even I can tell by his tone that there will be no bending on this.

The poor guy trying to do his job attempts to explain to him that I would be completely safe riding in the ambulance but there is no use. Axel and all his stubbornness have spoken and there will only be one way for me to get to the hospital tonight.

Begrudgingly, he stops his protest and asks Axel to sign off that no further treatment by the paramedics is preferred. He gets my head cleaned and applies some gauze to my back, telling Axel that he needs to keep pressure on my head until I get to the hospital. I get a few ice packs and hold one to my right eye and the other to my sore neck. After he has done all he can, the paramedics take their leave.

I start nodding off shortly after, listening to the voices around me explain the events leading up to my crying out from the porch. I attempt to answer the questions the officers have for me but my drowsy and confused mind keeps pulling me under. Axel rouses me a few times and I am able to tell them who attacked me, but after falling asleep again, I faintly hear Axel tell them to meet us at the hospital with any further questions. Despite his calm and strong tone, I can hear a small tremor of fear.

He adjusts me in his arms and begins to stand. I don't hear much after he tells telling someone to get the truck and drive him to the hospital. I let the safety of his strong arms and the comforting scent that only comes with Axel carry me off to the numbing blackness.

I wake up to the annoying sound of beeping and the nauseating smell of antiseptic and cleaner. Death—I've always thought the hospital smelled like death. It's a smell you never forget and one I have always hated.

I try to open my eyes but they don't obey my commands. I try to open my mouth and demand answers but nothing comes out. It's like my body has decided to play dead.

"The doctor says there are no internal injuries other than some bruising and a lot of old broken bones badly reset. Home job the best he can tell. I looked at the scans, Reid. It looked like she has had every rib in her body broken at one point. I would gladly kill that motherfucker if I got my hands on him." Coop. I've never heard him sound so pissed. He's usually the fun-loving one of the group. "Took ten stitches to close up her head, nothing too bad and should be fine.

Her neck is swollen. Fucker must have had one hell of a firm grip on her. The biggest concern at this point is her concussion and assessing her vision after she wakes up."

The warm hand holding mine flexes and tightens a few times during my grocery list of injuries review. Even with my eyes closed and my mind hazy, I can feel the energy in the room grow heavy. It feels alive, making the hairs on my arms and neck stand on end.

"He's fucking dead, you hear me? I'll kill that sick fuck myself." Axel releases my hand and I feel it return, pushing the hair back behind my ear. "It guts me to know she lived like this for so many years. Knowing this wasn't even close to the worst…slices me fucking deep."

"I know, Reid."

"Where's Dee, Greg? Both—either. I don't care." He must have his head turned because it's hard to make out his question. I'm shocked that Dee isn't already by my side.

"Beck made her go get something to eat, said she wouldn't stop pacing and was shaking something crazy. Last I saw Greg, he was about to pop some hemorrhoids he was holding it in so tight. You sure there isn't more there? They seem pretty tight."

"Just friends," he says. "Doesn't matter. He isn't touching her."

His hand returns to mine and he brings his lips down for one small kiss to my hand. So tender and unlike the Axel I've been dealing with for the last month.

"I feel you. I'm going to step out and see what Locke found."

A few minutes pass. He has his forehead resting on my hip, his lips resting on our joined hands. I can feel his mouth moving, warm breath caressing my skin, but I can't make out his whispered words.

"Izzy, please wake up. Please, please, Princess." I don't know what shocks me more, his gentle pleading or the single warm tear that hits my hand.

I don't know how long we pass time just like that. A few of the others come and go asking Axel some questions, asking if he wants to leave and take a break. The cops come to see if I've woken up yet. Nurses come and check my IV bags and vitals. All the while, I am struggling to make my body listen, to wake up.

Dee is back in the room, and I think Beck and Greg are too.

To my horror, they are discussing the abuse I lived. I can hear Dee explaining to Axel what happened that night she came to save me, telling him how long I was forced to stay in the hospital to heal and how much worse the injuries were then.

"Jesus fucking Christ," I hear Axel say when she tells him how many broken bones I had then. He starts to speak but stops short when I finally force a whisper past my lips.

"Dee..."

"Oh God," she cries out before rushing over to my side. I crack open my left eye and take in her face. She's a mess, mascara running down her cheeks, her eyes red rimmed and swollen. With just the sound of my voice, she is a blubbering fool. "Oh, Iz...I was so scared!"

"Okay, I'm...okay."

I look around the room and notice that it isn't just Dee, Beck, and Greg Axel was speaking to. Maddox and Coop are standing off to the side, faces set in stone. When I meet Axel's eyes, they are bright and full of compassion.

"Hey, Princess." That's all it takes for me to join Dee in a fit of hysterical crying.

The nurses come in shortly after and start checking all the machines, poking around my body, changing the dressing on my head, and applying some ointment to my right eye. A doctor who looks like he is well past time for retirement comes in next and attempts to clear the room to discuss my injuries, but Axel puts his foot down again and refuses to budge. The fight would be futile, so I just shake my head and wait for the doctor to go over everything.

"Ms. West," he begins, looking over at Axel with worry. He must assume that he is the reason for my injuries. "How are you feeling?"

Even though I know it's going to hurt like a bitch, I can't hold back the laugh that bubbles up.

"Like I was hit by a truck, thrown a few feet, then run over by a bus."

"Well. This is no joking matter, Ms. West. I understand that you had an altercation late yesterday evening?" Did he just say *yesterday*?

"Um...yes. Yes, sir. My ex-husband."

"Right. I'm going to let you go home later this afternoon. I was assured by your roommate, Ms. Roberts, that you will be monitored and she will return you to the emergency room with any signs of concern. She has the list of what to watch out for. You need to keep your head dry for the next forty-eight hours. After washing your hair, dry as best as you can. Your back needs ointment applied every six hours. Keep the open wounds covered and watch for signs of infection. I've given her all the prescriptions for your home care. Antibiotics, as well as some pain medication. Do you have any questions?" Obviously Grandpa doesn't specialize in bedside cheer.

"No, sir."

"Ms. Roberts has already signed all of your discharge paperwork. Try to be more careful in the future, Ms. West." That earns a low growl from Axel. I squeeze his hand to make sure he keeps his mouth shut.

Five hours later, I am being wheeled out to the entrance and loaded up into Axel's monster truck. Dee has already left with Beck and Greg to go get my medication filled. Maddox and Coop climb into the back and we head off, away from the disgusting smell of death.

A few minutes down the road, I realize we aren't headed in the right direction of my house. "Axel, where are you going?" I roll my head to the side with the help of the backrest and look over at him with my one good eye.

"My house," he replies as calm as can be.

"I don't want to fight with you, Ax. Please take me home. Dee can take care of me just fine."

"Not taking you back there, Princess. Not until I know that fucker is no threat."

"Take me home, Ax. Please. Just take me home." Tears start to prickle against my lids. If I had the energy, I would probably be throwing my attitude all over the cab of his truck.

"No." That's all I get in return.

"Axel. Take me home. Now."

"Izzy, get me now, that motherfucker walked up to your door. Walked right up. There were three trucks in the driveway, not to mention Maddox's bike right up against the walkway. He walked right up to your door like there wasn't a problem in his life, attacked you right under our noses." He is gripping the steering wheel so tight I start to worry he might snap it right off. "I will not send you back into a house that he has no fear of strolling right up to and risk him put his hands on you again. No, not fucking happening." He looks over at me and his eyes are blazing, his nostrils are flaring, and I can see the blood pounding through his veins. He looks like a rabid beast. "Never again will I allow you to be harmed when I can do something about it, so pitch your fit another time."

"Please..."

That earns me another harsh snap of his neck and death glare. "NO!" he booms.

I sigh deeply. "Maddox?"

"Yeah, girl?" His grumbled response comes from behind me.

"Take me with you, please?"

He pauses for a second and I can feel the vibes coming off Axel go from pissed to nuclear. "Yeah, girl."

"Thanks, Mad."

"Fuck!" Axel bites out, slamming his fist against the wheel. "We will have words later, Locke."

Other than Coop's soft laughter, the rest of the ride back to Axel's is passed in tense silence.

CHAPTER 13

I'VE BEEN at Maddox's apartment for two days now. When we first got here, he set me up in the guest room and spent the night watching stupid reality TV with me. He helps me keep my wounds clean and dressed and makes sure I take my medication when needed. Surprisingly, he is a great nurse. What I hadn't expected was the late-night screaming waking me up from his room. I know he has demons, but I didn't realize they were this bad. It was almost like we have an unspoken pact not to speak of his late-night terror.

Axel has been a daily guest as well. He isn't happy about losing control of the situation, but I'm not sure I can handle being in his space for so long. Coop and Beck left to drive back to Bakersville and check on Brandon's whereabouts. We get a call early this morning from the detectives on my case; Brandon has an alibi. His girlfriend says that he spent the weekend at her house, in her bed. There isn't much more they can do since he has a witness backing up his story. I have to admit, at this point, I don't feel safe going back home but I know my welcome is becoming an issue with Maddox. It isn't that he doesn't want me here but that he *fears* my being here.

I can't understand his fear. He lives in a secure apartment complex, doorman at the entrance and a security system that would put the pentagon to shame. His house is probably the safest place for me to be. No, his fear seems to be related to whatever demons plague him at night. Demons he doesn't want anyone to know about.

We sit down for dinner on night two when I decide to ask him.

"Hey, Mad? Can I ask you something?" I ask him hesitantly.

"Yeah, girl. You can ask but that doesn't mean I'm going to answer." He looks over, and despite his teasing, I can see the wariness behind his eyes.

"I know, I just… I just want you to know I'm here if you want to talk. I hear you, you know? I know what it's like to have your nightmares chase you out of your dreams. I guess I just wanted to know if you wanted to talk about it?" I keep my eyes level with him, wanting him to know that, even with my problems, I can take on his issues. I want to help; I want to be there for my friend.

"Nothing for you to worry about, girl. Things better left alone, yeah?"

"All right, Mad. But if you want to talk, I'm here." I pick up my fork and return to my salad.

"Izzy?" he asks. He startles me, not because I can hear the question coming, but because I don't think I have ever heard him call me my name.

"Maddox?" I tease.

"What happened between you and Reid?" He looks at me with concern written all over his face. Sympathy for my situation and compassion for me and my pain.

I don't know what makes me open my mouth, but I know that whatever demons are chasing me, his are worse. For once, I don't feel the stabbing pain that normally comes with thinking about the old Axel and Izzy. For the first time, I want to talk to someone, want to have someone else understand why I am firm on keeping him at arm's length.

"All right," I start, placing my fork back on the table and pushing back in my chair, "how long have you known Axel?"

"Close to ten years. I know about you. He used to talk. I just don't understand how you are the same girl he always talked about. I can't seem to understand his anger and your heartbreak."

"Ten years, huh? So not long after he joined. Did you know I was supposed to be by his side ten years ago? We had it all planned out, like stupid kids. We thought that nothing would ever get in the way of our stupid plans. I was seventeen when he left for basic, still had one more year of school left, but he was coming back. I had this tiny speck of a diamond promise ring from him, so tiny you couldn't even really see it was there…but that ring was worth more to me than all the riches in the world. He left for basic and was coming back for a visit a few months later. The plan was for me to make it to graduation.

Then we would have a small wedding and I would join him wherever the Marines took him. He broke those plans. Broke them and never looked back." I stop picking at the table and look up to meet Maddox's blank stare.

"He broke them?" he calmly asks.

"Yeah. Never came back to me." I can feel the emotion start choking me, but I am determined not to go there.

"Izzy, you're sure? He never came back home?" He seems so confused by this.

"I don't know if he ever came back home," I start, earning another confused frown from Maddox. "Two weeks after he left, my parents were killed—drunk driver. Still being a minor and with no other local family, I was sent to my grandparents' in North Carolina."

"Did Reid, Axel... Did Axel know this?"

"Yes, he would have known about my parents the second he rolled back into town. Small-town living means everyone is always in your business. There is no way he didn't know about their passing."

"Not what I mean, girl. Did he know where you were?"

"Um, yes. I left my grandparents' address with his foster mother. I wrote him and wrote and wrote some more to the base he was supposed to be stationed at, but all the letters came back to me. June, his foster mother, she had all my contact information. It wasn't like I was hiding, Maddox."

His normally blank face looks so different when he allows emotion to filter through his tightly locked walls. His nose is scrunched up, eyes are narrowed, and his lips are pulled tight. He looks distressed, mildly confused, and constipated all in one.

"Girl, there seems to be some major wires crossed between you two." He keeps his weird look. "Is that all? Seems to be a little more than just some foiled plans with all this shit."

"Yeah, Mad...there's a lot more."

He sits there, silently waiting for me to continue. It feels oddly liberating to get this off my chest, knowing that I won't be judged and that someone else will understand where I am coming from.

"Mad, I get you're trying to be there, but this might be different with you being his friend and all."

"His friend. Your friend. Don't see how it makes a difference who I share my cookies with at snack time." His attempt at lightening up this conversation works, earning a giggle before I shake my head and look down at my clasped hands.

"You know I tried to get in contact with him, so many letters... It was ridiculous how blinded by love I was. Never once did I give up faith that he would come to me. I saw everything, even with the pain of losing my mom and dad, with a little extra sparkle knowing he would come back for me." I laugh lightly, looking up and meeting his serious eyes, "Never once did I give up that hope. It wasn't until almost two months later when I started panicking and worrying." With a deep sigh and a wobble in my voice, I look back up before continuing. "He hadn't been gone long, so I didn't really have much cause for concern. I knew it wouldn't be easy to talk often, but I thought for sure he would call, find a way to reach out to me when he found out about my parents. God, was I stupid. So stupid..."

I don't realize that I have zoned out, staring off into space, until Maddox coughs, clears his throat, and interrupts my mental trip down memory lane. "What happened next, Izzy?"

I turn my head and look into his deep, dark eyes, just look into his understanding face for a few moments before I whisper my biggest sorrow. "What happened? I finally had some light brought back into my life and more motivation to find Axel. I was pregnant, Maddox. Seventeen, alone, and pregnant with a baby I loved more than anything in this world. Even with as much as I missed Axel, I was finally smiling again because I had a small part of our love growing inside of me. I was happy. Even without my parents and without Axel physically by me, I was able to feel whole."

His mouth is wide open in shock, eyes large and bugging out, and the wheels are turning so fast, I worry he might start flying off track. I have stunned this big man.

"Uh..."

He coughs a few times, pausing to collect his thoughts. Or maybe he is picking up the pieces of his mind I just blew all over the room. Not what he was expecting to hear, I'm sure. Greg was shocked, and he didn't even know who my Axel was then.

"Pregnant?" He looks down at my stomach like he is expecting me to still be pregnant twelve years later. "Izzy, what happened to the baby? You sound like you wanted the pregnancy, and forgive me if I'm wrong, but I don't remember seeing any babies." His tone is light, and I know he doesn't mean to cause the sharp pain that jolts through my body. I can't help the flinch that rocks me back in my seat. I feel like he slapped me, and even though I know he didn't mean it, I can't help the tears that rush to the surface.

Smiling sadly at him, I continue my story. "No, you didn't see any baby. I lost my little miracle when I was three months pregnant." The tears are flowing now. As much as it hurts to talk about this, I start to feel a little lighter from finally letting someone else in.

"Oh, girl...come here." He pushes his big body from the table and holds his arms open to me. I crawl into his lap and hold on tight, letting out the sorrow of my loss, letting him take in the pain, and purging the grief from my system.

We stay like that for a while. He rubs my back and becomes my anchor while I just let it out. He doesn't push, doesn't ask me any more questions; he is just there. I know in this moment that Maddox will forever be part of my 'family.'

I finally calm down and am just starting to get up when he clears his throat. I look over at him, shocked by the moisture in his eyes, the unchecked sadness his face holds. "Izzy, you have to be one of the strongest chicks I know. Hear me when I say this, and please don't take this the wrong way. I feel you, girl. I feel your pain. Cuts me deep, you and Reid. But you two need to talk because I promise you...he has no clue. Not my story to tell, but girl, no clue. That wire I thought was crossed is more like a ball so fucked up that if you don't sit down and work it out, you might never get it unraveled. You two hurting, and hurting for no reason... A shame girl. A damn shame."

Sometimes it sounds like he is talking in riddles. I don't see how this could be misconstrued. It's pretty cut and dry if you ask me. I know Axel doesn't know about our angel, but he can't play dumb about not following through with our plans and coming to me.

"I don't know, Mad. I think if there were something else at play here, he would have tried harder to find me. I'll think about it, but no promises okay?"

"All I can ask. Can't hold that shit in forever. Might have been easier when he wasn't around, but now, not going to be able to hold it in."

"Mad, you know… You know you can talk to me too, right? I won't push, but I know something is eating at you, and I would guess it's something big." Maddox is always so closed off, and I know that this moment of sharing my past is big for him. I just wish he would let me in, let me help him.

"Know that, girl. One day, but that day isn't today. Won't be to-morrow, but maybe one day."

And that is that. I go to bed that night feeling lighter than I have in years. Dr. Maxwell was onto something when she told me to open up and let people in. All these years, I was afraid to let my guard down, and one big bad ex-Marine finally let me feel close to normal again.

I sleep for the first time in years without dreams, an almost peace-ful sleep full of promise…until Maddox's terrifying screams wake me up a few hours later.

THE NEXT morning, I'm making breakfast for both of us when a sharp knock sounds at the door. Maddox is still sleeping. I heard him screaming out a few times throughout the night. Whatever haunts him was doing a bang-up job last night. My heart hurts for my friend.

Glancing over at the clock above the stove, I note the time—7:00 a.m.; too early for normal company.

I have to remind myself that this isn't my place and it probably is wise for me to go wake up Mad. After all, I am here for a reason. The knocking continues, so I go up to the door and check the peephole. I jump back like the door bit me when I see who is on the other side.

Axel.

Just who I don't want to see bright and early in the morning. Well, I didn't *want* to see him, but a small part of me is jumping up and down like some stupid cheerleader just by seeing his handsome face.

"Hold on, hold on…" I mutter under my breath while I disarm

the security system and throw open the door. "Good morning, your assholiness. To what do I owe this esteemed pleasure?" Throwing a snarky smile on my face for good measure, I look up into wide, shocked eyes.

"What the fuck are you wearing?" He growls.

Uh, oh.

Looking down, I notice that I am still wearing my bed clothes—a tank top and panties, which are doing a bang-up job of hiding nothing.

Shit.

"I just woke up, Axel. What do you expect me to sleep in? A snowsuit?"

"I expect you to not walk around naked in another man's home."

"Excuse me? What does it matter to you what I wear when I am *sleeping!*" I need some serious caffeine before I can be expected to deal with his bullshit this early. "Idiot," I grumble under my breath and turn to walk back into the kitchen.

I take the eggs off the burner, plate the bacon, and grab the toast out of the toaster. I set up two spots at the table, effectively ignore Axel, and walk down the hall to Maddox's room. I can feel Axel burning his eyes into my back. Just to piss him off, I throw some more swing than normal into my hips. His answering groan is all I need to hear to bring a small smile over my face.

Knocking softly, I call out to Maddox, "Hey, you want to eat something?"

Wide awake and hollow, his voice calls back through the door. "No."

I knew he wouldn't be in a good mood this morning, but I really hoped I could help him. Even by just being here.

"You sure? I made you breakfast." I turn the knob and peek in.

Maddox is sitting on the side of his bed with his elbows braced on his knees, his head folded down into his big hands. It breaks my heart.

"I'm here if you need me, okay? Even if that's all I can offer, I know how important it is to have someone waiting to help carry your burdens."

"Yeah, girl. Go eat. I'm good." He looks up at me, his dark eyes seeming to see right through me. It would seem that Maddox is still very much trapped in his head.

"All right, Mad. Axel is here, and he is fuming at the top, but what else is new."

I turn around and immediately draw back. Axel is standing directly behind me, and with no warning, I end up pressed tight against his hard body.

We both suck in sharp pulls of air. I can feel my body instantly becoming aware of his being this close. Every single inch of my exposed skin that presses tightly to his denim-and-cotton-covered body is tingling. And just with this small press of our bodies, I can feel my panties become soaked in seconds. His eyes are dark with desire and his breathing has picked up; at least I'm not alone here.

He shifts closer, pressing his thick erection into my stomach. I let out another sharp gasp, not even realizing I was holding my breath this whole time. My nose fills with his hardy scent immediately. Mouthwatering. My nipples pebble and my heart is pounding.

His big, strong hands reach out and grab both of my small wrists. Slowly, oh so painfully slowly, he starts caressing his way up my arms, my skin breaking out in millions of tiny goose bumps along the way. When he reaches my shoulders, he brings his hands up, one going to the back of my neck, fingers lacing into my hair. The other travels up to the side of my face, holding my cheek and part of my neck tenderly. My body is on fire. The skin he touched is burning, and the overwhelming need to *feel* him has consumed my every fiber.

"So. Fucking. Perfect," he whispers against my lips, bringing his head down the final few inches and finally crushing his lips to my own.

He nibbles and bites at my lower lip, tracing the same path with his tongue to soothe the ache before taking my bottom lip between his teeth and pulling. My gasp of surprise opens my mouth long enough for his demanding tongue to work its way in. Desire is coursing through my veins, my heart is surely going to explode, and my soaked panties are going to melt off my body.

As our kiss continues, getting hotter by the second, he runs the hand holding my cheek down my back, his fingers gliding over the bandage on my spine before reaching my ass. With a firm hold, he pulls my body even further in to his own. There isn't a single inch of my body not stuck to his. Turning my head to the side, he continues to lick and caress every solitary spot of my mouth. Our tongues are dueling together, both overcome with the feelings this kiss is provoking.

The hand behind my head follows the path his other hand just traveled, and when he reaches my ass, he flexes his fingers, digs both hands in, and lifts. Instinctively, I bring both my legs up and wrap them around his body, driving my core flush with his hard erection. Just what my body is craving, demanding to take what it needs.

I don't realize we were moving until my back meets the cold wall. I break away from his mouth and push back a little. This does nothing but help rub my swollen pussy against his denim-covered cock. Biting back the moan, I look into his green eyes, so dark and hooded with desire.

"We shouldn't be doing this," I weakly try to protest. I want this. God, how I want this.

Right or wrong, this feels like heaven. Even chocolate is no match for the full body electric tingles that are shooting through my system. Every hair is standing on end, and my core is clenching with anticipation of the orgasm that is just within reach. God, please don't let him take my comment seriously.

He brings his face back level with mine, rubbing my painfully neglected nipples against his shirt. I dig my hands into his sides, moaning again when I feel how solid and warm his hard body feels under my fingertips.

When he speaks, his words tingle my lips, reminding me of our kiss, making me groan all over and rock my pussy against his hard length.

He sucks in a deep pull before speaking, his voice thick with lust. "Oh, Princess, I can't think of anything that we should be doing more. You feel that? You feel how fucking hard I am for you? I can feel your warm fucking cunt hugging my dick even through my goddamn pants. You are on fire for me."

He brings his hips forward, rocking against me and supporting my body against the wall. We both moan, my head falling back and thumping against the wall. He brings his left arm under my ass and supports me while bringing his other hand up, running it along my hips, making me gasp when he tickles my sides on his way to my swollen breast. His fingertips brush softly against the swell of my breast before pulling the tank down and under, pushing my tits up high. He lightly runs his fingers down and circles around the barbell in my nipple; I am panting now and can feel my orgasm building.

When he pinches my still tender nipples between his thump and finger, I let out a soft cry, grinding down against his cock again. "Still sore?" he questions, sounding like he is standing at the end of a tunnel. "Hmm…can't speak, huh, baby? Just think how good it will feel when I bury my cock deep inside that warm pussy, when I fuck you so hard you will feel me for days. Going to make you drown in pleasure, fuck you so good, so fucking good." He drives that home with one more rock of his hips. I close my eyes, too overcome with everything he is doing to my body to even act like I understand.

His hand releases my breast, and right as I am ready to protest, I feel the warm heat of his mouth. His tongue traces the outline of my nipple, nips at the soft skin under my breast, and licks his way back up before closing his lips around my nipple and barbell, giving a hard pull.

"Oh God, don't stop… Please don't fucking stop," I beg, fanatically moving against him, desperate to reach my orgasm.

His fingers play against my stomach as he dances them down my torso. He splays his fingers wide and pushes his thumb hard against my clit. "Soaked… Fucking drenched. Can't wait to have my mouth down there licking all that wetness up." He rolls his thumb and crushes his lips back down on mine, swallowing the cry of satisfaction I scream out as the waves of the most powerful orgasm come crashing down on me.

I feel like my whole body has just lit up, coming to life with each roll of pleasure that rockets through me. His tongue tangles with my own; this kiss is full of ecstasy. Our tongues mate together while he slowly brings me back down to earth with small rolls of his hips against my still pulsing pussy. He is reminding me that he is still very ready to continue when I feel the thickness brush against me again.

"Fuck, baby…you feel so good in my arms again."

I look up into his eyes, trying to focus on his face long enough to make sense of his comment. The harshness I have grown accustomed to seeing mar his beautifully handsome face is gone, and in its place is pure affection. He looks like the old Axel, the one so full of love for me that nothing else matters. In that moment, I can almost believe it, almost believe that we can get back there again, and after all we just shared, I realize that I want that. I want Axel back. I want us and our love back. It has never felt like that before, not even with him. Time might not have been on our side the last few years, but right now…I can almost hope that fate has decided to love me and give me some happiness for a change.

"What are we doing, Axel?" I ask, tightening my arms around his neck and bringing my forehead down to his chest. What are we doing? I have no answers myself, but I hope he doesn't look at this as a mistake. That might just kill me.

"I don't know, Princess. I don't know. But it feels way too fucking good to ignore." He brings his hands back up to either side of my face and pulls me up to look at him. "We got some shit to figure out, Izzy…but after this, I won't let you go until we figure it out. Not happening. Do you feel it? Every single thing we ever felt for each other… It is still there, Izzy, and I won't let you push me away. We walked back into each other's lives for a reason."

I nod my head, because really, what can I say? He's right. I just have to believe that when we sit down and bring back all those memories he will still want to hold me so tight. "Okay, Axel. You're right. We do need to talk."

The white flags are waved. I bring my head back down and rest against his chest. His heart is pounding rapidly against my ear and his scent, which is now mixed with my arousal, is invading my senses. I bring my arms up, wrap them around his torso, and pull tight. His sighs softly, adjusting my body so that he can pull me closer and just enjoy the moment of our hearts being together again.

Peace. Even with the fear of telling him everything, my soul is at peace.

A deep throat clearing brings me back to earth. I lean up, look over Axel's shoulder, and meet Maddox's laughing eyes. It's such a rare sight that I am momentarily speechless. He looks so different when he allows his emotions to come out, youthful and approachable, completely different that his normal hard, cold staring.

"Interesting. Live porn. Think you could at least take this reunion behind closed doors? Or maybe your own fucking house?" His eyes might have been laughing with me but his question to Axel was full of unspoken warning. It looks like I have earned myself another big bad brother.

"Sorry, Mad," I whisper over Axel's shoulder and give him a wink.

"Sorry? Fuck that shit, Izzy." Axel lets my feet fall to the floor and holds on to my hips to make sure I have my balance before he gets ready to address Maddox. He leans down and, with a growly whisper, says, "Don't you move, Izzy. I won't have Locke looking at you half naked with that just-fucked glow about you. Damn...mmmm. I can't wait to be deep inside you."

I get one chaste kiss before he gives me his back and makes sure his big body is completely covering me before addressing Maddox.

"My bad, brother. I won't apologize that it happened. Hell fucking no. Best breakfast I've ever had." His laughter is vibrating his body. I dig my hands into his shirt and push my heated face into his back. How embarrassing.

"Funny. Just hilarious. Fucking shit, I need to get laid. Asshole." Maddox walks past us and into the kitchen. He's wearing some worn sweats, which are hanging low on his hips. It's a good thing I don't have the hots for him, because this view of him scratching his ass while searching the fridge is not his best look.

"Classy, Mad!" I call over to him, unable to keep my giggles in. "You shouldn't have any trouble with the ladies if you keep digging in your ass!" I'm laughing harder now, feeling like the weight that was pushing down on my body is almost gone.

Axel turns around, gives me a small smile, and wraps me in his arms again, lifting me off the floor so he can easily whisper in my ear.

"Missed that sound so fucking much." His lips kiss a line from my shoulder to my ear. His tongue comes out and licks along the shell, causing me to shiver in his arms and moan his name.

"You two need to either get the fuck out or get behind closed doors. Don't need to be seeing that shit this goddamn early. Go reunite somewhere else. Serious as fuck right now. I get it, and I will only say this once—about fucking time," Maddox says matter-of-factly like while he butters his toast.

I pull away from Axel and just look into his eyes. I notice the adoration that still shines bright. I hope I'm giving him just a small sign of what I'm feeling when I smile up at him.

Maddox was right last night. I can't hold it in anymore, and when I have Axel back in my arms, the uncertainty isn't as terrifying. With everything else that is a mess right now in my life, I feel like this is one thing I might be ready to deal with and move on from. Hopefully I'm making the right decision here, but I can't hold on to the past anymore. I can't hold that pain in, and more importantly, I am ready to let him in. Let him in in the hopes that we can find a way back to each other that isn't just about this sexual buzz roaring around us.

"Go get cleaned up, yeah? And please put some fucking clothes on. As fine as that body is, I don't want anyone else enjoying the view."

"Sure, Axel. I'll go get cleaned up, but I don't understand what your issues are with my clothes! Most bathing suits show a whole hell of a lot more than this. Maddox doesn't care, and he doesn't see me like that." I try to reason with him, and it might have worked if Maddox would have kept his mouth shut.

"Just because I'm not pushing you up against walls and humping you like a fucking animal doesn't mean I can't appreciate the view. You just haven't caught me looking." He laughs—LAUGHS—between mouthfuls of his breakfast.

"Ugh, pig!" I yell and run off to the room I have been staying in.

"Izzy, get your shit packed up. I'll be back around lunch to pick you up. This fucking sleepover party bullshit is over now. You're coming home with me, got it?" he yells down the hall.

Ready or not...time to find some of that locked-down courage and face the facts. Ax is back and we are about to have a 'make it or break it,' 'come to Jesus' talk. For the first time in years, the thought of opening up those old wounds doesn't terrify me.

CHAPTER 14
Axel

FUCK ME, I think as I walk out of Locke's apartment and climb into my truck. I sit there for a second, trying unsuccessfully to calm down, shifting slightly to try and ease some of the discomfort in my pants. My cock is so hard that I might have permanent indentions from my zipper.

I rub my hands over my face, trying to bring my heart back to a normal speed. *Fuck*. I can still smell her, her arousal still clinging to my fingers, making my cock even harder. Swear to Christ, I have never been this ready to explode, not even when I was a horny teenager getting a fucking hard-on for every single female I looked at.

Damn.

Even better than I remember. Iz came alive under my fingers. Just one kiss and everything else ceased to exist. She consumed me. Her breathy moans, her soft skin, her delicious fucking kisses, and that warm fucking pussy just begging for me to take her.

It wasn't my intention when I got here to go there. Not yet, at least. I have been slowly going insane since Saturday when the ex showed up. Knowing she was hurt was one thing, but knowing I hadn't been there to protect her was enough to keep me on edge all week. I haven't gotten shit done around the office, but if Greg noticed, he didn't say anything. He was just as worried about Izzy but his had the added fear that he still didn't have her whole friendship back. I know they talked before the game Saturday, but they haven't since, with the exception of a few calls to check in. He might be having a hard time not being able to protect her too, I don't fucking know. I haven't asked, but I do know one thing. Even if they are best fucking friends, exchanging friendship necklaces and shit, he won't be the one in charge of protecting *MY* Izzy anymore.

I have been struggling with the desire still very much there between us for a few months now. Even when I'm not in her presence, I know she is there, just within reach, and I have finally come to the realization that I'm not ready to let her go. Not again. And if I'm being totally honest with myself, I haven't ever gotten over the fact that she was and always will be 'it' for me.

I don't have any delusions. We have a lot of shit to work out, but I am ready to fight and not just fight for us but fight anyone, including that piece-of-shit ex-husband.

Shaking my head, I start my truck and head off to run some errands. I need food if I expect Izzy to stay with me, and I need some condoms. There is no way, especially after that shit back at Locke's house, that we will be able to spend time alone and not end up naked. I am ready to make my girl mine again.

A few hours later, I have a fully stocked fridge with more food than we will ever need and the biggest boxes of condoms I could find. Three boxes might be excessive for a normal man, but for me, that;s just making sure I'm prepared. I plan on making a huge fucking dent in those boxes as soon as possible. My cock is still standing at attention, and at this point, I'm starting to fear my balls might fall off.

Desperate for some relief before I go back for Izzy, I climb the stairs and make my way into my bathroom, stripping as I go. Turning the water on, I step in and start cleaning my body, making a point to avoid my throbbing dick. When I finish soaping up and rinsing off, I lean my hand against the far wall and let the water rush over my tense shoulders. I wrap my hand around my cock and let out a sharp hiss. Stroking a few times, I bring my hand down and caress my balls then guide it back up, and firmly taking hold of my cock. Only a few stokes are needed before I feel my balls pull up tight. My hand picks up speed, going from root to tip in a slow, steady, and firm rhythm. All I can picture is Izzy's face when she came this morning, and with the memory of her cry of pleasure, I still my hand and let the orgasm take over my body. My abs tense with every jet of come that shoots from my body.

I rinse off again and leave the shower. I quickly dry off and throw on a pair of jeans and a black tee before setting off to claim my woman. Just thinking about whom I am going to pick up later and the night I have planned for us has my dick rearing back up and back to life. I lock the door and climb back into my truck with the anticipation and knowledge that in just a few hours, God willing, I will have her tight, hot body underneath mine again.

Smile on my face, rock-hard dick in my pants, and some peace in my heart, I feel like I can take on the world and win. Time to hurry these errands up so I can get her back in my arms.

Get ready, Izzy, because here I come.

Izzy

AFTER AXEL leaves, I'm in a complete daze. If it weren't for the buzzing still running through my body, I would have thought I dreamt the whole thing. Well, that and the fact that Maddox hasn't stopped smirking at me for the last hour. Cheeky little bastard.

"You think this is hilarious, don't you?" I ask him, after losing a ten-minute-long staring contest.

"No, girl, not hilarious. I knew this shit would happen. You two... You two have that once-in-a-lifetime type of shit that will always triumph. Try as you might, there was no avoiding that. Meant what I said last night. There was no way you two would be able to hold that back. You can forget how it was, being apart from each other, but that kind of passion? It never dies." He turns away from me and walks off towards his room.

Guess he thinks we are done here.

"Hey, wait a minute. What am I doing here, Mad? Am I making a huge mistake?"

"You're always going to make mistakes in a relationship, girl. The trick is to make sure you communicate and learn from them. The

152

way I see it, the only issue you two have right now is communication. You need to tell him what you told me last night. He might take it well, he might not. But you have to buckle up and be ready to ride that wave when it comes. You want him? Fight for it. Be honest. That's all you can do."

"What if he hates me?" I whisper, not making eye contact with him.

"Izzy, look at me." When I meet his eyes, he continues. "I don't know how he will react. You can't go into this in fear. Told you last night, both of you have your wires so fucked up. Not just crossed, they might as well be on different sides of the globe. If he doesn't take it well, call me and I'll come get you, but don't go into this with the mindset that he will hate you. Fuck, girl, you were a child."

It makes sense, what he is saying, but I am so scared to let Axel in again, only to lose him all over. I know without a doubt that he will be upset, but I worry he will blame me for losing our baby.

"All right, Mad. I promise to keep an open mind, but you better come if I need you."

"Any time, girl."

We go our separate ways after that. Maddox gets ready and leaves to get some work done, whatever that means. I still am not exactly sure what these boys do. It doesn't take me long to pack. I don't have much here since Dee has been bringing me more as I need it. I don't think either one of us is ready to admit that I might be gone for a while. There isn't anything we can do about Brandon because of his alibi, so right now we are just watching, waiting, and praying he is done with me. I'm not stupid enough to believe that just yet.

I take a shower, apply the ointment to my back the best I can, and place some bandages on the worst of the wounds. My eye is looking better. Well...better if you count that I can open it but it has that nasty yellowish brown color to the bruising. It is still a little swollen but not as bad as it was three days ago. There really isn't anything I can do to fix my mess of a face so I pull my hair back into a messy bun and finish removing all traces of myself from Maddox's guestroom.

Realizing I probably have quite a bit of time to kill before Axel gets back, I decide to give Maddox's house a good clean. I grab my iPhone out of my bag and hook up my earbuds. When One Republic's 'Feel Again' fills my ears, I can't stop the smile that takes over my face. I bet I look ridiculous, just standing in the middle of Maddox's kitchen with bleach in one hand, a scrubber in the other, and a big, blinding smile on my face.

Deep down inside, I hope this is another sign that fate is finally on my side.

I just finish up cleaning Maddox's bathroom when I hear a knock at the door. Butterflies immediately start fluttering inside my stomach. I actually reach down and press my hand against my stomach to see if I can feel them. Laughing softly at my ridiculous actions, I put away the cleaning supplies and brush off my pants.

Deep breath in.

I check the peephole and see Axel's handsome face filling the viewer. He looks like he's changed his clothes and attempted to clean up a little bit. Even through the small hole, I can see the cocky smirk on his face and the bright twinkle in his emerald eyes. He looks like he stepped off the pages of some sexy cologne add.

Another deep breath in.

Disarming the alarm and turning all the locks, I open the door and just look at him. My eyes travel the length of his body, up to his face and back down again. His jeans are molded to his legs, cupping his impressive bulge and doing nothing to hide the fact that he is literally about to burst through the zipper. I lick my lips. I don't mean to but when his strangled moan reaches my ears, I look back up to his face. His eyes are on fire, so brilliantly bright. He clears his throat and reaches down to adjust his pants.

"You keep looking at me like that and we won't make it out the door, Princess."

I'm so turned on right now that just the sound of his gravelly voice makes me squirm. I could probably come right now; all it would take would be one brush of his skin on mine.

"Serious as shit right now, Izzy. You keep looking at me like I'm the last drop of water left after a long-ass drought and I will take you right here in the doorway. Jesus Christ, I'm so fucking hard right now, I think I really could hammer nails." He sounds angry but I'm pretty sure he's more frustrated at our current location than he is mad that I am currently eye fucking him hard. "Shit, baby, I want you so fucking bad," he whispers before pulling me into his arms. He bends down and nuzzles his nose into the crease of my neck, inhaling deep. "Smell so fucking good."

I've been wearing the same perfume for years, ever since Axel bought me my first bottle of Light Blue. It has been something that, at times, I wasn't even able to wear, but it was also something that gave me some strength with one inhale. I would remember Axel and what we shared all those years ago with just one whiff.

When I feel his hot, wet tongue start tracing my collarbone before making its way up to my ear, I am once again brought to my knees with the overwhelming hunger that takes over my system. We have got to get out of Maddox's house. Now.

Pushing on his shoulders reluctantly, I open my mouth to speak but am halted when he brings his head up and softly presses his lips against mine. This isn't a kiss like we shared earlier. That was full of lust and pent-up rapture. This kiss is full of promise—the slow, torturing kind. He takes his time, gently stroking his tongue against my own. With one last swipe, he pulls back and looks down at me with hooded eyes.

"Wow," I sigh. "It gets better every time." Even to my ears, I can hear the wonder in my tone.

It was always passionate between us as teenagers, but never with the knowledge of an adult's sexuality. I think we both know deep down that whatever will come next will blow every single coupling we have had in the past together, and with others, out of the water.

"As much as I would love to drag you back into that bedroom and take you now, I want time to play. If I got started here, I would only have to stop when Locke got home. I want you alone in my house, where only my ears can hear you scream."

Oh boy.

"Where are your bags?" he questions.

I just mutely point to the two bags sitting on the kitchen table.

He laughs lightly before walking over and picking them up. I set the alarm and lock the door. Before I can pocket the key, Axel reaches over and takes it from my hand. "You won't be needing that again,

Princess. I'll make sure he gets it back." He winks, pockets the key, and reaches down to lace our fingers together.

I don't even remember the walk to the elevator and through the lobby or how I got into his ridiculously high truck. One second we are still standing in Maddox's living room, the next we are pulling into traffic and on the way to his house.

I'm sitting here thinking about the night to come when the sound of my phone ringing interrupts my steamy thoughts. Damn. Squirming in my seat, I look down at the display and smile when I see "Dee Calling" and her smiling face.

"Hey, you," I answer, looking over at Axel out of habit. I have to remind myself that he isn't Brandon and a phone call from Dee doesn't even register on his radar.

"Hey back at ya! Aren't you just a dirty little ho bag!?" she sings into my ear.

Jesus, I'm going to freaking kill Maddox.

"I don't know what you're talking about." I hedge, figuring it's best to just play dumb. Dee is going to burst over this new development. There is no telling just what she has heard either.

"Don't you act like you don't know what I'm talking about, missy! I had a visit from a tall, dark, and lickable man today. You might know him. He goes by the name Axel? Called me himself bright and freaking early, and I might add that he sounded way too smug for it being before my morning coffee! Anyhow, he called, asked me to wait a second before heading off to the office. He was coming by and wanted me to pack a bag. A big bag, Izzy. Now, want to tell me why AXEL would be calling me to ask for a BIG bag of your clothes?" Little shit is laughing at me. She is enjoying this way too much.

"Yeah, yeah. Like you don't already know. Let me guess, Maddox came by or something?" I ask sarcastically.

"Maddox? Why would he come over?"

"Seriously, Dee? You didn't talk to him?"

"No. Axel really did call and ask for me to get your stuff together. His words were something along the lines of, 'Me Tarzan, taking Jane to tree house where she won't wear clothes and we will play bedroom aerobics for the rest of the days.' Then he took four of your biggest bags and packed almost all of your stuff up. So, now, do you want to tell me what's really going on?" She sounds nervous now, like she isn't sure if she did the right thing by letting him pack up my stuff.

"It's complicated, Dee. I'm okay, promise. We are… We are working on things. But I will admit that four bags does sound a bit excessive." I look back over at him when I hear a deep rumble of laughter. "This is not funny," I hiss at him.

"Baby, it is fucking hilarious. You really think that once I bury myself deep within your pussy and feel your tight walls squeezing the come right out of my dick that I will ever want to let you go again? You must be out of your fucking mind, Princess. I won't even be able to let you out of my fucking bed until we make up for every single day we have lost." He leans over and lands a smack on my lips before smiling back at the road.

"Oh…my…God…" Dee says softly into the phone. "I think I just came. That was seriously hot, Iz."

She's not the only one who might have just had an orgasm. And if all it takes are his words to get me this turned on, I'm seriously starting to get nervous for what is to come.

CHAPTER 15

I MUST HAVE been really out of it the last time I came to his house because I don't remember anything like what I am looking at right now. His house is ridiculous. Why one man needs *this* much house is beyond me.

"Ax?" I ask, looking over at the man climbing down from the big black truck. "Why exactly do you need a six-bedroom house again?" He has no family; it was just me back in the day. So unless he's picked up a few kids along the way, I just can't understand this. The very thought of him having a family with someone else causes my heart to tighten up in anguish.

He almost looks embarrassed by the answer, and before he even speaks, it all makes sense. He had a bedroom as large a small walk-in closet when we were in high school. To a man like Axel, this is all about feeling comfortable and knowing that he isn't that person anymore.

"Had enough of living in a box. I promised myself a long damn time ago that I would never have to worry about space again. Or not having it." He walks over to me and pulls me into his arms. "You know what it was like in June and Donnie's hole of a room. I had even less when I was enlisted. Doesn't make sense to many, but you know." I give him a squeeze, silently voicing my understanding.

"Right, let's go get settled before I fire up the grill and cook dinner. You're going to need your strength tonight, Princess."

Heat flushes through my body, and the desire to skip dinner and go straight to the bedroom cranks up to almost unbearable levels.

"Although," he continues, "it might be nice to skip the steaks and have dessert first."

Quivers of arousal shoot through my body, and if it weren't for his strong arm around me, I melt right here on his driveway.

He parks in front of the house this time instead of the garage, so when we walk inside I am met with a bright and very empty entryway. There is a large staircase right smack in the middle of a very empty room. To my left, there is another empty room, and to my right, there is another. There are two hallways on the sides of the staircase, but I have a feeling they lead to more emptiness. I apparently only saw a fraction of the house when I was here before.

He is looking at me intently and seems to be waiting for something.

"It's…um, nice?" Damn. Of course it would come out as a question. Real convincing, Iz!

"Nice, huh? Is that your way of saying you hate my house?"

"No?" I'm sure my embarrassment is all over my face. Even after all this time, I still can't lie for shit to this man.

He lets out a loud laugh before slapping my ass, shaking his head, and letting out some soft laughs. He bends down and picks up my bags before heading up the stairs. "Come on, Princess. Let's get you settled before dinner."

I follow him up, and up, and up. When I get to the top, there are two hallways in either direction. He starts off to the left, passing a few open doors along the way. Every single room is empty except for the one I used to escape from him. Eh, how embarrassing. I hoped he wouldn't ever have to witness one of my episodes, but it seems like the more I'm around him, the more they are triggered.

He walks into his bedroom and drops all the bags next to the closet. When he turns back around, I quickly jerk my eyes up to meet his, which sparkle with amusement. I was just busted checking out his very nice ass.

He smirks.

I blush.

He winks.

I lick my lips.

His smile is instantly wiped from his face and a long and low groan fills the silence between us.

I smirk.

And just like that, he's on me.

"Thought I could wait," he says before picking me up and throwing me onto the mattress.

Before I can even blink, he is on top of me, his large frame pressing me into the soft mattress. My legs open without hesitation and his hips meet my own. Now I'm the one who is letting out a strangled moan.

"Thought I could get you here and enjoy some dinner without having to be inside your wet heat. Fuck, baby, I can smell you from here. I bet your pussy is soaked, fucking sopping wet and ready for me."

He trails his tongue from my shoulder to my ear before taking it in his mouth and biting down. He licks the sting away and braces his body with his elbows on either side of my body. Taking both of his large hands and placing them on either side of my face, he leans down and places his lips to my ear.

"Can't wait, baby. I'm going to rip those tight-ass pants from your body and bury my face between your creamy thighs. I want to feel that sweet cunt around my tongue. Going to make you scream, Princess, and then when you can't take it anymore"—he pushes his denim-covered hips hard into mine, his thick erection rubbing my clit in the most delicious way—"then I'm going to lick my way up this sweet fucking body and finally I'm going make you mine." He rolls his hips, and I gasp, so close.

"Oh God," I pant, looking up into his bright eyes. He looks into mine, seemingly satisfied with what he sees, before bringing his lips down and devouring me.

There are no other words for what he is doing with his tongue in my mouth. Our lips are moving together in a wet dance. I move my hands to his back and pull him closer to me, relishing in the feeling of his hard, tight body pressing me farther into the mattress. I can feel the bundles of corded muscles underneath my fingertips, and I am suddenly desperate to feel his skin against my own.

With awkward and jerky movements, I rip his shirt up his torso, letting go of his lips long enough to pull it over his head. He lifts up and trails his fingers down my body. His rough and callused hands pull on the soft silk of my blouse before reaching the hemline and slowly pushing it up my belly. I lean up and help him remove my blouse before reaching behind my back and ripping off my bra my-self. I don't even have a second to bring my arms back around before his lips are closing around one of my tight nipples and giving a strong pull.

"Oh yes," I moan, threading my hand through his hair and pull-ing his head closer to my breast. "Feels so good, Axel." I'm so close to coming it's embarrassing. With Axel, it has always been effortless.

His answering groan against my skin causes wetness to gush from my core.

As he switches to the other nipple, his hand travels back down my belly, unsnapping the button on my jeans and thrusting his hand inside the waistband. His thick finger enters me with one swift thrust and instantly I am coming, coming so hard I swear I am floating in the air. My vision is dimming and the scream that rips from my throat echoes through the room.

He brings his head up from my chest, and with a wickedly arro-gant smile, he brings his hand out of my pants and licks my essence from his finger.

"Fuck me, baby. Not even a second and I had that tight cunt milking my finger. I can't wait to get inside your body. Nothing tastes better than your fucking cunt—nothing." He pulls me closer to his body and kisses me hard.

My naked skin rubbing against his only makes me burn hotter. I need this man, need him more than I have ever needed anything in my life, and if I don't have him naked soon, I might just die.

He jumps off the bed and pulls his jeans off his body. He takes his boots off and pulls off his socks. He stands next to the bed, my feet brushing against his naked, hairy thighs. No shame. But then again, why would he? His huge body is ripped and hard with muscles. His tan skin, ink, and every inch of his large cock are on display for me. Taking my time, my eyes travel up from the erection pressing against his toned abs to his small, dark nipples and then up to his heated eyes. My mouth drops open when I see the desire swirling in his hooded emerald eyes.

"Dreamed of this for so fucking long, Izzy."

He makes quick work of pulling my tight jeans from my body, and my drenched panties come with them. He tosses them behind his kneeling body onto the floor. He grasps my ankles and, with slow tortured movements, runs his hands up my legs. When he reaches my knees, he brings his hands underneath and throws them over his shoulders, kissing my left knee and then my right. With a small smile, he turns to run soft kisses down my left thigh, skipping my throbbing center with just the barest breath before continuing up my right thigh with the same small kisses. His hands fall down to my hips and roughly pulls me to the edge of the bed and towards his waiting tongue. I squeak out a sharp cry of pleasure, my hands fisting the comforter and pushing my feet into his shoulders to bring my pussy closer to his mouth. He laughs and the vibrations rip through me, causing another rush of wetness to meet his tongue.

He nibbles his way around my lips, tracing every inch of my tender skin with his tongue before latching on to my swollen clit and pulling deep. I bring my hand up and press against his head, bringing him closer to my body. I can feel him bringing his hand around but the ribbons of pure unadulterated bliss that are firing through my system prevent me from tracking his destination. His thick finger rims the outside of my passage before thrusting inside. He gives me a few shallow thrusts before picking up speed and twisting his thick digit. Immediately, my pussy clenches down hard and I can feel another orgasm coming fast.

"Oh my fucking god, Axel! Don't stop. Please don't stop!" I scream.

He hooks his finger and starts to press against my G-spot, applying just enough pressure to have me shooting off like a rocket.

"Oh, Axel...baby, oh god. Feels so fucking good... Oh, god... Never felt anything better than with you," I moan, my head thrashing back and forth against the bed.

He lifts off my clit and I look down at his face between my thighs. "Princess, you need to let go of my head so I can finish eating this sweet pussy."

Oh. My. God. Just like that, I am ready to go again.

"Right," I whisper huskily and reluctantly remove my fingers from his silky locks.

With a wink, he is right back at it, licking every inch of my swollen pussy and every single drop of my come before thrusting his tongue deep within me. I cry out and scream his name, the sound bouncing off the walls of his bedroom. I can't talk much more. He is slowly killing me with pleasure.

"Please, baby, let me love you," I gasp out.

"Not yet," he says against my skin, making me shiver. "Give me one more. I want one more, Izzy. Then I'm going to fuck you so hard you won't be able to walk when I'm done." He dips his head and thrusts his tongue deep within my pussy.

I scream.

He moans.

I cry out his name.

He brings his hand around my hip and presses his thumb against my clit, thrusting his tongue in and out in a steady rhythm.

"AXEL!" I yell out, coming all over his tongue before my body falls back limply against the mattress.

I am just returning to earth when I feel his wicked mouth kiss the insides of my thigh, trailing soft kisses up my belly. He gives each of my painfully hard nipples a few licks and bites before continuing up to meet my lips. I hungrily kiss him back. My tongue dancing with his. I can taste myself on him and groan into his mouth at how turned on that makes me. Never would I have thought I would enjoy tasting myself on a man. But with Axel, everything is a turn-on.

His hands hook me under my arms and drag me farther back on the mattress as he settles his hard weight on top. My pussy lips open wide to hug his cock. He moans into my mouth and rocks back and forth, sliding his hard length through my wetness.

Together we twist and move against each other's sweaty skin. I trail my hands down his back and grab his tight ass in both hands, pulling him closer to my body. I bring my arms up and wrap them tightly around his back and my legs around his waist.

"Please Axel, I need you inside of me," I gasp against his lips.

"Soon, baby. So fucking soon." He pulls back from my lips and looks in my eyes. His lips are swollen from our kisses, his face is flushed, and his eyes are dark with wanting. "It will be over before it begins, baby. Just have to cool off... Want you so fucking bad."

He crushes his mouth back down to my own and tangles his hand in my thick hair before bringing his other hand slowly down my side.

He caresses my heated skin before reaching between us. He pulls his hips back slightly, giving just enough room to take himself in his hand and align his broad head to my core. Rubbing my clit a few times, he dips into my pussy only to travel back out and coat my juices around my pussy lips. He repeats this a few times while I whimper into his mouth. He groans right with me and I know he is just as tortured with this slow process as I am.

"Feel so good...so wet, so hot. Can't wait to be deep inside your tight cunt, baby," he says into my neck, kissing and sucking the soft skin where my neck meets my shoulder.

And with that, he gives one swift thrust and he is instantly fully inside my waiting body.

I scream out. The shock of his swift entry and the tightness two years' worth of abstinence has given me bring a biting pain I wasn't prepared for.

"Fuck! Princess, you okay?" he bites out harshly as he stills inside me. "God damn, you're so tight."

I nod my head that I am okay, but words escape me.

"Baby, I need the words... I need to know you're okay."

"Fine..." I whisper, my words trailing off when I feel him twitch inside me, and I moan when the tingles of pleasure travel through my womb, causing me to clamp down on him.

"Shit, baby...this might be over before I move if your warm fucking walls hug my dick any tighter." He groans, bringing his lips down to mine and giving me a tender kiss.

"I'm okay," I gasp when he moves back slowly and inches back inside my waiting body. "Just been a long time. I'm good, so good... Please don't stop!"

That is all the reassuring he needs, because he starts to pick up speed. He keeps his eyes level with mine, his gaze burning into my own. Our moans are tickling each other's lips and our heated breaths mingle together.

I dig my nails into his back and move with his body, bringing my hips up when he drives his down. We move like we haven't been apart a single day, like our bodies were made for each other. I can't help the tears that slowly roll out of my eyes. This connection, this love that is between us never died. My heart suddenly feels like it might explode.

The claws of another, more powerful orgasm start climbing up my spine and I can feel his rhythm falter when I clench around him.

"Come on, baby. I'm going to come and I want you with me."

I moan when he slams into my body, rubbing against my clit with just enough pressure to send my body into an orgasm so powerful my toes curl, my breath stalls, my eyes roll back into my head, and my skin feels like tiny needles have been injected. The most delirious orgasm I ever experience.

"AXEL, oh…God…AX!" I scream.

I feel his grunt of completion against my neck. He thrusts a few times before bringing his hips hard against my own.

I can't tell you how long we stay like that, his body molded tight against mine. His cock is still inside my body and I am still twitching in aftershocks. I can feel his lips against my neck as I rub small circles across the wet skin of his back.

With tears still falling from my eyes and the vulnerability that rushes into my system, I can't help the sob that breaks past my lips. He is immediately up, bracing his weight on his arms. His still-hard cock pushes back into me and it causes us both to groan.

"Baby?" he questions.

I shake my head and another sob escapes.

"Izzy? Princess, did I hurt you?" He looks tortured.

I shake my head again, reach up, and bring my hand to the back of his neck. Tangling in the hair that curls at the end of his skull, I bring his lips down to my own, hoping to express all of the emotions flying around my body.

I still love him. This man who I have thought was forever lost to me. If I am completely honest with myself, I never stopped loving him. But all this knowledge shouldn't scare me. The teenage love we shared over a decade ago has grown with such a power that it will kill me if I lose it again.

"I…missed…you…so much," I sob out, gasping as the emotions over take me.

"God Princess, you have no idea. No fucking idea," he says, rolling to the side and pulling me closer to his hard body. "Never letting you go, Izzy. Never," he whispers into my hair, squeezing me a little tighter.

I let him hold me while I purge myself of the overwhelming emotions our lovemaking has brought forth.

"I need to clean you up, baby. Don't move." He rolls up and off the bed, padding across the large room and into the bathroom. I roll over and look up at the ceiling, hugging myself tightly. I can hear the toilet flush and the water running. He walks out of the bathroom, completely unconcerned with his nudity, right up to the edge of the bed. "Open up, baby, and let me clean you up." I let my legs fall to the side and watch, in shocked amazement, while he cleans our joint come from my pussy. The warm wash cloth causes me to jerk a few times when he touches my tender skin.

After a few seconds, he throws the towel in the direction of the bathroom and falls back to the mattress, pulling me into his arms again.

"Talk to me, Izzy. What was that?" He doesn't sound mad, just confused.

Sighing deeply, I reply, "It was just so much, Ax. So much emotion flooding through my system at once. Never in my wildest dreams did I think we would be here again, and trust me, I dreamt of this moment plenty." I take another deep breath before continuing, looking into his questioning eyes. "You have to understand, Ax. I don't know what it's been like for you all this time, but I thought you were gone, Ax. Not just gone, but dead." I hiccup a sob and take a moment to collect myself. My wet eyes meet his shocked ones. "I lived in hell for six long years, but those years were nothing...absolutely nothing compared with the pain I felt thinking you were dead this whole time."

"What?" he asks, so softly that I would have missed it if I weren't been looking into his handsome face.

"I don't understand what you don't get about that, Axel." I really am confused now. He seems completely baffled. How can he think I would think any differently! He disappeared out of my life, vanished! How else would someone take that?

"Baby," he chokes out, "please explain that to me. What do you mean you thought I was dead?"

I turn my head to the side and study him. I am beyond confused. His brow is winkled, his lips are pinched tight, and his eyes... His eyes look pained.

"Can we get dressed please? Maybe get something to eat before we have this conversation?" I weakly ask him. I need to take a second and figure out what is at play right now.

He shakes his head, as if clearing the fog, and nods. "Sure, Princess."

We get up and he throws a tee at me from his dresser before pulling some sweats up his narrow hips. Walking over to where I'm standing, he pulls me back into his arms and holds me tight. Almost too tight.

"I know you felt it, baby. No way had something that fucking powerful skipped your attention. Hear me now, and understand me. We will talk, but nothing you say will change the fact that you and I are happening. I won't let you go, Izzy. Never. You're mine, you got that, Princess?"

Do I? Can I so easily give my heart back to this man, knowing he has the power to destroy me? Yes. I can. If I walked away from him now, I might as well pull the trigger myself because I would be dead anyway.

"Yeah, I understand. But, Ax?"

"What baby?"

"I always have been yours, you know that, don't you?"

And with a bright smile that reaches all the way to his beautiful eyes, he pulls me tighter and places a soft kiss to my shoulder, my neck, and my ear before whispering, "Oh yeah, baby. I know."

CHAPTER 16

I HAVE BEEN standing on the back deck watching Axel flip the steaks on the grill and enjoying the view for the last ten minutes. If I hadn't understood what motivated him to buy this large waste of space before, it is all clear now. While I look out at the vast sparkling water his house sits on the shore of, I get it.

He has a very large deck—with of course no furniture or seating. But he does have one large gleaming grill. There is a nice-sized grassy patch of yard before it meets the pebbled path to the dock. And then there is the lake. There are no other houses that I can see. Just woods and a lot of water. It is absolutely stunning.

"You almost ready to eat, babe?" he asks, coming up behind me and handing me a glass of wine.

I look over my shoulder and just drink him in. He is still naked from the waist up and his sweats are riding low on his hips. The sexy V that disappears beneath the material makes my mouth water. His abs clench and he growls low in his throat.

"Stop, Izzy. Stop right fucking now or I will take you right here on the fucking porch."

"Sorry, Ax, but you did ask if I was ready to eat," I tease.

"Shit!" He throws his hands up and walks over to the grill.

I laugh and turn back to enjoy the view while he grumbles behind me about me needing to keep my sexy fucking mouth closed.

We continue in a comfortable silence while he finishes up the grilling and I finish my reflecting. I follow his lead back into the house, plate the juicy steaks, baked potatoes, peppers, and onions, bringing them over to the bar and sit on the only pieces of furniture he owns in the kitchen. Barstools.

"Axel, you have got to see about getting some life in this house.

Besides your bedroom—your lacking bedroom—the only things I have seen are these stools, your mammoth TV, and one recliner." I point my fork at him after taking in a piece of this delicious steak. I moan over the succulent taste that explodes in my mouth before I'm able to continue. "You can't buy a house this big without something to take up some space."

I look up and meet his eyes after I notice the silence that follows my observations. Oops. Maybe I overstepped. I mean, this isn't my house and it really isn't my business. Blushing, I put my fork down and stare at my hands in my lap.

"Why are you doing that?" he questions.

"Doing what?" I hedge.

"Acting like you're ashamed for asking something, even if you are being a nosy little brat." His tone is light, teasing.

"I…I don't know?"

"Can't fool me with that question bullshit either, Izzy. You forget I know you. Might have been years since I've had you, but I know you."

Sighing, I look up into his eyes. He doesn't look mad, just confused. His gaze is searching. "It's not something I do consciously. You have to understand, Axel. I can't turn off years of conditioning. I have lived a certain way for so long that sometimes I just kind of fall back into the old me. Well, I mean the old me after you."

"I can understand that, I can, but what I can't understand is why you seem to be afraid of *me* sometimes. A lot has happened, but you know—you have to know—I would never fucking hurt you."

"No, you wouldn't hurt me physically. I know that," I reply as I look back down at my hands.

"Izzy? What do you mean by that? Did we not decide that this is happening? I get you're scared, but hear me, really hear me. I am NOT going to hurt you. There isn't one goddamn thing that will tear us apart again. Lost too much time already, Princess. Too much time that I should have had you right here in my arms." He reaches over and pulls me into his lap. He has one arm around my back and the other across my lap. He takes one of my hands in his own before continuing. "There wasn't a day that went by that I didn't miss this, right here. I spent so much time, so much fucking time, thinking you were happy, thinking that you were better off without me. God, baby…" He trails off and brings his hand up to cup my face, bringing my eyes level with his. "It's killed me every day since you walked back into my life, knowing I could have done something to save you from that bastard."

I'm beyond confused right now. What is he talking about? He thought I was happy? And like a bolt of lightning, it hits me.

"You knew where I was?" I ask, and I can't stop the bite of anger that colors my tone.

"Not for a few years. I finally found you right after you had gotten married," he says, and the pain in his eyes is heart stopping.

"What?" I whisper softy.

He brings his finger up and brushes it against my furrowed brow, sliding down the bridge of my nose and tracing along the line of my lips. He takes my chin in his strong hand, bringing my mouth closer to his, and places a soft kiss against me.

"Baby, I looked for you. Searched for you every single chance I had for almost four years. I followed every limited lead there was, but they never gave me anything to go on. Not a fucking thing. I know about your mom and dad, and baby, I know that was hard and I'm sorry I wasn't there to help you through that, but why? Why didn't you tell me where you were going? You have to know I would have come for you."

This big strong man is letting me in, and letting me see the pain he has felt all these years ago. I can't stop the tears even if I wanted to. I tried, lord I tried, but knowing the depths he went through to track me down washes through me and breaks what little thread of sanity I have left. My temper is set on a simmer now.

"I had just enough time when I got back home for my leave to find out about them and that you were gone. No one knew where your grandparents lived. The best I got was that you were in some small town in the Carolinas and no one knew which one. It wasn't for lack of trying, Princess. Please understand that. I just didn't have the resources or the time to track you down. It got to the point where I started to feel like if you wanted to be found, you would let me know. Hell, a breadcrumb trail, flares, Bat-signal… I would have taken any of that."

His attempt at humor misses the mark. I try to take in all this new information, all these facts that I haven't once considered over the years. He wanted to find me? How is that? I left my address with June. She knew I wanted him to find me; she knew I was waiting on him. I can't stand the anger that is slowly burning through my body. That fucking bitch!

"June!" I bark, getting off his lap and pacing around the large empty space of his kitchen. I turn back to look at him and notice the confused look blanketing his handsome face. I rush to explain. "That bitch, June. I gave her everything, Axel. Every-fucking-thing that you would need to find me. My grandparents' address in North Carolina, their phone numbers, and I wrote letters, so many fucking letters. When the ones to the base started coming back, I started writing them to June's house. I figured if there was any way for you to get them, it would be when you came home. Oh my God, Ax! All this time. All this fucking time. You have no clue, no fucking clue what that bitch kept from us, what she told me." My fury is a palpable thing, filling the room with its thickness and completely eclipsing the sadness that had preceded it. I am forced to stop my frantic pacing when I feel the unyielding bands of Axel's hands close around my biceps.

"Princess, stop," he says softly, pulling my back to his chest and closing his arms over my chest. "I can't fix this if you don't tell me what has you freaked out."

I pull out of his hold and turn around to look into his eyes. I have to look into his eyes. Be able to judge where his mind is right now.

The only thing I see is confusion and maybe, hopefully, a little love.

"Do you have any idea how much I needed you? When my parents died, you were the only thing that would take that pain away, but you weren't there. I was okay with that. Please know I never would hold that against you." I rush to explain when I see the look that crosses his face. "I was so proud of you, Axel. Not a day went by, even through all that pain, that I wasn't so proud of you." He reaches up and brushes the tear that leaks from my eye. "I had so much going on the week after they died. I was hurting, lost, alone… I felt completely adrift with no anchor. Gram and Pop, they were good people and they loved me, but they lost too and suddenly had a depressed teenager to deal with. Sometimes I wonder if they just didn't know what to do with me, but they tried. I had a week. One week to pack my things up and leave. Pop couldn't leave things back home for too long and Gram didn't want to be away. She hated traveling. That's why you never met her."

I walk away from him and over to the window that faces the lake, now dark with the soft glow of the moon reflecting in its rippling water. "I made sure I ran by June's to bring her everything you would need. I didn't know who else to give it to. You hadn't been gone long enough to let me know how to contact you. The only thing I had was the base you were going to be stationed at." A sob tears up my throat and interrupts my retelling. "I—I w-w-as so st-stupid," I cry.

I turn around to face him and find him right behind me, arms stretched wide and waiting. I rush into his hold and let my sadness flow. I let him be my rock, the rock I have needed for so long.

I bring my arms around his back, pull him as close as I can get. I feel his lips against my hair, his chest rising and falling rapidly and his heart racing beneath my ear.

"Baby...Jesus. I wish I would have known. I wish I would have been there. You're killing me, fucking slicing me open right now. Look at me, Izzy," he says, leaving no room for argument.

I look up into his pleading eyes.

"I would have dropped everything to save you from any ounce of pain. If it is within my reach to do that now, know that I will never fucking let pain touch your heart, baby. It kills me to know how easy it was for the world to rip us apart. For years, baby. I have spent years thinking you left me. That you chose to leave me. God..." He trails off and leans down to capture my lips.

This kiss is like nothing we have shared since coming back to us. This kiss is full of the sadness of what we have lost but with the promise of what we will have. His lips make love to mine.

"Not one day went by, Izzy, that my heart didn't belong to you. To this day, there has only been one woman who has and will ever hold it. Fuck, baby, but the love I have for you is so fucking strong sometimes, I wonder if it will crush me," he whispers when he breaks the kiss to pull me tight against his chest.

I still with his words. Love? I know how I feel about him, but the shock of hearing him say it to me is overwhelming. He can't love me. Not yet. Not without knowing everything.

Small panic bubbles up but I quickly squash it. I have to be strong. I have to be strong for him, because after this, I don't know how he will feel.

I press my hands against his chest and give a small shove. He looks down at me, confused that I'm pushing him away instead of pulling him closer. Or maybe the shock is because I didn't return his sentiments.

Oh, if he only knew the love that burns for him.

"I didn't finish, Ax. You have to let me finish," I desperately say, resuming my pacing just out of his reach.

I look over at him standing beside the window I left him at. He's leaned back against it, crossed arms over his chest. I can't read the emotion in his eyes. I know he is confused but he seems almost agitated with me.

"God…this is so hard," I whisper to myself. I should have known his stupid empty house would aid the words into his ears.

"Izzy, I don't know what else there could be. I already know about *him*," he spits out.

I stop my pacing and look back over at him. My heart is breaking all over again, remembering the night of my eighteenth birthday.

"I wanted it so bad," I whisper again.

"What?" he questions, pushing off the window and walking over to me, taking my arms in his hands again and forcing me to still in my fidgeting.

I choke down the nervous sob that starts up my throat but I am helpless to clench the tears that flow lightly down my cheeks.

"I wanted it so bad, so fucking bad," I choke out, trying desperately to communicate my pain.

"Princess, serious as shit right now, I have no idea what you're talking about," he says, his frustration causing him to give me a small shake.

I look into his handsome face, picturing for what has to be the millionth time, what our child would have looked like. Unable to take the vision of angelic perfection that crosses my mind, I crash my forehead into his chest and sob. Sob for everything we have unjustly lost.

"The baby," I cry into his chest. "The baby I loved with every fiber in my body and every single ounce of love for you I had. The baby that I wasn't able to even protect from my own body!" I scream hysterically into his chest.

My body gives out with the amount of agony and grief that invades my mind and I crumble to the floor before he can catch me. Emotions I have worked so hard to push back and lock away are flooding my system, causing great big powerful wails to escape me.

"No, baby...no!" I hear him cry over my breakdown.

I feel rather than see his body drop to the floor next to me. He wraps me tightly in his arms and begins to rock me, my cheek resting on his shoulder and my nose buried in the warm shin of his neck. I don't know how long we sit like that. It feels like hours but it could only be minutes. He just holds me to his body, his arms and legs wrapped tightly around me.

It wasn't until I feel the warm drops of his tears hitting my face that I look up to meet his eyes, eyes that must mirror my own right now. He is doing nothing to hide the evidence of his despair. Never in all the years I have known this man have I ever seen him shed one tear besides the one I felt when I was in the hospital. There are only a few tears that escape before he seems to pull himself somewhat together. His body is heaving with the effort of his control.

"Baby, fuck... Princess, I had no clue, no fucking clue." I take his face between my hands and wipe his tears away with my thumbs. "What happened?" he asks. I know what he is asking; he wants to know what happened to our baby.

I take a deep breath and finish what needs to be said. "I had just marked the end of my first trimester when I miscarried. Three months along and I lost our baby," I whisper, keeping my eyes on his while I tell him. "The doctors said there wasn't anything I could have done. It was just God's will." I shake my head and look back down, pressing my head against his strong chest. "It was my birthday," I say almost as an afterthought.

He stills at that. I can hear the wheels turning in his head, the pieces finally fitting together. "The club? That's what Greg was talking about, wasn't it." A statement. He knows. There really isn't any question about it. Of all the days he could have walked back into my life; that was the worst.

"Yeah. The club," I reply.

We sit there, him holding me in his arms, my legs brought in tight against my chest, and my arms thrown tightly around his body. His arms are around my neck and his legs are stretched out on either side of my balled-up form. We sit there and silently offer the only thing we can.

Each other.

It's hard for me to put myself in his shoes. I don't doubt that he is feeling the heaviness of the situation, but he hasn't had any time to even process the fact that there was a baby. We would have had a child, made out of love. Even with our young hearts, we both know that any child we would have made would have been our greatest accomplishment. A joy we would have welcomed, even being babies ourselves.

"I bet she would have looked just like you, that round, beautiful face with the softest of skin and the palest eyes you ever saw. Hair that would catch fire when she ran through the yard, laughter that would make even the surliest of bastards smile—the picture of fucking perfection," he says against my ear. The lightness in his tone does nothing to blanket the sadness. He's trying to reassure me when it should be me reassuring him.

"No, he would have been the spitting image of his handsome father. The strongest face you ever did see on any child. Hair so dark it would give midnight a run for its money and eyes so green you would have sworn we robbed a jewelry store. He would have been so brave and strong. Just perfect. And I would have loved him just as much as I love his father," I whisper, ending on a soft catch that gives me away.

We can try and lighten our sadness, but there is no getting around the fact that we both have lost and lost hard.

"Never again, Izzy West. I will never again let anyone take you from me. Or anything from us." His words hang between us both as a promise and a threat.

I know in this moment that this man would fight to the death to keep me by his side, protecting me from the world.

"I don't want to be anywhere else but here." I lean off his chest and give him the softest of kisses. It doesn't take long before we are using our desire for each other to erase the pain we still hold heavy in our hearts.

"Come on, Princess. Let's go to bed, yeah?" He helps to pull me off the floor and then, to my shock, lifts me into his arms and begins to walk through the house.

"I can walk, you know?" I joke, leaning into his neck and inhaling his intoxicating scent.

His arms tighten around me before he replies, "I know, but right now, I need this. Just be quiet and let me lead."

I can give him that.

I lean up from where my head was resting on his shoulder and look at his strong profile. This man, this incredible man, I never thought I would have again, is hurting. I can tell by the clenched jaw and the focus determination in his hard lines. Rightfully so, it isn't every day a man learns that he was a father. Even if the child never made it past a much-loved fuzzy ultrasound image—an image he didn't even know existed five minutes ago. A sharp pain shoots through my heart when I think of how much he would have loved our child. We had always talked about how much we wanted children.

"You okay?" I whisper when we hit the landing on the second floor. He ignores me for a while, and I have almost convinced myself that he didn't hear my question until he breaks the silence.

"No. But I will be. We will be."

He stops when we reach his room and gently lowers me onto the bed. I look up and meet his sad eyes before he breaks contact and pushes his sweats down his lean hips. I sit up, and pull the tee off my body, and throw it to the floor seconds before he presses his weight into my body, pushing me into the mattress. Every inch of our skin from shoulders to toes is touching. I open my legs and welcome his weight, his hips sliding against my arousal.

He presses his forehead to my own, his breathing fanning my lips and dancing with my own heavy pants. His hands, which are holding my head reverently, warm my cheeks.

"I need you, Princess," he softly whispers against my lips.

"You have me," I reply.

He lifts his hips and I help guide his heavy erection into my waiting body. He doesn't move his hands from my face or his weight from my body. His forehead comes off of mine so that he can press the most loving and tender kisses to my lips.

This isn't the heavy, fast sex we had earlier. This is pure love-making. This is two souls that have been adrift for too long finally coming home to each other. This is healing.

I bring my legs up, circling tightly around his hips. My arms curl up and around his shoulders and I hold on tight.

There is nothing fast about this moment. His breathing against my lips is coming in heavy pants, mirroring my own.

He rocks against me, not breaking his slow and steady rhythm for what seems like hours. It isn't until our tears start mingling together down my cheeks that he releases my cheek with one of his hands and brings it behind my knee to hook my leg higher up his side.

"Oh, God..." I cry as lights explode behind my eyes and my toes curl. My fingernails are digging into his shoulders, anchoring me against his powerful movements.

"Never. Going. To. Let. You. Go," he rasps out, punctuating each word with a hard thrust into my wet core. His pelvis is grinding against my clit in the perfect friction. I cry out once again when another orgasm hits me so close to the first.

He buries his head into my neck and, with a strangled cry, empties himself into my body. We lie there, covered in sweat and connected in every way possible, for the longest time. His body feels wonderful against mine.

My breathing slowly returns to normal and I feel like I am able to speak. Turning my head slightly so my lips kiss his ear, I whisper as softly as I can the words I have longed to speak to him.

"I love you, Axel Reid. I have loved you forever and I will never stop. Made for me, baby. You were made for me. Don't ever leave me. Never again. I would rather die than be without you again."

He tenses for the smallest of seconds before rolling our bodies so that he is taking my weight, my legs straddling his hips and my arms still wrapped around his shoulders. He brings his arms up and pulls me even closer to his body. I can feel our joint orgasms leaking between us, reminding me that we are still intimately connected.

"You wouldn't be able to get rid of me if you tried." I lean up and look into his face, memorizing each feature before rubbing my cheek against his. "It feels like my heart has been ripped from my body knowing everything that happened to you. I can't even begin to process all that we lost. This is our second chance, Izzy and nobody is fucking it up this time." His voice is soft against my cheek. His lips are warm when he presses a soft kiss against my ear before he rolls me back over and slowly slips from my body. I cry out weakly at the loss of him.

"Princess, that's twice now I haven't used protection. Promise you, I'm clean, but I can get you papers if you don't believe me. Is this going to be an issue?" He says this lightly, but I can tell by the way he is staring at my stomach he isn't talking about anything I can catch. "As much as I would love to have you carrying my baby inside you, we aren't there yet. We will be. But not until my ring is around your finger," he adds almost as an afterthought, leaving me stunned.

"Um…" I clear my throat a few times and look back up into his smiling eyes. "We're okay. I'm on the pill," I whisper.

"Good. Then I guess I don't need all those boxes of condoms, huh?" He laughs as he walks to the bathroom and shuts the door behind him.

I can't help but wonder what the hell just happened here. Was that some weird marriage proposal? No, surely not. We might have agreed to see where this goes, but marriage?

I am silently freaking out when he returns to the bed and tenderly cleans me off. He throws the towel off in the direction of the bathroom before pulling me into his arms and holding me tight. My head is resting against his chest and I can feel his heart beating slowly under my ear. I wrap my arm around him and hook my leg over his hip, brushing his still-hard dick in the process.

"Easy there, Princess. You might want that in working function later."

I laugh before I allow his warm body and steady breathing to pull me under into the most peaceful, dreamless sleep I have had in twelve years.

CHAPTER 17

I WOKE UP feeling the most delicious soreness between my legs and an ache in muscles haven't been used in years. Stretching out, I reach over expecting to find Axel's warm body next to mine but only meet cold sheets.

I open my eyes and look around the room. Empty. Climbing out, I pick up the shirt from last night, pull on a pair of yoga pants from my bag, and continue my search for Axel. The bathroom is empty and so is every room I check after. Not in the kitchen, not in the garage, but his truck is still out front.

I'm standing on the back porch, looking off across the lake at the sun just barely peeking over the tips of the trees. The lake is calm in the early morning hours, and the world seems to be asleep. I am about to give up my search when I see a slight movement down at the end of the dock. The path to his dock is covered slightly by a line of trees, and in the early morning hours, I am worried my eyes might be playing tricks on me. When I see the movement again, I realize I have just found him.

Tiny pinpricks shoot through my feet when I hit the cold pebbled walkway on the way down to the docks. I keep my eyes on his naked back. He is sitting at the very end of the dock, his legs are folded up, and his arms are resting against his knees. It isn't until I get a little closer that I realize his head is resting against his arms and his back is heaving with deep breaths. He has to have felt my footsteps against the wood of the dock, but if he did, he didn't change his posture.

"Ax?" I ask softly.

No response.

"Baby?" I try again.

Nothing.

Sighing deeply, I sit down and bring my body close to his. My legs fall open and the cold skin of his back hits my front. He must be frozen.

"Jesus, Axel, how long have you been out here?"

Nothing.

"Ax, baby, please. You're scaring me. What's going on?"

He's silent for a while. His body jerks slightly, giving away his silence for anything but what it is. My big strong man is breaking. I knew he was holding his pain tight last night, trying to be strong for me. Trying to keep his torment from showing.

I bring my arms around and lace my fingers together against his chest, his heart beating rapidly against my arm. His body stills when I place my lips against his back and whisper the only thing I can think of. "It's okay, Ax. You can't hold this in. For years I have and it doesn't help." Then I fall silent and hold him tight, hoping he opens up to me.

"It's my fault," he finally says, his voice thick with emotion.

"What? What is?" I question.

"Everything."

We fall silent again while I puzzle over his response. We were both victims here in fate's cruel game of keep-away. I don't understand how he can even begin to blame himself.

"Baby, you have to give me more than that. There is no way any of this is your fault," I plead.

He straightens his body but doesn't make the move to turn. Letting his legs fall to dangle from the end of the wooden path, he turns his head and looks over at the sun rising slowly above the tree line. He brings his arms up from their relaxed position at his sides and closes them over mine before pulling my arms away from his chest and clasping our hands together on his lap.

"The first thing I did when I left June and Donnie's was report them to child services. Between the conditions they forced us to live in, the food they refused us, and Donnie's creepy behavior with the little girls, there was plenty to shut them down. They lost every child the state was paying for. It's no fucking wonder she slammed the door in my face when I went on my search for you." He lets out a humorless laugh before continuing. "I wouldn't have even bothered, Izzy…

but I was fucking desperate to find you."

"She opened the door, and when she saw it was me, the bitch spit in my fucking face. I didn't even get a word out. She did manage to tell me about your parents. I will spare you the details on that, but I got nothing else. She must have loved knowing she had the key to my finding you, the key to keeping me from you."

When I feel wetness fall on the arm resting on his lap, I lift my cheek from his back and look up at the cloudless sky before realizing it was coming from him. My heart is breaking just a little more from knowing just how deep his agony is rooted.

"I never got your letters, Izzy. You know… You fucking know I would have come running. Not a single one. I wasn't at base long. I can't give you much but they scooped me up quick and I had to leave. Top-secret shit and I went dark, baby. I wrote you a letter that explained it all, but the timing of your parents… It makes sense you never got it. I had no fucking clue you were writing, trying to find me." He shakes his head as if that simple move can purge the bitterness of his memories.

"Baby…" I don't know what to say.

He squeezes my hands and lets me know that he needs this. He needs to get this out. "Fucking killing me, Izzy…to know that I was so close to you but so fucking far. Knowing that you and our… baby…" He pauses on a sob that catches his words, "Our baby, God, our baby… That baby would have been the most perfect child ever born." His big body folds over and he starts crying in earnest. Tears of my own are falling down my face and onto his back, but I just hold him tighter.

I give him the time he needs to get it out, holding him tight and whispering words of love against his back.

We sit there for a while. He lets out his anguish and I hold him, offering what strength I can. The sun is finally up when he sits back up and turns his head. His eyes are red and the tears are still falling silently. Seeing him like this is destroying me.

"I would have loved that baby, loved that baby so much, Izzy. We would have been so happy," he says, each word pushing an invisible dagger into my heart. I know it isn't my fault that I miscarried, and I long ago coped with the loss, but right now, in this moment, I feel as if it happened yesterday.

"I know, Axel," I offer. "I wish I knew what to say to help you, to ease this pain."

He turns his body so that he is sitting completely on the dock before opening his arms; I climb in. "All these years, I was so mad at you and I held onto that anger so I wouldn't feel the hurt. Fuck me, Izzy. I thought you were happy, that you had moved on without even a second thought. I don't even know how to begin processing this. I don't know how to grieve a child I never knew I almost had." His words are soft above my head as we sit there looking across the water that is lapping up against the shore. We silently mourn the past that was taken from us without our knowledge.

"When I lost the baby, I wasn't in a good place, Axel. It took me a while, a long while, before I started to feel human again. At that point, I thought you were gone, Ax… I thought you were lost to me forever, and when I lost that baby, it was like I lost the last part of love we had." I turned to look at him. "When I met Brandon I was vulnerable. I wasn't looking for someone, but he knew how to play the part and he made me need him. Looking back now, I know I never loved him. I needed the love that I thought he could bring me. I was so alone. I need you to know that I never once stopped loving you Axel. Please don't take that on your shoulders."

He looks at me like he is looking into my soul before placing a soft kiss against my forehead. "I know, Izzy. I don't know all of the details to your marriage, but I know you, and I believe that."

We sit down by the lake with the cold November breeze blowing and I tell him about meeting Brandon and the early years before the abuse. Axel handles it well, only tensing up a few times. When I start to get to the bad stuff, I can feel the rage building. I gloss over a lot of the bad stuff, but by the end, he knows everything. I think he is going to blow a gasket when I tell him about the letter from June.

"She fucking told you what?!" he yelled.

"Uh. She said that you were dead. I don't know why I believed her. I really don't. You have to know that I would never have given up on you and on us. But, Axel? She said you were dead and I had no other way of confirming if it was true or not. It was her way of making me think the worst, and I did."

AXEL

He looks mad. No, not mad. He looks bloodthirsty.

"I will kill that bitch," he grinds out. His eyes are flashing and his nostrils are flaring with each rapid breath.

"Seriously, Ax, can we just look forward now? No one wants to see her get hers more than I do but look where we are. We won. You and I, we are finally back to where we are meant to be. Don't let her win. Please." It takes a while but he calms down. We sit there in silence while he takes in everything I just told him. I can see all the emotions, from anger to resolve, cross over his face.

"I wish I would have tried harder. I keep thinking if I would have approached you when I finally found you that things would be different now. We might have more kids; I would finally have my rings on your finger. It kills me, fucking kills me," he says when I finish explaining everything the last twelve years has brought me.

"Stop it." I get off his lap and kneel in front of his relaxed form leaning against one of the posts supporting the dock. Taking his face between my hands and leaning in close, before I finish. "You can't sit here and play what-if. It has taken me a long time to realize that what-ifs will never change the past, Axel. Right here and right now, you have to promise me that we look forward. No more living with what we could have had. From this day on, we are the new Axel and Izzy."

A small smile forms on his face and some of the sadness leaves his eyes. I lean in and kiss him quickly before releasing his face and sitting back down next to him.

"Axel and Izzy, huh? That mean you want to be my girlfriend or some shit?" He laughs and it sounds like music to my ears.

"No, I just want to be yours. That's all I've ever wanted," I answer, reaching over and linking our hands.

"Princess, you have always been mine. Always. I can promise you to try, but this shit will sit heavy. You have no idea what I want to do to that motherfucker."

"I know, but can we try? Just try to take each day as the gift it is? I finally have you back, Axel, and for once in a long time, I feel like myself again. Baby, I feel strong."

His eyes flare as he pulls me close and plasters a kiss so full of love on my lips that the cold around us has been forgotten.

"Let's get inside. I'm suddenly starving," he says with a wink.

We stand up and walk back into the warmth of his empty house hand in hand.

Axel

I SLOWLY shift from the bed for the second time this morning after wearing Izzy out. Goddamn, crawling back into her tight fucking pussy was like coming home all over again. My dick starts getting hard just thinking about how rough we came together. All the emotions hung thick between us, but knowing that she was finally—fucking finally—my girl again had me feeling like I needed to mark her.

I look down at the angel sleeping in my bed and smile. She is passed out and I doubt an earthquake would wake her at this point. It's been three hours since we climbed back up to the house from our talk at the docks. Three hours of intense lovemaking that had us both screaming over and over. I don't even think there is a drop of come left in my balls at this point. She sucked me dry—literally. A few times.

I have to leave this room before the sight of her naked body, every creamy, exposed inch of her skin, has my dick begging for more. More importantly, I need to get this phone call over with before she wakes up.

Jogging down the stairs and into the kitchen, I locate my cell on the counter, where I tossed it last night, and walk out the back to place the call.

The phone rings a few times before I hear Greg's muffled voice come over the line.

"What, motherfucker?" he says

"Nice. Good morning to you too, asshole." It's 10:00 in the morning. Shouldn't he be doing something productive? "Long night?"

"What do you want, Reid?"

"Jesus Christ, are you always a little bitch in the morning? Forget it. I need you to get with Locke and run every fucking thing you can on Izzy's ex. I want the fucking dirt and I want it yesterday. Hear this, G. I want him so fucked that he will feel my dick in his throat. We need to find something that will lock this bastard up for-fucking-ever."

That got his attention.

"She finally opened up to you, huh." Not a question, but he would get an answer.

"I know everything, G. No secrets between us now. Once we get this motherfucker put away, I can finally give my girl the future we were meant to have. I might not like that you are so close to MY girl, but I am man enough to appreciate everything you have done for her when I couldn't."

"Yeah, I hear you."

"Do it. Call Locke, and you two do whatever needs to be done. Keep me posted, but I plan on locking my doors and burying myself deep in my girl for days. Do not fucking bother me unless you have something."

I hang up the phone to his laughter before slowly climbing the stairs, falling back into my bed, and pulling my girl close.

Finally feeling like my heart can beat again.

Izzy

I CAN feel the sun warming my skin. I love this blissful state between sleep and just waking. But I no longer relish this moment for being numb. No...now I relish this moment because it reminds me that I am alive.

The sun streaming through the big picture windows warms my back, and the hard warmth under my cheek is all radiating from Axel.

My Axel.

I sigh, slowly bring my head off his chest, and look into his sleeping face. He looks youthful in his sleep. The hardness that is normally present is wiped clean. All the heavy emotion from yesterday has been erased and the small smile that teases his lips reminds me of our promise. From this point, on there is no more pain of the past hanging between us. We are once again Axel and Izzy.

It's fucking beautiful.

Running my eyes down his long, hard body, I notice the tent pitching the sheets that lie loosely on his hips. With a naughty smile, I softly run my hand down his abdomen, enjoying the tensing of his abs as I caress each inch. I check to make sure he is still asleep before I slowly peel the sheet off his body. His thick cock springs up once free of the sheet, standing tall from his body and begging for attention, judging by the small drop of come oozing from the tip.

Jesus, I still can't believe how different his body is.

When my hand reaches his neatly trimmed pubic hair, I slide it under his straining skin and cup his warm balls. I roll them softly and test their heaviness before running my hand up and over the silky skin of his throbbing erection. More pre-come seeps from the tip, and my mouth waters at the sight.

Leaning up from where I'm resting next to his side, I bring my body down next to his hips, my legs folded under me, and lower my lips down towards his cock. I lick the drop of come off the tip before placing a soft kiss against his heated skin. He offers a soft moan and stirs slightly but doesn't wake. Wrapping my hand around the thickness of his cock, I notice for the first time just how large he is. *Is he even going to fit in my mouth?*

Licking my lips, I open wide and suck the mushroomed tip into my mouth, swirling my tongue around before releasing and running my tongue from tip to root. He lets out a louder groan and I see his hand fisting the out of the corner of my eye.

I continue licking and caressing his throbbing cock a few times before he lets out a loud curse and shifts swiftly, bringing his torso up roughly. The movement jars me enough that I lose my suction and he falls from my mouth with a loud pop that echoes through the room.

His eyes are dark with desire; the hunger is heavy in the room.

"Good morning," I offer with a wicked smile. "I got hungry."

"Fuck me. Got hungry, huh? Jesus, baby, you're going to kill me." He smiles before he reaches down and pulls me up his body. "Love your mouth on my dick, baby, but I love your pussy more." He grips me by the hips and lifts up. He needs no help persuading me to guide him inside my seeping body. I was ready for him the second I opened my eyes.

Our lovemaking is hard and quick. Before I know it, we are both crying out in our shared climax.

I fall back onto his chest, slick with his perspiration that is sliding against my own.

"Good morning, Princess," he mumbles into my hair.

We both laugh and I hold him closer, enjoying this new lightness between us. We cuddle there for a while before he gets up to clean himself off. I smile when he walks back from the bathroom with a washcloth in hand.

"You do know I know how to clean up myself, right?" I joke.

"My job. I like seeing my come all over your skin. Mine. This is my job." He continues to wipe me clean before leaning down and giving my sensitive skin a kiss that causes me to moan long and loud.

He laughs lightly, falling back next to me in the bed.

"We might want to get up at some point today," I note, looking over to the window. The sun is hanging high in the sky, letting us know we have missed a good portion of the day.

"I'm happy right where I am and have no plans of leaving this bed today."

"Hate to point out the obvious, Axel, but we might want to eat at some point." I look into his smiling eyes before continuing. "I mean, I don't know about you, but I plan on enjoying this fine-ass body some more today and I will need some fuel!"

His body shakes with silent laughter and I cuddle back down next to his side. Reaching out, I touch the hands of the angel tattooed on his other side. I can't see the body from here, but from what I remember of the tattoo, it was done in almost a loving and peaceful way.

"Why an angel?" I ask.

He is silent for a few seconds before answering. "Look closer," is all I get.

Puzzled by his answer, I crawl over his body and bring my face closer to the tattoo. I gasp when I get my first good look at her face. It's me. Holy shit, that's me.

"Um…" I offer lamely.

"I told you, you were the only person I have ever given my heart to. You have always been the angel in my life, Izzy. You came into my life when I needed you the most, always happy and so full of love for me. Not one day went by that I didn't know how you felt. I got this a few years ago. You might not have been by my side physically but I couldn't deny you were there mentally. Every day I was gone, it was the memory of you that pushed me, and even when I thought I had lost you for good and through that anger…" He trails off and I look up into his eyes. "Even through the anger of losing you, I still knew you were my angel. My light."

Oh my God.

"I love you, Princess."

"I love you, too," I croak and fall into his arms.

In that moment, I know that whatever was broken over the years has finally been put back together again.

I am whole.

CHAPTER 18

ONE MONTH LATER

A XEL AND I have been going strong since that weekend we spent locked in his house. It is sometimes shocking for me to think back to the scared and lost girl I was just months ago. He brought out the old me. And I am shining. We have new dreams and plans for our future, and for once, I'm starting to think fate is done with me.

I am happy.

I am loved.

I have overcome.

Over the last few weeks, we have spent almost every second together. Axel likes to joke that he is making up for lost time—a joke that often falls short because it would always remind me of the time we spent apart. Until he starts taking my clothes off. Our desire for each other is like an itch we can't scratch.

We haven't spent a large amount of time with our friends, but we have had a few nights out with them for dinner or drinking. I am able to do all of my work from Axel's house, and he spends the majority of his time doing his from home as well. The first thing we did when it became obvious that neither one of us wanted to part from the other was buy office furniture. We now both use the large library space as our dual office. His area takes up much more space. Computer monitors and other technical equipment are spread over every surface on his side of the room. I have a small corner, but that is all I need. We work in silence mostly, but we are together, and at this point, it is something we both need.

Another big purchase we made together was a kitchen table and comfortable couches for the living room. If you didn't know what his house looked like before, you wouldn't be so shocked, but slowly we are turning this large, empty shell of a house he bought into a home for us both.

We were back to 'us' for three weeks when he told me I was moving in. There wasn't any room for arguments, and honestly, I wasn't going to put up any. It might seem soon to most, but with all the time we had lost, it made sense for us. We made the pact to move forward, and that's what we are doing. Picking up the pieces we had lost and putting them back together.

Continuing with our dreams.

Axel has been hinting at marriage, but I'm not sure I'm ready for that yet. Yes, I know it will happen and I know it will happen with him, but we have only been back together a little over a month. Hell, he has only been back in my life for a few months. I feel like we need time. Time for what, I'm not sure, but when the time is right, we will know.

He isn't happy about that. I can tell he wants to have me married and pregnant as soon as possible. His argument? We aren't getting any younger and we both know it will happen, so why wait?

It is the only thing between us that doesn't feel settled.

It is Saturday morning and Christmas is just two weeks away. With my move to Axel's, I have missed my daily dose of Dee. I miss my best friend. I know she is way beyond happy for us and has been busy herself, but it is still an adjustment, going from being dependent on her for my only happiness to seeing her every few days.

We have plans to spend the day shopping, visiting Sway, and having dinner with the gang at Heavy's. Axel has some business he needs to take care of in the office and will be gone most of the day anyway. This is the perfect day to spend with Dee.

I have just finished getting dressed when I hear the doorbell echo though the house. I finish zipping my favorite brown leather boots up over my skinny jeans, and with one last check in the mirror, I run through the hall, down the stairs, and to the foyer.

Throwing open the door with a large smile, I have just enough time to brace myself before Dee is throwing herself in my arms.

"Girlfriend, I have missed you!" she sings in my ear.

"You just saw me the other day, stupid." I laugh and pull away, straightening my cream blouse back into place before looking up into her twinkling brown eyes.

My friend is happy as always, but now that *I* am happy, it is almost like she will burst at any second. Her happiness has hit nuclear levels.

"You're glowing, Dee. I swear to God, one of these days all that joy you keep inside you is going to come pouring out. Like some deranged leprechaun."

She laughs before following me through the foyer, and around the hallway, and into the kitchen.

"Let me grab my purse and we can get going. What time are our appointments with Sway?" I ask while searching through all the junk on the counter for my phone. I know I threw it down here last night when Axel and I had got home from dinner. He practically attacked me when we walked in the door.

"Noon. He said we needed to, and I quote, 'get our fine little skinny white asses over there with a quickness so Sway can get all the good gossip about our new man candy.' Her impersonation of Sway is disturbing.

"Okay, okay. Well, Ax is going to be in the office all day. He got a call from Mad early this morning and took off quick. Did Beck say anything about it?" I look over at her face, losing its smile slightly before quickly hiding the slip. "What was that, Dee? Are you and Beck having issues?" She has been 'dating' Beck for a few months now. From what I can tell, that just meant they were having regular sex because they never went out alone.

"Ahhh…" She looks down at her phone, trying to avoid my questioning eyes. "We decided to cool it for a while."

"Okay," I respond. I can tell she doesn't want to talk about it, and knowing Dee, if she doesn't want to talk about something, she won't. "Are you okay with that?"

"Sure I am." Her face takes on a fake smile. "It was my idea, okay? He wanted more and I am not ready for that. It's fine, really. You ready?"

Okay. Guess that means the topic is closed.

We climb into Dee's Lexus before heading out to do some much needed Christmas shopping.

I somehow manage to cool her shopping high down today and it is an almost pleasant experience. I pick up some clothes for Axel and a kickass black leather jacket that I decide he has to have, plus a few sexy pieces from Victoria's Secret for myself. I run into the local jeweler and pick up the piece I had commissioned out for his Christmas present.

I can't wait to give it to him. I had the jeweler custom make a dog tag necklace for him. I used the tiny diamond from my old promise ring he had gave me the day he left for boot camp and engraved a message for him underneath it. You could hardly see the tiny diamond until the engraver placed some marks around the spot, highlighting it perfectly. It was hard for me to part with that ring. It held so many memories and promises. Knowing that Axel would open his gift and know what that diamond meant is the only reason I was able to do it. I spent hours searching for the right words to engrave on his dog tag. It finally hit me one day and the words just popped into my head.

When you are with me, I am free.
My strength. My heart. My everything.
Our love now continues forever.
Amor Vincit Omnia

'Love Conquers All.' It is perfect. And it is us.

Axel has been secretive about what he has planned. He has gone off shopping a few times but never came home with anything. Something told me to expect a proposal, and even though it freaks me out slightly that it is too soon, I know I will never be able to tell him no.

He is my dreams.

He is my future.

It is almost time for our appointment with Sway, and I am both looking forward to and dreading the appointment. I just know that when Sway figures out who Axel is there will be a big flamboyant display.

"What's with the big goofy grin?" Dee asks, interrupting my

thoughts.

"I didn't even realize I was smiling. I was just thinking about how Sway will react when he realizes the giant hunk of sex in the building next to his salon is Axel."

"Oh my God! I completely forgot about that! Girl, this is going to be hilarious!"

"You are not kidding. I was hoping that he wouldn't find out, but when I told Axel the story, he thought it was too funny to pass up. Apparently the boys are coming over to say hello while we are there."

She looks over at me in shock before continuing the drive to the salon. I expected humor, but she looks almost panicked.

"Are you okay, Dee? I know we don't get as much time to talk as we used to, but you seemed fine the other night."

A slight frown crosses her face before she quickly clears her expression. "I'm fine. Just busy at work."

Liar. I make a mental note to ask Axel if Beck has said anything lately.

"All right, but you know if you need to talk, I'm here. I'm always here for you, Dee." Ever since I moved out, things have felt strange with Dee. I know she is happy for me and I know she loves Axel, but there is something going on. "I love you, Dee. I hate knowing something is bothering you and you don't want to talk."

"It's nothing." She sighs. "Just have some stuff on my mind, but I need to work it out on my own. Promise." She gives me one of her trademark smiles and it reassures me enough to drop it. For now.

We pull up at the salon fifteen minutes before our appointments. Sitting in front, looking at the rows of businesses in the small strip, I can't help but smile when my eyes hit the simple, bold words—Corps Security. The windows are blacked out so we can't see inside, but I know he's there. My man is close. As if my heart knows, it starts picking up speed.

We get out of the car and start toward the building. Dee looks beautiful in fitted jeans, a long-sleeved sweater, and of course, her pencil-thin heels. She attempted to get me to shed my old clothes, but I stuck with what was familiar. I will never have her classy style, but I am finally holding my own.

I can see Sway inside waving at us like a crazy person through the floor-to-ceiling windows that line the salon. He is dressed similar to Dee, with skin-tight skinny jeans and a long pink sweater. But his sweater flares at the waist and elbows. He looks like a giant cotton candy ball. His boots are up to his knees, but unlike my flat soles, his are sporting five-inch heels. He has his long blond wig pulled up into a sleek ponytail. Jesus, if I didn't love him, I would laugh.

"He looks wound up today." Dee laughs.

Right when my feet hit the landing in front of Sway's salon, the door to Corps opens wide and Axel is standing in front of me, his arms crossed over his wide chest and a smirk firmly in place. I am frozen with my hand outstretched to open the door and Dee bumps into me from behind.

"Oh wow," I hear her mumble behind me. Oh wow is right.

His dark denim jeans are molded to his powerful thighs and his long-sleeved green Henley is stretched tight. His thick black hair has the same look that it did this morning when I had just gotten done running my hands through it and holding him tight to my pussy. Those green eyes I love so much shine bright.

My panties are instantly wet.

"Get over here and give your man some love," he rumbles out, causing another surge of wetness to hit my panties.

I throw my purse into Dee's arms and run over the short distance to Axel. Jumping up slightly, he catches me under my ass and hauls my body up his own. I can feel every hard inch rubbing against my front. I let out a soft moan before sealing my lips to his and diving into one of the best kisses ever.

He gives my ass a squeeze before releasing my lips and smiling down at me. "Hey, Princess."

"Hey, baby."

And that's when the shrieking began.

"Oh my honey Jesus. You did NOT tell Sway that you knew this fine mountain of a man, no you did NOT. Holy goodness Lord above, I need a cold shower after that, girlfriend. You get your pretty little self into my chair and you tell Sway all about it. Every single delectable thing about it, if you know what I mean. Sweet heavens, I need a drink."

I turn my head from my perch in Axel's arms and laugh down at Sway. He is standing in the doorway of the salon fanning his face.

"What is that?" Axel asks softly into my ear so only I hear him.

Turning around with a bright smile, I say, "That is Sway."

He laughs. "I don't know if I should laugh or run."

"I would run, you big beautiful hunk!" Sway yells over my laughter. "Oh my lawd, I would run. In fact, take that shirt off when you do…sweet lord, yes!"

I laugh harder and almost fall out of his arms. When I finally control myself, I look up into his smiling face. His smile is so wide and his eyes are full of love. "Love hearing you laugh, Princess. Most beautiful sound in the world."

He drops me softly down onto my feet and holds his hand out to Sway.

"Holt Reid, nice to meet you."

"Oh, honey, the pleasure is all mine…all mine. Sway's the name but you can call me whatever you want." He places his hand delicately in Axel's big paw and bows.

This time, Dee joins me and we laugh at Sway's antics. Looking at the two of them together is one of the funniest things I have seen in a while. Axel is six foot six of pure, raw masculinity, and Sway, with all his short, round fatness stuffed in tight women's clothing, looks ridiculous next to him.

"Yo, Reid… We going to finish this shit up or do you plan on being here all fucking day?" I hear the deep baritone of Greg call from inside the open door behind Axel.

"Oh sweet Lord in heaven…there are more?" Sway asks, looking over his shoulder at me, his long ponytail slapping against Axel's chest. I can't answer because the look of horror on Axel's face has me in fits again.

"Come on, Sway. Let's get you and giggles-a-lot inside," Dee says with a soft chuckle. She pushes me and I stumble sideways before composing myself. "If you don't help me get him out of here before the rest of them file out, we might be here a while. He's panting, Iz."

"All right, Sway. Dream about my man later. Love you, baby!" I call over my shoulder as we usher Sway back into his salon.

"Oh, Izzy, girl, how do you let him get dressed? A shame, oh it is a shame to let that man ever put clothes on."

The rest of our trip turns out much the same. Sway doesn't shut up for a second and really loses it when he sees Greg and Maddox walk by the front windows. They both wave in greeting to Dee and me. Sway starts jumping up and down and goes on and on for the rest of my appointment about what an injustice it is that not one of those 'hunk pieces of sex with legs' is gay.

When we (finally) finish up with Sway, it is almost five. Axel's truck is still in the front, so Dee and I walk over to the office. The front reception area is done in black and gray. There is a reception desk in the middle with the Corps Security logo in the center of the wall behind it in large block letters. The office is simple but professional. I smile at Emmy, the secretary, and ask if Axel is busy.

"Not at all, or at least he wasn't a second ago. He's been itching for you to finish up next door, but between you and me, he was too scared of that little blond guy to come check."

I like Emmy. She is soft spoken and somewhat shy, but according to Axel, he wouldn't be able to run this place without her. She is around twenty-five with long blonde hair, light brown eyes, and a face full of freckles. She is the perfect image of the girl next door. I can't help but notice that every time all the guys are around she is silent, but her eyes? They are always following Maddox around.

"Do you mind if I go on back?" I ask.

"Go on ahead. Beck and Coop are around here somewhere. Greg and Locke left a while ago." I can't help but smile when she blushes. Yup, this girl has it bad for Maddox.

"I'm waiting here," Dee says. I look over at her, and she is expressionless and the walls are up. There is definitely something going on with her, and I would bet it has everything to do with Beck.

"All right, be right back."

I walk down the long hallway in search for Axel. Passing the many open doors of the other guys' offices before reaching my destination, I can't help but smile at how successful Axel has become. I always knew he was destined for greatness.

Loud and very infuriated tones reach my ears before I can knock on Axel's door, causing me to pause.

"What the fuck do you mean you can't find the motherfucker?" he asks in a low and lethal tone. One that means he has lost all patience. Uh oh. Silence. "He what?" Silence. "Fuck! No, I don't want you to sit there and play with yourself, dumbass. Find him. I want to know where that bastard is." Some more silence follows and then there's a lot more of Axel yelling before he finally slams the phone down in the cradle. I wait a little longer before pushing open his door with a soft knock.

His enraged gaze hits me and the tension is so thick I can't help but take a step back into the hallway. I let out a small squeak when my back hits someone standing behind me. Whipping around, I see Coop there, and Beck is standing farther down the hall. Coop's normally playful eyes are hard and determined. Beck doesn't look like the carefree guy I am used to.

"Everything okay?" I question.

The guys share a pointed look before Axel answers me, and when I look back over at him, he has carefully masked his fury.

"Yeah, Princess. Get over here. And Coop?" He looks over my shoulder with a scowl. "Get your fucking hands off my woman."

God, I love it when he gets all possessive.

Coop laughs and scoops me up into a big hug and kisses my cheek, earning a deep growl in warning from Axel.

"You do realize he is armed right, jackass?" Beck asks with a smirk.

Armed?

I look over at Axel and don't notice anything out of the ordinary.

"Back holster, hanging behind the chair. My guess is he has at least five knives on him right now and an ankle holster," Coop whispers when he notices my unspoken question.

"Three and no ankle holster today," Axel says with an evil glint to his eyes.

Oh boy.

"Right. Well, if you two are done pissing all over the floor, are you ready to go? Dee is in the lobby and we're ready whenever you are." I walk over and offer him a quick kiss, knowing that if we don't get going we won't get to dinner for a long while.

"Let me finish up in here. I need to brief these two idiots and then we can leave. Go wait with Dee in the lobby." I can tell he means business. Whatever I had overheard before was starting to weigh heavily the air again with his temper.

"All right, baby." With one more kiss, I leave the office and shut the door behind me.

I brush off his mood and continue down the hall. I know they don't handle small things here, and most likely, whatever has him heated up is just a normal kink in their day-to-day operations.

With a smile, I walk back into the lobby and sit with Dee and Emmy. Before I know it, we are in a heated debate on the pros and cons of sexting. I make a mental note to send Axel some fun pictures the next time he comes into the office.

Heavy's is packed by the time we get there. Saturday is normally a big night for them, but tonight they are slammed. Maddox and Greg got here before us and held a table. We talked Emmy into joining us, so by the time everyone arrives, we are already getting loud and rowdy.

We are sitting in the back corner, all eight of us squished around a small table. Food and beer are littering every surface. We have been laughing and having a good time for the last two hours. Once dinner is over, Axel pulls me into his lap and starts whispering all sorts of naughty things he plans to do to me later in my ear. I am trying to pay attention to the friends around us, but the only thing I can think of is getting back to the house.

"What the fuck?" I hear Dee gasp over the rock music pumping through the bar.

I have to work at clearing my mind. Between Axel lust and the beer, I wasn't following her sudden change of mood.

She is staring across the room, where Beck and Coop are at the bar getting the newest pitchers of beer. Coop is flirting with the bartender, but Beck currently has his tongue shoved down the mouth of what we liked to call a Heavy Slut. Bar regular and downright trash. This wasn't normal Beck-style either. It doesn't take a genius to figure out that this is about getting under Dee's skin.

"That stupid little fucker. I hope his dick rots off!" she yells in my ear. Axel starts shaking with laughter before I elbow him in the ribs. I give him a hard look before studying Dee. Now that the alcohol has loosened her up, I can see that, under the anger, there is hurt. Something happened between her and Beck.

Before I can open my mouth and ask her what is going on, she is on her feet and across the bar.

"Uh oh, looks like drama is about to start flying!" Greg yells across the table from his corner next to Maddox and Emmy, who is wide eyed and a little intimidated by our rambunctious group. "What's her issue, Iz?" he asks.

"No clue. She wouldn't talk about it. I thought they had been spending time together?"

"Not since last weekend. I don't know the details, but he showed up at my place pissed as fuck and itching for a fight."

We all watch as Dee walks up to the bar and grabs the Heavy Slut by the roots of her badly dyed blonde hair, pulling her from Beck's hold. I can't hear the words but her face looks horrible. I don't think I have ever seen hatred like that coming from my little ball of joy.

What the fuck?

I make a move to get off Axel's lap and go help but he tightens his arms around my waist.

"No."

One word but no bend. He isn't going to let me wade in.

"Ax, I have to."

"No. Not your fight. They need to work this shit out themselves."

We watch for a few more seconds. To my fascination, Dee throws all her strength into a move that would make any badass proud. She pulls her hand out farther and literally throws this woman across the room. I think everyone at the table is shocked, but then she jumps in Beck's face, giving a few stabs of her finger to his chest and a lot of words before he gives her a feral smile. She cocks her head to the side and shrieks loudly when he jumps forward and throws her over his shoulder.

Before anyone can blink, they are out the door.

"What the hell just happened?" I ask.

"Oh my God!" Emmy gasps.

Maddox is silent, but Greg barks out a loud laugh.

"Princess, that's what happens when shit festers and bitches act like bitches." I turn on Axel and give him a hard glare. He pulls both his arms from my body and holds them up in surrender.

"Shut up. Is she going to be okay?" I ask, all joking aside.

"Yeah, baby. My guess is she will just be well fucked in the morning."

"I'll second that," Coop says when he slides into the seat Dee left. "That was some crazy shit. Who knew that little Miss Cheerleader had it in her!"

All the guys laugh, but I can't help my worry that Dee might be in over her head with Beck.

The night continues with more beer, great food, and a lot of laughter. Even Emmy starts to come out of her shell a little, yet with one look at Maddox, she is right back in there. Axel started rubbing his hands up my legs thirty minutes ago, and I am about to come out of my skin.

"You almost ready, Princess?" he ask against my neck, biting the skin softly before letting me turn my head. "If you say no, I can't be held responsible for my actions. I'm so fucking hard right now I'm ready to throw you down on the table and take you in front of everyone."

And blast off.

"Let's go."

He smiles and we quickly say our goodbyes before heading home.

We didn't make it two steps into the house before he had me against the wall and screaming in pleasure.

CHAPTER 19

OH GOD. I throw my head into the pillow and moan loudly. My stomach lurches when I feel Axel move next to me.

"You okay?" he questions, rubbing his hand down my naked back.

I shake my head. That does nothing but make my stomach protest.

"You didn't drink that much, baby. What's got you upset?"

"Stomach," I croak.

Oh shit. I jump out of bed, and run naked across the room, and slam myself onto the floor in front of the toilet. Everything from last night comes rushing up. I feel Axel come behind me and gather my hair before pressing a cold cloth to my neck.

"Just let it out, Princess. I knew all that BBQ was going to bite you in the ass."

"Shut up," I grumble before letting out a few more heaves. There is nothing left in my body but my stomach is still in knots. Just the thought of all the food I consumed last night causes more heaving to rush up the back of my throat.

Axel stays with me until I feel well enough to get up. I brush my teeth and let Axel carry me back to bed.

"Better?" he asks, the worry clearly dancing over his face.

"Yeah, I'm okay. I guess stuffing the last two plates in my mouth last night wasn't the wisest decision, huh?"

He offers me a weak smile before kissing my forehead and standing from the bed. For the first time in months, the sight of his naked body doesn't immediately make me want to jump him. No, not today.

"Let's try some toast, okay?" he asks. I can tell he is about to crawl out of his skin. He is so concerned something is wrong.

"I'm okay, baby. Just ate something wrong last night. I'm good."
I offer him a weak smile before pressing my face into his pillow and
pulling in his scent. My nerves calm instantly.

He stands there next to the bed for a few minutes to make sure
I'm okay before walking off. I hear him rummaging through the
dresser, assumingly to get dress.

"Be right back, Princess."

"Okay," I mumble, already falling back to sleep.

Axel returns after a couple minutes carrying a tray with dry toast
and ginger ale. He smiles shyly at me when I look up at him.

"God, I love you." I say.

"Love you too, Princess. How's the stomach?"

"Better. At least it isn't protesting the sight of food."

We sit there for a while and I slowly eat the breakfast. Everything
seems to be staying down and I see the concern start to leave Axel's
eyes.

"What's your plan for today?" he questions, clicking the channel
over to the local news.

"Not much. Just catching up on some clients that needed a few
things." I actually planned to finish wrapping up his presents, but he
doesn't need to know that.

"I need to tell you something and I'm not sure how you're going
to take it."

I don't like the sound of that at all. I put the tray on the table next
to the bed and shift to look at him.

"Okay...I'm listening?" I can already tell I won't be happy by
the way he keeps looking at me with dread. "Axel?" I prompt.

"Okay. So I want you to remember that everything I do is to protect you. Got that?"

I nod my head, narrowing my eyes.

"Right. So I've had the guys keeping tabs on that fuckwad for
a while now. So far, we haven't had an inch to go on until last week
when Locke finally found some irregularities in the company reports." I go to interrupt him but he just shakes his head. "Do not ask
me how we got those. You don't need to know the particulars. Anyway, he's been combing over those reports day and night and final-

ly put it all together. Deep, baby. He's been pulling thousands—I'm talking hundreds of thousands—right out from under the old man's nose. Two days ago, Locke followed that trail right into Brandon's pockets. Long story short, Locke sent a nice care package to dear old dad outlining and showcasing all the evidence. The last thing I heard from my inside guy was that old man went balls-to-the-fucking-wall mad. Police were called in and warrants sworn out for Brandon." He studies my face, looking for any sign of displeasure with him for disregarding my wish to just let it all be. He won't find any. As upset that I am at him for keeping his thumb on Brandon, I know why he did it—respect it even.

"And..." I add. "I know there is more, Axel, or you wouldn't be sharing." My tone is neutral but my body is wound tight.

"I had a guy on him. Not one of our men, but one who I know and trust. Brandon, at this moment, is unaccounted for. Police are looking for him. The boys are looking for him. I'm looking for him. He won't hide from me. Hear me now, baby, I will find that fucking shit. But I need you to be safe. Stick close this week, okay? I know you aren't happy about this, but it needed to be done."

I reach out and grab his hand, giving him a small squeeze. "I understand. I'm not mad. A little upset maybe, but I understand where you're coming from. If I'm honest, I don't think I would feel safe knowing he was floating around there." I give him a small smile, noticing that the worry lines have left his face.

"I'll find him." A threat. There will be no mercy from this man if he gets his hands on Brandon.

I snuggle into his side, and we spend the rest of the morning in our bed watching TV and just enjoying being together.

The rest of the day passes uneventfully. Housework and catching up on some of the things I have put off throughout the week.

I have been calling Dee all day but so far haven't heard from her. Axel tells me to leave it be for the day. Chances are she isn't able to come to the phone anyway. He tries to call Beck when I wouldn't leave him alone but just gets voicemail. With a smile and a shrug of his shoulder, we go about the day. I decide to take his advice and just let her call me when she is ready.

I am still not feeling back to normal, so the night ends with us watching movies in bed before drifting off to sleep.

Monday morning starts off much like the morning before. Axel gives me a kiss before the sun is even up and tells me that he needs to go into the office for a few hours but will be back for lunch.

Rolling over slowly, I try to calm my stomach but am unsuccessful and dashing off for the bathroom a few minutes later. I spend the next thirty minutes dry heaving into the toilet before I am able to crawl back to bed. I drift off to a restless sleep not long after my head hits the pillow.

I jolt awake when a chill climbs up my spine. Throwing off the covers, I run down the hallway and stairs before crashing into the office. Pulling up my calendar, I start doing some math in my head. It doesn't take me long before I am dropping heavily into my desk chair.

Holy shit. It can't be.

I sit there staring out the window above my desk, watching the trees sway in the breeze and the water down by the lake ripple with the wind. It makes sense. That was been the week after the attack at my house. I remember taking my pill every day like clockwork but I was also been taking some heavy antibiotics.

Holy shit. I drop my forehead on the desk for a few minutes and allow myself a few seconds to freak out.

I pick up the phone on my desk and try calling Dee again but have no luck. It is still early, so I leave a message for her to call me as soon as possible. I disconnect the call before picking the phone up again and calling my doctor, making an appointment for a few hours from now.

On shaking legs, I make the climb back up the stairs and quickly get ready. I don't even bother with my hair or makeup. I just throw on some jeans and a sweatshirt before dashing out the door.

I make it to the doctor by 9:30 and quickly sign in. I don't have to wait long before my name is being called. I go through the motions with the nurse and then sit, wait, and silently freak out.

An hour later, it's confirmed.

I'm pregnant.

Holy shit, I'm pregnant.

"When was your last menstrual cycle, Ms. West?" the older man asks.

"Um…I don't know. I think it was October, maybe early November?" I have no clue. I'm still in shock. "I don't remember. I'm sorry," I mumble lamely.

"That's all right, dear. Let's go down to the ultrasound room and take a look, okay?"

I don't answer him. I just follow behind him as he guides me into a dimly lit room.

"This is Jane. She is going to do your ultrasound, dear. We can talk when she finishes up." He offers a kind smile before stepping out of the room.

I turn my shocked gaze to Jane. She looks like Nurse Hatchet.

"Undress from the waist down. Sheet goes over your legs. I'll be right back." And then she's gone.

I follow her instructions and sit gingerly on the edge of the exam table. My heart feels like it is going to pop right out of my chest. I have no idea how Axel is going to handle this. Besides the brief discussion by the docks that day, we haven't discussed children. I knew he was still having issues with the loss of our first child, the child he didn't know about until recently, but this is different.

This is our fresh start. This is our new beginning. I place my hands over my stomach protectively.

A baby. We are going to have a baby. I allow myself a small smile but slip my hands from my stomach when a brief knock sounds and Jane walks back in.

She rolls a condom over the probe and asks me to spread my legs. I blanch but do as she asks. After one awkward, slow thrust, I look over at the monitor and stare in fascination as the tiny, grainy dot appears.

"Well, there you go," she says, and for the first time, she sounds almost sweet. "That dot there is the fetus. Looks like you are about five, almost six weeks along, which puts your due date at August 3rd." She prints off a small picture of the baby blob and hands it over into my shocked fingers.

I quickly get dressed, not once taking my eyes off the picture of our baby.

Our baby. As I stand there in the middle of the ultrasound room, the biggest sense of peace settles around me. Axel and I are going to have a baby and I can't wait to share the news. I am scared, but I know deep in my heart that he will be happy. Placing my hands back over my flat stomach, I promise to protect this little bean with every-thing I have.

This baby is so loved already. The love is overflowing into my body and I am walking on cloud nine.

Heaven. Absolute heaven. This is what it feels like to have the world.

I get home a little before lunch, quickly hiding the ultrasound picture away until I find the perfect way to tell Axel. This has to be special. He wasn't there the last time, never got to experience the shock and joy of learning that he was going to be a parent. I can't wait to experience that with him this time. With only a week to go before Christmas, I know the perfect way to let him know.

Axel gets home shortly after I do. We enjoy a nice lunch before he carries me upstairs for dessert.

I love afternoon dessert with Axel.

Luckily for me and my anticipation, the rest of the days before Christmas are spent with Axel trying unsuccessfully to locate Bran-don. I am not focusing on that right now, because I know that tomor-row I will be sharing my news with Axel.

It is Christmas Eve and we have decided to spend the night in and watch old movies. I finally got ahold of Dee two days ago. She has basically disappeared since Beck carried her out of the bar. She was short and, I could tell, frustrated. We made tentative plans to ex-change our gifts tomorrow, but that was all.

I drift off to sleep with a smile on my face and butterflies in my belly. Tomorrow is the day I make one of our dreams come true.

"Good morning, Princess, Merry Christmas," I hear whispered lightly in my ear followed by a soft kiss behind my ear. "Time to get up. Breakfast and Santa," he says with a smile.

"If you're playing Santa, can I sit on your lap first?" I reply, roll-ing over and rubbing my throbbing nipples against his chest.

He lets out a groan before bringing his lips down to my own. He trails slow kisses and nips down my neck and across my collarbone and then drags his tongue across the swell of my breast before taking a painfully hard nipple into his mouth. He sucks deeply and flicks the tiny barbell with his tongue, bringing up his hand and pinching my other nipple between his fingers. I feel the sensation all over my body.

"How ready for me are you, Princess? Is your sweet fucking pussy dripping for me yet? Begging for my dick?" He trails his hand down my stomach, and my oversensitive skin screams for the feelings only he can bring me. "Huh, Princess? Want me to make you fucking scream?

"Oh yes, please, Axel, please… I need you so fucking bad," I beg. My pussy is begging to be filled filled and fucked hard.

"Jesus Christ, Izzy, you're fucking soaked." He brings his hand up and I can see my juices glistening on his fingers. He licks his fingers clean before taking his rigid flesh in his hand and rubbing it against my clit. The most exquisite shocks shoot up from my core. My womb clenches and I groan loud and shamelessly. "My girl wants my dick, doesn't she?" he asks. I nod my head; speech is beyond me now. I can feel the claws of my climax climbing up my spine; every inch of my skin is on fire.

I feel his broad head stretching my entrance before he gives a slow thrust, seating himself deep within me.

"Oh my GOD!" I scream and clench down on his dick.

He hisses and holds still and deep. "Baby, got to stop or I'm going to come right fucking now. Goddamn your tight pussy loves my dick." He drops his head to my neck and clamps down before moving his hips.

He starts off slow, building the friction until I almost can't take it anymore, and gradually builds up speed. Before I know it, I am screaming his name and he is slamming into my waiting body. He brings his hands down and lifts my hips up to meet each one of his powerful thrusts. My hands snake around his body and my nails bite the skin before I throw my head back and scream. I swear the house is falling around us, lights are exploding, and the world is shaking. With one more powerful thrust, I feel the warm jets of his orgasm empty into my body.

We lie there for some time while our bodies return to earth.

Rubbing my arms back and forth across his sweaty back, I kiss the side of his face. "Merry fucking Christmas," I whisper, enjoying the feeling of his semi-hard dick moving with his laughter inside of me. Tremors are still shooting through my body.

"Merry fucking Christmas is right, Princess."

He slowly pulls out of me and we both let in a sharp pull of air at the loss of each other. He makes quick work of cleaning me off before we get dressed and make our way down to the living room, where we set up Christmas.

I busy myself with making breakfast while he sets up the living room. He starts bringing in boxes from all over the house and, with a devilish smirk, joins me in the kitchen.

"Where did all of that come from?" I ask in awe.

"Been busy, baby," he says sitting down and starting in on his pancakes.

"Obviously." I smile and join him, making quick work of breakfast so we can get down to gifts.

He doesn't stop smiling the whole time we eat, and by the time we finish, we are both sporting ridiculously happy grins.

We start with his gifts. They start off small, some new design programs for my computer I have been looking for, earrings, some barely there garments that earn a slap from me, some odds and ends things I have been raving about for the house, and finally, a large but flat package is pulled out from behind the tree. When I look at him with a question, he just gestures at the package. I walk over from the recliner I was lounging in and start to gently pull the paper off. When I finally get it off, I notice that I am looking at the back of a very large canvas of some kind. He is looking at me with patience but also a small bit of fear. I wrinkle my brow at him before turning it around.

When I see the picture looking back at me, I almost lose it. It is beautiful. The old me would have looked at this picture like I had so many times over the years and let the painful memories consume me. But now, with Axel by my side, I can look at it and smile. I can look at this picture and see the overwhelming love two young kids had for each other.

"It's stunning, Axel. I love it." My words are so soft they are barely audible.

"You aren't mad, are you? You left that box of pictures out a few weeks ago and I got the idea." He seems to be walking around on eggshells, worrying that I won't like it—or worse that, it will cause me pain.

"God, no. It's perfect." And it is.

The picture is of Axel and me the day he left for boot camp. I still remember the day my mom brought it back from the store. She had a smile on her face and tears in her eyes. They had framed it and given it to me the same day.

In the picture, Axel was hanging out the bus window, one hand hanging on to the window frame and the other reaching down and holding mine. You can just see his broad shoulders dressed in his camouflage and his newly shaved head. I still remember taking my father's clippers to his silky locks the night before he left. I was standing on the tips of my toes, stretching up as tall as I could and meeting his waiting lips in a sweet kiss. I had bought a new soft yellow sundress to wear that day and it was hanging beautifully from my youthful body.

There was so much love, promise, and sadness in that picture. It is us. It is our past and our future and it is absolutely perfect.

With tears rolling down my face, I carefully lean it against the wall before throwing my arms around his neck and peppering his face with kisses. "I love it, Axel. It is the best gift I have ever received. I love you so, so much."

"I love you too, Princess." He kisses me softly and wraps his arms around my back, holding me tight to his body.

We stay like that for just a second, soaking in the peaceful contentment that swirls in the air.

"My turn?" I ask into his neck.

"Not yet, Princess. One more." He loosens his hold on me, placing my feet back onto the floor, and takes a step back. Reaching into his pocket, he pulls out a small blue box before dropping to one knee in front of me. The tears that stopped from before are back with a rush.

Oh. My. God.

"Izzy, from the first moment our eyes met, I knew you would be mine forever. There wasn't a day that passed that you didn't hold my heart. Everything I have ever done in my life was with you in mind, even when I didn't think this moment would ever come. It was all I prayed for. We might not have had the easiest road to get here, but know, from this day forward, I will do everything within my power to ensure that there is nothing but perfection. The happiness and love we deserve, baby. Will you do me the greatest honor and become my wife?" When he finishes, I can hardly see him through the tears gathering around my eyes, blurring my vision before falling down my face.

"Yes. Yes, a million times over!" I yell and drop to the ground in front of him, throwing my arms around his neck and kissing him with so much love and exuberance. "Yes!" I scream, throwing my head back and smiling wide.

He laughs and opens the box. Inside is a stunning ring. A large round center diamond is set high on the thick platinum band. On each side of the center stone are three rows of more diamonds, the center row being slightly larger than the two on the outside.

It is the most beautiful ring I have ever seen in my life.

He slips it on my finger and brings the hand up to his lips for a soft kiss.

"You're finally going to be my wife," he says against my hand, his warm breath tickling the skin.

"You're finally going to be my husband." I smile back.

I give him another kiss before pulling away and looking down at my hand.

I can't help but just think finally, finally, FINALLY.

"Okay, this will be hard to top."

He offers an arrogant smile before walking over to plop down on the recliner I just left. "Oh yeah, Princess. There is no way you are topping that," he replies pointing down at my hand.

I smile to myself and start handing him the boxes. He laughs when he gets to the Victoria's Secret lingerie. "Great minds think alike." We laugh together and he places the box off to the side.

I hand him the box with the dog tag and watch his face when he opens it. He sits there for the longest time just looking into the box.

His face is void of emotions.

"Jesus," he chokes out. "Izzy, Princess, this is fucking amazing."

He looks at it for a few more minutes and asks me what the line at the end means.

"Love conquers all," I reply with a smile.

He fingers the necklace lightly and notices the diamond for the first time. "Is that..." He trails off.

"Yeah. I kept it. Locked away but I never let that ring go. I thought it was perfect."

"It is... It is perfect," he whispers.

He looks up, and the emotion in his depths causes me to stagger a bit. "Wear it always... Never coming off," he says, pulling it from the box and pulling the chain over his head, dropping it to setting against his chest.

"One more," I say, the butterflies picking up speed in my stomach. "You kind of helped me pick this one out actually," I add, walking over to the tree and pulling out a small box.

The smile on his face is one of pure bliss. This day has been perfect, and I pray this will be the icing on the cake.

He starts tearing off the paper and opens the lid on the box before pulling out the mug. He has it backwards at first and looks at me with a perplexed expression that turns to a questioning one when he notices my nerves. "Spin it," I say, twirling my finger in a circle.

He takes the coffee mug and spins it around. I watch when the clouds clear and his jaw drops in shock. He looks up at me, down at the coffee mug, to my belly, then back to my face before returning his eyes to the mug he is holding reverently in his hands. He sits there, his head bowed, and just looks at the mug. I picture it in my mind, knowing what he is seeing, and a small smile tugs at my lips.

The gray mug has a copy of the first ultrasound picture on it, and underneath the picture, it says, '#1 Dad – Coming This Summer'.

He is silent for so long that I start to worry. Oh God, I didn't think what I would do if he isn't happy about it. I can't stand the thought of being without him, but if he doesn't want our baby, I would have to learn.

"Axel?" I question.

He sets the mug down on the coffee table before climbing to his feet. I don't catch his expression before he wraps his arms around me softly and holds me close. I still can't judge his mood or feelings about becoming a father. The worry inside me is starting to take root and I feel like I might be sick.

"Princess…" he whimpers. His giant body starts to shake slightly under my arms, and I realize he is too overcome with emotions to talk right now.

I hold him and he holds me. I can feel his tears wetting the skin through my shirt. My own are coming freely. He leans back and looks into my eyes, bringing his arms around and wiping his eyes clear.

"A baby? You're having my baby?" he says in astonishment. "We're having a baby?" he repeats, a huge smile coming over his face. "We're going to have a baby!" he booms through the living room and picks me up in a tight hug before spinning me around.

I laugh at his liveliness.

He drops me to my feet again and slams down to his knees, pulling up my shirt and pressing a soft kiss to my flat stomach. Splaying his hands wide across my belly, he whispers to the skin, "We're going to love you so much, little one."

I hiccup on a sob and run my hands through his hair. He looks up at me with his bright emerald eyes full of peacefulness and blinding love.

"We're having a baby." He wraps his arms tightly around my middle and holds me close with his head against my stomach.

I hold his head to my skin and echo back to him, "We're having a baby."

CHAPTER 20

I STILL CAN'T believe it. Not only am I engaged to be married, but our baby is growing inside my body. Once Axel was over his shock, we spent the rest of the day in bed, celebrating as he said. I can't say no to him. He is over the moon, and I want that closeness only he can give me. We fell asleep well after midnight, his arm draped over my stomach, holding my belly with his large hand.

My phone starts buzzing the next morning, reminding me that I set my alarm so I could get up and over to Dee's before it got too late. Axel and I have plans to go to dinner tonight and celebrate—with clothes on this time.

I lift Axel's arm off my belly and walk across the room to the bathroom. Pausing to look over at his sleeping form, I see that the dark sheets are riding low on his naked hips. He has one arm over his abdomen and the other stretches out under my pillow. The desire to crawl back in bed and cuddle close is strong, but I need to hurry so I can make my plans with Dee and be home early enough for dinner. Once Dee and I get talking, I know I won't be home anytime soon.

I pull on my favorite pair of black leggings and an oversized knit sweater. Grabbing my black boots, I walk out of the closet and almost collide with Axel. I look him over from head to rock-hard dick to toe. Good enough to eat.

"You're killing me, Ax! You know I have to get going before Dee starts knocking the doors down here. It should be illegal for you to look that good in the morning." I brush my hand down his stomach and grab ahold of his dick, stroking him lightly a few times. "I love how hard you are for me." I kiss the corner of his lips and step away before he can grab me.

A low rumble sounds from his lips. "You remember this moment tonight when you're begging me to let you come. Going to keep you right on the edge for hours. Hours, baby." He swats my butt before walking into the bathroom and turning on the shower. "Call me when you get there!" he yells over the spray of the shower.

"Will do. Love you!"

My phone rings on the way over to Dee's house. I answer and press speaker before placing the phone back down. "Hey, you! Merry Christmas."

"Merry Christmas, baby girl." Greg's deep voice comes through the line. "Missed you yesterday."

I feel a little bad about closing our friends out yesterday, but with it being our first Christmas back together, plus one that was so full of special moments for us as a couple, it didn't feel right to open it up for everyone.

"I know, G. I missed you, too. I'm on the way over to Dee's house now if you want to come meet us for lunch. I've got your gifts in the car. Plus, I've got some news for you." I smile when the line goes silent. I know Greg. Right now he is probably picturing every kind of 'news' I could possibly have for him. He might correctly guess one, but there is no way he would guess them both.

"Wouldn't miss it, baby girl. I got some work to finish up before I head over. Give you and Dee some time to do your thing."

"Sounds good. I'm glad I get to see you today. I was just telling Ax last night that we needed to have y'all over for dinner."

"Something tells me Reid didn't want to share your time, right?"

"Ah...something like that." I laugh, and we continue with the small talk before hanging up.

I try calling Dee to let her know Greg is coming but she doesn't answer. I brush off the flicker of worry that floats across my skin. Knowing Dee, she is still in the bathroom with the music cranked up to ungodly levels while she gets ready.

I pull up into the driveway of my old home with Dee and climb out. It is a beautiful morning. The sky is clear and blue, and the winter chill is blowing softly. There was talk of snow this weekend, but knowing Georgia weather, it would change a few times before the weekend hit and there would be no snow. My hair flies around my

AXEL

head when a strong gust hits my face, causing me to shiver. Pulling my coat tighter to my body, I walk to the back of my car.

I gather all the gifts I have for Dee, leaving some for Greg to get later. My hands are full enough with the things I have for Dee.

Walking up the small walkway, I pause to pull my keys out of my pocket. If she were up, she would have already come running out the door like a cheerleader on crack. I drop a few of the packages in my arms before I am able to pull my keys out of my waistband. *Shit*! I forgot to call Axel. Pulling my phone up, I press his name and wait for it to start ringing as I push my key in the lock. It clicks, but before I can open the door, it swings wide and I meet the disturbing brown eyes of my ex-husband.

"Hey, Princess," I hear coming through the line.

Brandon smiles his cold and evil smile.

"You there?" I hear calling from far off. My body is frozen in terror.

"Hello there, Isabelle," Brandon says. There is so much control in those three words, but they are heavily laced with menace.

All of the packages fall from my arms, joining my phone on the front steps.

"Izzy!" I hear right before Brandon reaches up and slams his fist into my temple, causing the world around me to fade into black.

God! Why does my head hurt? Shit. I roll over but stop when my head starts to pound. Why don't I remember what happened?

"Ah, Isabelle. Glad you could join us."

My eyes snap open and I look around Dee's living room. It all comes rushing back, and my blood turns to ice when I look up and see Brandon standing over Dee. He's got her arms tied behind her back and a piece of tape slapped over her lips. Her eyes are wide and terrified. I can already see a bruise forming around her cheek and her hair is pulled to the side of her ponytail.

She tries to stay strong but there are dried tear tracks all over her face.

"This little bitch was nice enough to invite me in. Nice to know her manners aren't lacking. I was just asking her a few questions about my lovely wife when you drove up. Thank you, Isabelle, for

215

making it so easy to find you." He shakes his head back and forth and begins pacing in a tight line behind Dee. I move my eyes from his face to hers and check on her again. I can see her pleading with me not to do anything stupid. Her eyes are wide and she keeps shaking her head softly.

"Your little boyfriend has been causing some trouble, Isabelle. I warned you what would happen if he didn't back off. I wonder how long it will take that motherfucker to come riding to the rescue, hmm?"

His pacing continues, and when Dee lets out a soft whimper, his hand shoots out and backhands her hard across the face. She falls back off the couch and doesn't move.

That was all it took to snap me out of my shock. "You bastard!" I scream and go to move from my spot on the floor but stop short when he trains a gun on me.

"Oh no, I wouldn't do anything rash. My dear wife seems to have forgotten her place in the world. We can't have that now, can we? You sit the fuck down and shut up, you stupid whore."

I pause in my motion but quickly scan the room. There has to be another way. I won't let him win. He controlled me for too long and I am finally happy. Fate is finally on MY side. I steady my resolve and straighten my spine. I will win.

I go to get up again when he walks quickly over to me and grabs me by my loose hair. He bends down and brings his face right up to mine. His words are harsh and he spits all over my face when he speaks.

"You little slut. You think you can run around spreading your legs for another man. You are mine! Do you hear me, Isabelle? I won't let that bastard touch what is MINE!" he screams. My hair feels as if it is being ripped from the roots when he begins to pull me to my feet.

"Please, Brandon. Please leave us alone. What do you want? Money? I can get you plenty. Please leave," I beg. My only thought is getting free and getting Dee and my baby safe from his insanity.

He swings his wild eyes on me and throws his head back. The sound that comes out is animalistic and has me scared out of my mind. The chill of dread rocks through my body, all the way to my bones.

"You think I'm going to let him have you? Oh no, Isabelle. What you need to understand is that you will never get rid of me. He thinks he can take you from me? He can try, but he will be swimming through a sea of bullets before I let him get those vile hands on MY WIFE!"

I can see the control in his eyes snap and it's like watching a light go out. This is not my ex-husband. The irrational madness has taken over any common sense and chance of reason I could have made with him.

"I'm going to make him watch you when I bend you over my knee and punish you for all the shit you have caused. I'm going to rip your clothes from your body and make him watch me take you for all the shit HE caused. That's right," he says when my eyes widen. "You think I don't know it was him who had the police barking at my heels? And then do you know what will happen next?" He doesn't even blink when he pauses. That malevolent smile forms and his face is transformed from his normal somewhat handsome look to one of pure evil. "Then I'm going to put a bullet through your fucking heart while he watches. While he is helpless to stop me."

Even with the fear coursing through my body, I know I have to get away from him. He's blocking the hallway to the front door but not the one off to the kitchen. It's risky, but I might be able to get away quickly enough to hide. I know Axel is coming and that has me more afraid than the madman standing in front of me with a gun.

A low moan sounds from the couch and I see Dee start to stir. Shit! I can't leave Dee.

"Why, Brandon?" I ask, hoping to distract him from Dee. I have to keep him focused on me.

"Why? Because that motherfucker ruined everything! I was finally going to have it all and he had to ruin it all! I won't let him take you too! YOU ARE MINE!" he screams. He brings his hand up and starts pulling at his hair, and banging the handle of the gun against his forehead before leveling it back on Dee.

He's completely lost it. There isn't an ounce of humanity left in this man.

His pacing continues. He moves slightly from the open hallway but he doesn't move his gun from Dee's body. I see a shadow cross the threshold, and my heart picks up speed when I realize who it is.

Greg.

Oh God no! I'm going to lose everyone I love in one moment if Brandon sees him. He holds his finger up to his lips. He taps his wrist and then cocks his head toward the kitchen, silently telling me to run when he makes a move.

My heart is going to stop. There is no way it can beat this rapidly and not just give out. Dee's eyes are wide. She looks over at me and I can see the fright in her alarmed brown eyes.

I bring my hand to the side and motion to her to wait then bug my eyes toward the kitchen. Her legs aren't bound, and if she can run, we might be able to get out of this room.

We wait in stone-cold fear while Greg inches closer to Brandon, but before he can reach him Brandon spins around. He seems to pause for a second in confusion, and that's all it takes for me to jump up, grab Dee by the arm, and pull her with me as we run into the kitchen. I hear the sounds of them colliding behind me as we take off.

The sound of the gun going off causes me to falter. I push Dee behind the island and look around for some form of protection. Damn! The knives are by the open doorway we just ran through. The only thing I can see is the cast-iron frying pan left on the oven from Dee's breakfast. Thank God! Picking it up, I test the heaviness of the metal out in my hand before holding it down to my side. I bend down and check on Dee. She is shaking but seems okay.

"Get under the desk and don't you move," I tell her. I make quick work of the knot behind her back before letting her move from my side.

I watch her scurry around the far side of the island and burrow under the desk built into the wall. I push the chair in behind her and cover her body the best I can.

Moving back to the center island, I brace my legs apart and wait. I don't know who is going to come around that corner but I'm ready. I won't let him win. I won't let him take my happiness.

It's time that I remember what is important and fight for the future I want.

The future I deserve.

The future I have earned.

A future with Axel and our baby.

With an evil laugh, I hear him and my fears are confirmed. Oh,

God. Greg!

"Oh, Isabelle? Come out, come out, wherever you are!" He laughs again before stumbling into the kitchen. "Where is that little bitch friend of yours, Isabelle?" He cocks his head to the side, and I notice that his left arm is hanging at an odd angle and the gun is missing.

I feel slightly better knowing Greg was able to put up a fight. The fear for Greg bubbles back up, but I push it back and straighten my shoulders.

I won't let this man win.

Never again.

"Where is Greg?" I ask, shocked that my voice sounds strong and sure.

"Don't you worry about him, Isabelle." He takes a step forward. There are only a few more steps before he will have rounded the island. "Come here, bitch." he spits out.

"No." My voice sounds powerful in the stillness of the house.

"You're going to be sorry for that."

He lunges forward but doesn't make it far before I swing wide and crash the frying pan against his skull. He looks into my eyes in confusion before crumpling to the floor. I throw the frying pan to the side and jump over his fallen body.

I run into the living room and almost fall to the floor when I see Greg's still form and the pool of blood forming under his chest. Choking on the sob that escapes my mouth, I begin to frantically look for the gun. I get on my knees and search under all the furniture before finding it in the far corner of the room tucked under the couch.

I try a few times to reach it before I finally succeed. Right when my hands wrap around the handle, I hear him. Before I can straighten from the floor, my hair is gripped in his strong hands and he throws me towards the far wall. My body collides with Greg, who doesn't move even with the force of my weight slamming into him. His warm blood soaks through my side.

I look up into Brandon's disturbing face and smile when I feel the cold medal of the gun still in my hands. He takes a step forward but stops when I raise the gun level with his chest.

"Fuck you!" I scream and pull the trigger, empting every bullet into his chest.

I can hear Dee screaming from the other room, but before my arm falls back down, I overcome with the overwhelming fear running through my veins and let the numbness take over my body. I vaguely hear the gun hit the floor before I slump back against Greg's body and the darkness rolls back in.

Axel

"IZZY!" I scream again into the phone. I run down the stairs and jump into my truck. When I heard her ex-husband's voice coming through the line instead of Izzy's, I thought my mind was playing tricks on me. For days we have been searching for him. Not one god-damn clue to where he has been, and the second she is out of my sight...the worst possible situation is playing out and I am helpless. There is no way I can get there quick enough.

I grab my phone while I tear out of the driveway and call Greg, the only one I can think of who will be close enough to save my girl.

"What's up, Reid? Just talked to —"

"Shut up. Where the fuck are you?" I interrupt.

"Damn. On my way to Dee's house. Izzy ca—"

"Brandon is there," I interrupt again. I don't have time. Izzy doesn't have time.

"What?" All teasing has left his voice now.

"Just got a call from Izzy but it was him I heard over the line. I didn't hear her once, Greg." I take a second to calm down before I'm able to continue. The fact that I don't know if she is okay is not lost on me. "I'm too far out. Get there. God, please get there and save my girl." I don't even realize that tears are rolling down my face until I hear the anguish that colors my words.

"Be there in five. I'll get her."

"Don't let him take them from me," I plead.

"Got it." He takes a deep breath, and I know... I know how much he is holding back right there.

Greg loves Izzy, and for the first time, I realize just how powerful their bond is. He was her family and support when I couldn't be. If anyone else can understand what my panic feels like at this moment, it is Greg.

I have to trust that he can make it in time. There is no way she can be taken from me twice.

I break every speed limit and every traffic law to make it to Dee's in half the time it normally takes, pulling my truck right into the grass in front of her place and throwing it in park before jumping out and sprinting towards the door. I notice Greg's truck off to the side parked at an odd angle. I check but don't see him outside. The front door is wide open and there is no movement inside.

Silence.

Silence and sobbing.

Pulling the gun out of my ankle holster, I slowly walk through the threshold and down the long hallway. The sobbing is getting louder, and for the first time since arriving, I breathe. That is a female sob.

Hope flares to life and I rush around the corner but stop dead at the scene before me. The first thing I see is Brandon's lifeless body in the opening to the kitchen. I don't need to check to know he isn't breathing. No way would he survive with that many holes in his chest. Dee is on the floor next to the tangled mess of Izzy's and Greg's bodies.

"NO!" I roar, running towards them, slipping on the blood that covers the floor around them. "Oh God, Izzy!"

"I c-c-called 91-1," Dee stutters out next to me. "It isn't hers," she whispers.

"What?" I sob, running my hands down Izzy's still body, looking for any sign of injury before moving her gently to the side. Her chest is rising and falling normally and her color is just slightly paler than normal. Besides a few cuts and bruises, she doesn't appear to be harmed.

When I turn to Greg for the first time, her words register. "Fuck!" I roll him over and notice the wet hole on his side. "FUCK!" Ripping my shirt over my head, I press it against his belly and hope I can do enough to keep him stable before the ambulance arrives. "Check his pulse," I say to Dee, but when I look over, she is weeping over Izzy's body. My heart stills for a second when I look again at her still form. Why isn't she moving?

Bringing my attention back to Greg, I bring one hand off his wound and check his pulse. Slow but there. I hold my shirt against him and wait.

We wait for what seems like an eternity before the paramedics start running through the house. Greg is quickly loaded up and taken away with Dee in the back with him. I drop down next to Izzy, where the paramedics are working on her.

"Sir? Sir? I need to ask you some questions," the officer off to the side asks.

"Not now." I run my hand over her hair and pray. She has to be all right. She has to survive. "Why isn't she waking up?" I ask the paramedic next to me.

"I don't know. Looks like her body's way of protecting itself. All her vitals are fine, great actually, considering." He gives me a look full of compassion. "She's going to be fine."

I let out the breath I didn't realize I was holding, drop my head to her shoulder, and cry.

"She's pregnant," I whisper to the man beside me. "She's pregnant with my baby." My words sound odd to my ears, and I know I won't be able to hold it together for long if I don't see those beautiful pale eyes soon.

"Got it. We're going to load her up now. You the husband?" he asks.

"Yes," I answer and quickly follow them out to the ambulance.

"Sir. We need your statement," the officer says, running behind us.

"Not. Now," I repeat. "You want a statement? You get in your car and follow me to the hospital. I am NOT leaving her side. You hear me?"

The young officer stops short and seems shocked at the heat behind my words. Not what he was expecting. I can tell he is gearing up to protest, but I quickly interrupt him.

"Look"—I pause to check his nametag—"Officer Benson, I'm not trying to fucking run off. That woman is MY life and I won't be letting her out of my sight after this shit. Can you just try to understand for a fucking second what I am going through and follow to the goddamn hospital, yeah?" I say but turn around and climb in without waiting for his response.

The ambulance pulls off, and I take her hand in my own and bend down to her ear. "I love you, Princess. Wake up now so I can see those eyes looking at me. Let me see that love, baby."

I keep my head down to her ear and whisper everything and anything I can think of to let her know that she is safe and I'm here. The ten-minute drive to the hospital comes to a halt, and before they can roll her out, her eyes flutter open and she meets my gaze.

"Hey there, Princess," I say, the emotion thick in my voice and the relief rocking me to my core. "Hey, my love."

"Axel...love...you," she says weakly before closing her eyes and drifting off again.

I jump out and follow the gurney into the emergency room, finally breathing easy for the first time since I answered her earlier phone call.

Izzy

THE FIRST thing I notice when I wake up is the quiet humming. Opening my eyes, I look around the dimly lit hospital room, trying to orientate myself to my surroundings. I feel a soft tickle on my arm and move my head to the side to look down.

Axel is sitting next to my bed with his chair pulled as close as he can get it. My right hand is held firmly in his and his lips are pressed against my skin. The humming I keep hearing is coming from him, his soft whispering against my skin. He is speaking low enough that I can't understand the words, but the tone is light and loving.

"Ax-xel?" I say, my throat dry. It hurts to get the word past my lips.

His head shoots up and his red-rimmed eyes meet mine.

"Princess..." he whispers. Tears are forming in his eyes and a small smile tugs at the corners of his lips. "My girl, my brave girl," he says, and a few tears fall over his lids. He closes his eyes tight and more spill over. "I thought I had lost you. When I walked around the corner and saw you...saw you lying in all that blood..." He trails off but not before his words hit my ears.

Blood? I wasn't bleeding. Was I? Oh no! The baby!

"The...the baby?" I whisper hoarsely. "Please..." I shake my head back and forth violently, tears of my own streaming down my face. Not our baby! Please, God, not our baby!

"What? Oh, Izzy, no baby. The baby is fine. You are fine. I'm so sorry I didn't mean your blood. Princess, stop crying, I promise, our baby is fine." He is quick to reassure me over and over telling me that our little miracle is safe and fine.

When I finally calm down, I look into his eyes—his beautiful eyes. "We're okay?" I ask.

"You're both perfect," he responds smiling before giving me a soft kiss.

"Greg? Dee?" I ask when he moves away to sit down on the side of my bed.

"Dee is going to be fine. She's shaken up. Shaken up pretty fucking bad, but she will be okay. From what she said, Brandon had just tied her hands and taped her mouth. He had only been there for about an hour before you showed up. I think the worst of her injuries are where he clocked her when she opened the front door and a split lip. She's fine, baby."

"Where is she?" I ask, looking around the room again.

"Beck made her leave. He is taking her back to his place for a while. She said she was putting the townhouse on the market."

I take that in and try to process it. I understand. I wouldn't want to be there anymore either.

"I offered for her to stay with us for a while, but she said she would have to think about it."

I scrunch my nose at that. "Why would she need to think about staying with us?"

"I don't know, Princess. That's something you will have to ask her yourself."

"What about Greg?" I ask, almost afraid to know.

"He's going to be okay. He came out of surgery a little while ago. It wasn't anything serious even though it sure as fuck looked like it. Bullet went straight through and missed everything important. He's one lucky son of a bitch."

"He's really okay? There was so much blood, Ax. And he wasn't moving. He wasn't moving at all." My panic is coming back again, at remembering the way Greg looked—lifeless. He looked dead. "Axel, I need to see him!" I yell.

"Hey, hey…calm down, baby. I promise he's okay. He's in recovery, but I'll see what I can do about getting you on a field trip, okay?"

I look up and catch the slight concern that crosses over his eyes before his quickly masks it. I know he has to be a mess over everything that happened, but he is holding it in and being strong for me.

"Okay. I just really need to see him, Axel. I need to see with my own eyes that he is going to be okay."

"I understand, Princess. I'll make it happen." He leans down and gives me a gentle kiss. "Got room for one more on there, baby? I need to feel you close." His mask slips slightly for me to see the vulnerability simmering under the surface.

"Yeah. Yeah, I do," I respond and shift slightly so he can lean his body close to mine.

His feet are hanging off the end and a good portion of his body is hanging off the edge, but he wraps his arms tightly around me and I cuddle close, breathing him in and letting the peace only he can give me wash over my body.

"I never want to feel that fear again, Izzy," he whispers into my hair and squeezes me tightly. "Never been so scared in my life."

We lie like this, together and entwined, until the nurse comes in. She fusses until he moves back to his chair. I can't help but laugh at the pout he is sporting while she finishes up her vitals checks. When he hears me, the look is instantly gone and he looks over with a huge smile.

"Love that sound, Princess. Most beautiful sound in the whole fucking world."

I stayed in the hospital overnight. There wasn't anything wrong with me, but they wanted to monitor my vitals and make sure that my head wound was okay. Luckily, I came out of the whole ordeal with only a small bump right next to my temple.

When I'm released, Axel and I make our way to the floor Greg is on. Maddox and Coop are in the room when we get there. Greg is awake but groggy. I walk into his room on the arm of Axel, who hasn't let me go once since I woke up. Greg looks up and a small smile forms on his pale lips.

"Baby girl," he said with a tear falling from his eye. "Baby girl, you are a sight."

I walk over to the side of his bed and push Coop out of the chair he was sitting on, pulling it close to his bed. "Hey." Yup, that is all I have before I break down and bury my head in the bed next to his hip. Axel comes up behind me and rubs my back.

"Baby girl, I'm okay. Nothing I can't handle."

"I thought you were dead, G!" I cry harder into the bed. "Don't ever do that shit again!"

He laughs but agrees, and I sit there holding his hand while the conversation continues around us. Coop tells Maddox about all the good-looking nurses who keep popping in offering sponge baths and how he might have to get shot if that is what's waiting for him. Maddox was shakes his head, but his eyes never leave mine.

"You okay, girl?" he asks when Coop finally shuts his mouth.

Axel gives my shoulder a squeeze in support, and I climb to my feet and walk over to Maddox. He opens his arms when I get closer and I wrap mine around his back. "I'm okay," I say into his chest.

"Good. That's good," he says and gives me a small squeeze before releasing me.

"Get over here, Izzy," I hear Axel say behind me. I roll my eyes at Maddox before turning around and walking back to Axel. "Mine," he says to Maddox and pulls me into his body.

We get a rare laugh out of Maddox, and just like that, the tension in the room is lifted and we are able to breathe easy again.

Greg and Dee are fine. The baby and I are fine. And Axel's arms are around me.

Life is good.

CHAPTER 21

4 MONTHS LATER

"**Y**OU ALMOST ready, baby?" Axel asks, sliding his arms around my waist and rubbing his hands over my swollen belly. I started to really show a few weeks ago. My small pouch went gone from making me look slightly overweight to a definite baby bump. I love it, but I love it more when Axel comes up behind me and places his hands over my small bump.

When I have moments like this, just Axel and me, I am reminded how lucky we are. It's been a hard road for us both since that day with Brandon. I have been plagued with nightmares, and Axel has been dealing with his worry about my mental state. About two months after Brandon's attack, I made an appointment with Dr. Maxwell. We both knew I wasn't dealing with taking his life well. Finally, four months later, I have come to terms with everything that happened. My nightmares are few and far between, but I am alive and so are the people I love. I have become stronger and stronger every day, and it is all because of this man.

I continue to fix my make up while he rolls his fingers around my skin. "We need to get going soon if we're going to make your appointment."

"Okay, I'm hurrying. I would have been ready by now but there is nothing that fits anymore." I put down my mascara and turn in his arms.

I step up on my toes and wrap my arms around his neck, burying my hands into his thick hair. I look at myself in the mirror and can't help the small smile that forms. My hair is hanging in long waves down my back. My makeup is done in neutral tones to match the soft yellow color of my sundress. The material stretches across my ample chest but flares out against my belly.

"Worth it, baby. I love seeing you carrying my baby." He brings his hands down and pulls me up by my hips, placing me on the counter.

"Be careful, Axel. Right now you're asking to be really late," I warn, opening my legs up for him to walk closer to my body. My dress pushes higher up my thighs.

My belly pushes into his hard stomach. He barks out a laugh before pressing his lips to mine and making my toes curl with the heat of his kiss. "Princess, I could take you right now and you wouldn't even fucking care if we missed that appointment, and don't think I don't know you've been crossing the days off until this one."

He is not wrong. We have our twenty-week baby appointment today and we are finally going to find out if we were having a boy or a girl. Axel is firm that it is a boy. I keep going back and forth, but deep down, I hope it is. I can just picture a little version of Axel running around the house.

I curl my hands into the fabric of his shirt, humming my agreement, and lean in for another kiss. Right before his lips hit mine, there is a sharp kick against my belly. Axel snaps back and looks down in complete shock. We have been trying to get him to feel the baby kick for weeks now, but either the baby wasn't having it or Axel just wasn't there when the baby was active. Either way, this is the first time he has felt any movement.

He looks down at my rounded stomach and then quickly back up to my eyes. The look of pure wonder in his eyes brings a smile to my lips. He is completely transfixed with this little person in my belly.

I reach down and grab his hands before placing them on the center of my bump. The baby kicks a few more times. I keep my eyes glued to Axel's face, watching the emotions play across his handsome features. Shock, awe, and enchantment. He is fascinated with this feeling—feeling of our baby.

"What are you thinking?" I ask him after a few minutes.

He looks up at me with his smile wide and his eyes bright. "How fucking lucky I am." He leans down and gives me a kiss, not once removing his hands from my active belly.

"Hey!" we hear Dee yelling up the stairs. "Where are y'all?"

Axel groans and helps me down from the counter. He might have offered for Dee to stay with us, but I can tell she is starting to get under his skin. She has a knack of knowing right when things are heating up. I love her, but right now, she is my little happy cock blocker.

"Play nice, Daddy." I laugh and slap him on the ass before walking around him and out of the bedroom.

I slide my feet into some flip-flops and walk down to meet Dee in the foyer. She looks stunning in a long orange maxi dress that fits tight to her body.

"You suck, you skinny bitch," I say and smile up at her. Of course she towers over me in her four-inch heels. I'm the midget around the giants. These days, the only thing that feels good is flip-flops.

"Whatever, Iz! You look beautiful! Doesn't she, Axel?"

He snorts but keeps walking down the stairs.

"Where's G?" I ask them. It's debatable who was more excited about the baby when we told everyone, Dee or Greg.

We told everyone together when we had a small 'family only' party at the house to welcome Greg home. He had stayed in the hospital for almost two weeks after the shooting but was one hundred perfect healed now. When we told them, Dee broke down in tears, Maddox gave me a rare smile, Coop praised Axel on his super swimmers, and Beck offered a polite congratulations. Greg, however, had hollered his excitement and pulled me into a big hug, which earned a growl from Axel. Greg just laughed and hugged me tighter.

From that day on, he's called daily and checked on my progress. He has bought baby books and is constantly filling us in on baby info. I knew he would be happy for us, but he is over-the-moon excited to become an uncle.

"He said he was running late. Something about an appointment and would meet us at the office," Axel calls from the kitchen.

I look over at Dee and she just shrugs her shoulders.

I follow Axel's voice and find him in the kitchen checking his emails on his phone. He looks up and I stop when I see the hunger in his eyes.

"Look good enough to eat, Princess. Can't wait to get back here so I can drag you back to the bedroom. Need to be buried deep, baby."

"Oh my god, Iz! That was seriously hot!" Dee says from behind me. I close my eyes and hear Axel let out a string of curses.

"How's the house hunting going, Dee?" he asks, and I laugh at her puzzled expression.

"We love having you here, Dee, but have you thought about finding a place yet?"

She looks down and goes silent.

"Dee?" I prompt.

"I don't know if I can do it yet," she says after a few seconds of silence.

I give Axel a pointed stare, and he gets it. Dee's been struggling since the Brandon scene. She has trouble feeling safe and usually sticks close to one of us. She has been working more and more at Axel's desk in the home office than he is.

"Okay, Dee, we get it. Promise."

She looks over at me with a frown, and I can see the fear in her eyes.

"Stay as long as you want." Axel offers.

She nods her head and then leaves the room to grab her purse.

"You okay with that, Ax?" I know he is ready to have his house back, but he just gives me a nod with nothing but understanding swimming in his green eyes.

We leave the house a few minutes later and make the short drive into town to the ultrasound clinic. Axel holds my hand the whole way and a content smile plays at his lips. I smile over at him and thank my lucky stars that he is back in my life.

When we pull up in front of the office, I see Greg standing outside the doors with his phone to his ear. He looks up when he hears the rumble of Axel's truck and quickly says his goodbyes. I look over at Axel, wondering if he caught the abrupt end to Greg's call.

"Stay out of it, Izzy. He wants you to know, he will tell you, yeah?"

I grumble but stay quiet while he walks around the truck and opens my door before taking me gently around the hips and bringing me to my feet. I hear his moan when I brush against his cock.

"Do not get my dick hard right before I go see my baby," he

laughs but can't disguise the strain in his voice.

"Later," I promise and walk around him to give Greg a big hug. Dee hangs back but comes up to give Greg a hug, too.

"You ready, baby girl?" he asks with a smile.

"God, yes. Last-minute guess on your niece or nephew?"

He smiles and looks over my shoulder at Axel. "Boy, baby girl. That is definitely going to be a boy."

"Why do all of you seem so sure it's going to be a boy?"

They both laugh loudly, and Dee and I just look at each other with confused faces.

"Baby girl, look at him. There is no fucking way he made a girl. No way." He is still laughing when we walk into the reception area and I sign in. I shoot him a few dirty looks before sitting down next to Axel and thumbing through a baby magazine.

We wait for about fifteen minutes before they call me back.

"Is it okay if my family comes back, too?" I ask the technician.

"Sure, honey. The more the merrier."

We follow her down a long hallway before entering the ultrasound room. It's a large room with a couch off the side and a large recliner next to the ultrasound machine. The only other thing in the room is a large projector pointing down from the ceiling. When I sit down in the recliner, I notice that the large wall in front of me is a screen for viewing.

"Here you go. Place this sheet over your lap. That way we don't flash everyone in the process." She laughs and helps me cover up.

I look over to Axel and see the nervous anticipation on his face. He smiles at me and grabs my outstretched hand.

"Love you," he mouths to me.

"Love you too," I return.

"All right Ms. West. Let's get you ready."

I smile at Axel one more time when I see the frown on his face over the use of my last name. He was not happy with me when I told him that I wanted to wait for the baby to be born before we got married. He grudgingly agreed when I bribed him with sex.

It wasn't that I didn't want to be married to Axel, just the opposite. I couldn't wait to be Mrs. Axel Reid, but it just felt right that our baby be there with us. When I sat him down and explained my reasons for wanting to wait, he wasn't so upset anymore, but that didn't mean he was happy about it.

"I'm just going to do some measurements before we take a look and see if this little one wants to make an announcement today, okay?"

I nod my head, too engrossed with the image of our baby on the large screen in front of us. Axel squeezes my hand, and I hear him let out a shuddered breath.

"Amazing," I hear Greg whisper to Dee, who is too busy sniffling in her tissue to answer.

When the baby's heartbeat fills the room, we all seem to pause in amazement. It never fails to fill my heart with joy to hear that fast-paced beating.

"You ready, Mom and Dad?" she asks us with a smile.

"Yes," Axel says quickly before I can open my mouth.

I look up at her and smile. She gives me a wink before turning her attention back to the screen.

"Well, will you look at that? Someone isn't shy at all." She laughs to herself, and we sit there all looking at the moving little image on the screen.

It doesn't take long for us to see what she was talking about. Right there, larger than life, is my son just letting it all hang out. Axel lets out a loud whoop and jumps up from his chair. He leans down and gives me a kiss before slapping hands with Greg. I laugh at their antics and wipe the tears from my face.

Axel comes back to my side and leans over me. Taking my face in his hands and pushing his nose up to mine, he rubs his nose against my own, and the smile that takes over his face makes my heart speed up.

"We're having a boy," he says. "You're giving me a son." He places a soft kiss to my lips and briefly closes his eyes. When he opens them, they are so full of love and happiness. "Making my dreams come true, Princess. Making my life worth living. Love you so much, baby."

I grab his head, and push my face up to his, and give him a kiss that I hope expresses my feelings.

"I love you, Axel."

The rest of the appointment passes in a blur. Axel continues to hold my hand and shake with his excitement. He is itching to get out of this room so he can scream to the world that he is about to have a son.

When we finish, the technician hands us some prints and he scoops them up before I can even take them, thanking her while looking down through the images. He is like a kid with a new toy. Completely enamored.

I go up to pay and Axel steps outside, immediately jumping on the phone. Chances are, the whole state will know when he is done that we are having a boy.

I finish paying and turn around to find Greg standing behind me. "Happy, baby girl?"

"More than you could even imagine."

He smiles and throws his arm around me and gives me a quick hug.

Axel turns, sees him, and pauses in his conversation. "Hands off, Cage!"

Greg laughs and drops his arm.

"Let's go! The gang is meeting us at Heavy's to celebrate my boy!" he yells across the parking lot.

The only thing I can think of is that I put that peacefulness in his tone and together we are finally where we are meant to be.

EPILOGUE

5 Months Later

Axel

I HAVE BEEN running around all day trying to make sure every-thing is in place for tonight. It's Izzy's birthday, and between anx-iously waiting for our son to decide to come and dealing with the memories that still plague her around this day, it was turning out to be a nightmare.

So far, the only highlight of today was seeing the blinding smile on her face when she woke up. Other than that…anything that could have gone wrong has.

The caterer is late, the cake hasn't shown up, and the birthday girl will be here in an hour.

I am officially losing my shit.

This day has to be perfect. Dee took Izzy early this morning to spend the day at the salon next to the office. I avoid that place. I don't care how many times Izzy tells me that weird little man is harm-less—I'm not buying it. The other day, he pinched my ass, which Izzy thought was hilarious. I couldn't even be mad about it when she was standing there laughing. Her large belly was bouncing with each breath. It was almost worth asking him to do it again if it got that kind of reaction from my girl.

The last few months have flown by. We have spent every sec-ond getting the nursery ready and finally filling my house with more furniture than one person should ever own in one lifetime. It keeps a smile on her face and it makes her happy. I would bend over backwards if it means that smile stays on her face.

These last few days have been harder on her. Not only has she been dealing with an overdue baby, but the Georgia heat is making her miserable. We all do what we can to make things easier, but I can tell it is getting harder on her.

Yesterday was a bad day. She spent the day in bed crying and wouldn't let me leave her side. She would say things about our angel baby missing out on his little brother. It killed me to hear her talk like that, but I would be lying if I said the thought hadn't crossed my mind too. We have worked hard to overcome our loss, even going to therapy a few times to talk about things that were still painful. We are closer than ever, but that doesn't mean that things don't still sit heavy on our hearts.

"Yo! Reid, got the cake. That bitch at the bakery tried to tell me that you didn't tell her you needed it this afternoon. Got it, but damn that shit wasn't pretty." Coop comes through the door with the stupid fucking cake I have been screaming at the bakery over for the last two days. Idiots.

"Dee just called. She said Sway was finally done rubbing all over Izzy's belly and has just started her hair. Should be another two hours now. Good news is, we can figure out where those fucking caterers are," Greg says, coming into the kitchen from the deck.

I'm about to pull my fucking hair out.

It isn't even a big party. All the guys are coming, and last time I checked, even Maddox is bringing a date. Emmy has been here since Izzy left, helping me set up the streamers and balloons. Dee's current boy toy, and newest 'piss off Beck' ploy—is here helping also. I don't know him very well, but Izzy says that he is nice enough. I wish those two would stop their fucking games and just admit that they want to be together. I've talked to Beck a few times about it, but he would just change the subject and say that it wasn't his idea. I think I understand where Dee is coming from, but I am sick of playing monkey in the middle.

"Where's Locke?" I ask. Doesn't matter who answers me at this point.

"He went to pick up Daisy," Emmy says softly next to my side.

"Or maybe it was Candy." She smirks and walks away.

I shake my head, thinking, once again, it would be nice if someone stopped making me feel like I am stuck in the middle.

Walking back into our living room, I push aside the balloons that seem to be floating in every direction and stand in front of the fireplace. Hanging dead center is the picture I gave Izzy for Christmas. Immediately, a sense of calm rushes through my body. I take a deep breath and remember what the point of this massive headache is.

My girl.

My girl and returning her birthday to a day of happiness and not one of heartbreak.

With a new determination, I turn and walk back to out to the porch, where we are finishing up with the decorations.

There are pink and white balloons flying from every available banister. The path down to our dock is lined with torches, and there are lights streaming from the branches of the trees that line our yard. It looks like it is raining white lights.

Emmy spent hours littering the yard with pink and red rose pedals. Coop and Beck had a good laugh over the roses. Laugh all they want, but when they find their women, they will be pulling out all the stops to make sure that life is perfect, too.

We set up tables across the yard and to the side for all the food. My backyard has been transformed into a princess's dream. I can't wait to see her face when she takes it all in.

"Greg!" I snap, yelling into the house for him. "Any word on those motherfuckers with the food?" This is what I get for hiring out a big company to cook some fancy shit. Should have stuck with Heavy's. It is all she craves these days anyway.

Fuck, Heavy's!

I cut him off before he can even open his mouth. "Call those assholes and tell them since they couldn't show up on time to forget about it. Coop, get your ass in the truck and drive to Heavy's. Buy the place out. Everything you can think of and get it here." I throw my wallet at him and turn back to Greg's smiling face. "What the fuck are you smiling at?"

He holds his hands up and walks off laughing.

"You need to calm down. I haven't heard you this uptight since last fall," Emmy says, sneaking up to my side again. I swear that chick floats. She is always popping up out of nowhere.

"I am calm." I'm not calm. I'm losing my fucking mind.

My girl is sad, trying hard to keep it hidden, and I can't fix it. My son refuses to come out, and if one more thing goes wrong today, I'm going to say fuck it and kidnap my woman and drag her up to the bedroom. At least I know I can keep her happy there.

"You aren't calm, but you will be," she says before she vanishes again.

I look around for her before I stomp back in the house and grab a beer.

By the time Dee calls to tell us that they are leaving the salon, things have finally calmed down. Coop gets back with so much food that it looks like he has, in fact, ordered everything Heavy's has to offer. Locke has finally arrived and gotten the rest of the sound system running. Emmy is running around, making sure all the tables have flower arrangements and that all the bubble machines are still hidden from sight but functioning. Coop is somewhere with his date and Beck is bringing out all the coolers with drinks and dragging them down to the yard.

You can't see the lights yet but the torches are lit and the rose pedals against the green grass make it look like there is a blanket of pink and red. The balloons are rocking back and forth in the slight breeze. It is perfect.

Nothing else could go wrong today.

"They're pulling up the driveway!" I hear Greg yell through the house.

We pulled all the cars behind the garage and down a little ways on the property. She won't see them from where she would park. If she comes through the garage, she won't notice the balloons invading the living room either.

"Be right back," I say, handing my beer to Locke before walking into the house.

I wipe my sweaty palms on my shorts and walk into the kitchen to get my girl. She comes walking out of the garage looking like the angel I've always thought she was. She's wearing a long white dress that hugs her tits and large belly. It flows around the rest of her body, making it look like she is walking on air. Her skin is still glowing from all the time we spent down at the lake this summer. Sway did whatever it is that Sway does on her hair and it is hanging long, thick with curls.

"You look beautiful."

"You don't look that bad yourself, baby," she says, walking into my arms and giving me a kiss. I can feel my son rolling against my stomach.

"Feeling okay, Princess?"

"I'm feeling great. Sway pampered me good. He even made one of the shampoo boys massage my feet!"

I bite back the displeasure I feel about another man with his hands on my woman. She needs today to be perfect and my being a possessive ass won't help.

"Can Dee stay for dinner? I told her we were going to grill out and she said she would love to spend some more time with me."

"Sure, baby." I give Dee a hug and start walking Izzy out to the deck.

I hear her gasp from behind me when her eyes take in everything in front of her. Our friends all yell, "Surprise!" and I feel her jump through our joined hands. Her hand squeezes mine tightly and I go to turn around. She looks shocked but not about her surroundings.

"Um...Axel?" I hear Dee call back from inside the house. She is standing behind Izzy and looking down at the ground with an odd expression across her face.

"Yeah?"

"Oh boy," she says, looking up to meet my eyes, and I note the apprehension.

Izzy squeezes my hand, harder this time, and whispers my name. "Axel?" It comes out so light I almost miss it.

Shit, she must hate it.

"Baby?" she tries again.

I turn to look into her eyes and frown when I see sweat beginning to gather around her temples and worry lines across her forehead. "Izzy, what's wrong?"

"HOLY SHIT HER WATER BROKE!" I hear Greg yell from

behind me.

I look down, and sure enough, there is a small puddle of water between her feet. Her handle on my hand hasn't lightened up, and I know that my girl is in pain.

She gives a small, strained nod and waits a few seconds for the contraction to ease up before opening her eyes and looking into my own.

"He's coming," she whispers with a brilliant smile.

Everything moves fast from there. I quickly usher her out to the car. We had stopped using the truck months ago when it became too uncomfortable for her to get in and out. Dee and Greg run to his truck and the rest of the gang files out. Emmy yells that she will stay behind, make sure everything is turned off, and meet us at the hospital. I don't care. Let the house burn down. My son is on his way.

We make it to the hospital in good time, but by the time we arrive, Izzy is in more pain than before. Her contractions are coming quick and she keeps screaming out in pain. It kills me to hear her hurting and know there is nothing I can do about it. I start telling her how much I love her and try to reassure her with my words until she looks over at me with fire in her eyes and tells me to shut the fuck up. As soon as the words leave her mouth, she is apologizing. My poor girl. If I could do this for her, I would in a heartbeat.

I pull up to the front of the hospital and, without even shutting off the car, sprint over to her side and carry her inside.

Someone will move the car. If they don't, then they can tow it. There is no way I'm leaving my girl.

They get us checked in and into a room quickly. Izzy is hooked up to a million different monitors and machines. I'm told that they all monitor her and our son, but I am too busy worrying about her to even pay attention to the nurses. They seem to think we have all the time in the world. Why isn't anyone *doing* something? Anything!

We have been here for about an hour when she lets out the loudest tortured cry. The sound stops my heart, and I look around frantically for help. The nurses all spring into action and start shoving the bed around, turning on different machines and barking orders at me.

I hold Izzy's hand and try to help her, but looking at her beautiful face breaking down in agony is almost too much.

"You're doing great, Princess. He'll be here soon."

She tries to give me a smile but it's cut off when she lets out another scream.

"You're fully dilated, ma'am. Let's have a birthday."

Izzy starts pushing at the doctor's commands and I start slowly dying inside. My girl... I can't handle her being in this much pain. My mental distress for her continues, but I try to hide it and be the support she needs. I rub her forehead with the wet cloth one nurse thrusted into my hands. I curl my arm around her back and help her lean into her pushes, holding hold her leg open with my other arm.

Thirty minutes later, at the end of a long push, I hear the most magical sound I have ever heard. My son is taking his first breath and letting out a loud, healthy cry.

"Would you like to cut the cord, Daddy?" the doctor asks.

I nod my head lamely and take the scissors. The nurses take him off to the side after I finish.

I look down at Izzy and kiss her forehead. She meets my gaze and, with tears in her eyes, says, "Hey, Daddy." That is all it takes for me to drop a few tears of my own.

"Thank you, Princess. You've made me the luckiest man in the universe."

We both watch in awe as the nurses weigh and measure our son and bundle him up tight in a blue blanket. His head is covered with a tiny blue hat. They place him into Izzy's arms. Seeing her there with our son makes my skin break out in chills and my heart speeds up.

"Perfect," she whispers. I look down into her face and think that she is not wrong.

He has a tiny round and chubby face. His lips are small and form a perfect bow. He makes little mewing sounds and puckers his lips, showing off a dimple in his right cheek. I lift the cap up and see a full head of jet-black hair.

"He looks just like you, Axel." And he does.

We sit there until the doctor is done cleaning her up and the nurses start leaving to go make another couple as happy as we are.

This moment right here makes every day we were apart worth it.

Complete. I feel complete.

Leaning down, kissing my son softly on his small head, and

breathing in his baby scent has me choking on my emotions again.

"We've been waiting on you. Just as perfect as we knew you would be. Love you, little man." I kiss him once more before moving my lips to Izzy's. I kiss her twice before kissing away each tear that has escaped her eyes. "Love you so much, Princess."

Izzy

WATCHING AXEL fall in love with his son is the most beautiful moment.

"I love you too, baby. So much."

Axel has refused to leave our side to go tell everyone that the baby is here. We have just been moved into our private room when they start filing in. I'm impressed they made it that long. I'm starting to get tired, but the desire for our friends to meet our son keeps me from falling asleep.

"Oh my lord! Look at him! He is perfect!" Dee says with an excited whisper.

Congratulations are thrown around, and we enjoy sharing this moment with our family. Each and every one of the most important people in our lives is here. I am watching Axel hold our son close to his chest and thinking that he looks like a little football in Axel's large arms when I hear someone ask what his name is. Axel looks over at me with a smile and gives a small shake of his head.

I look over and meet each one of our friends' faces when I announce, "Nathaniel Gregory Reid." When I reach Greg's eyes, the tears gathering in the corners shock me for a second.

He walks over and gives me a small kiss on the top of my head. "Thank you, baby girl. That means the world…means the world to me."

I smile at him and wipe my eyes dry.

Axel comes over and hands me Nate before climbing into the bed next to me. We all sit there and enjoy the moment until the baby starts to cry. Axel looks worried, but I lean over and whisper in his ear that it's time to feed him. With some quick (Maddox, Beck, and Coop) and reluctant (Dee and Greg) goodbyes, our family leaves and Axel comes back over to me. He puts his arm around my shoulders and I lean into his body, settling Nate so that Axel can look down into his angelic face with me.

When I settle Nate on my breast and feel him give the first timid pull, I smile down at him and think to myself that fate finally loves me. Fate is welcoming me into her arms and shining her bright rays of love onto our family.

It doesn't take me long to drift off to sleep, safe in Axel's embrace with the gift of our love in my arms.

THE END

KEEP READING FOR SOME DELETED SCENES FROM AXEL.

NAMING THE BABY

"ARE YOU happy?"

The question seems so bizarre coming from her lips. Does she really doubt my happiness?

"You must be out of your mind, Princess, if you for one second think I'm not."

I look up and meet her green eyes from where my head is resting on her lap. My fingers are still caressing her swollen stomach, every few seconds getting a solid kick in return. Almost as if my boy is letting me know that he feels me.

Every time I look at her and see her body changing with our child, I almost lose my mind. It feels like my heart might burst. This is all part of the dream we shared all those years ago, but I would be lying if I said I wasn't terrified that it will all just vanish.

"Seriously, Axel. I can't help but wonder what life would be like if we hadn't lost all those years. I almost feel guilty being as happy as I am, knowing how much we lost."

Without breaking eye contact, I fold myself up and take her face between my hands. "Izzy, no doubt we were dealt a shit hand…to start with. But we found each other again. Nothing, and I mean nothing, can take this happiness from us. Me, you, our son, and any other children we have."

I press my lips against hers briefly, but with just enough strength that she starts pulling me more firmly against her. We both laugh when we feel our son kick. His strong kicks against my stomach feel a hell of a lot different against my hands.

"Come here, Princess. This little man needs a name." I go to pull her towards me but pause when I see her bite her lip. "Izzy? What's going on up there?" I tap her temple lightly and smile, knowing that whatever is rolling around up there has been weighing heavy.

"I've been thinking…" She trails off and looks away. "I don't just want to name him anything. I don't know how to explain it, Ax. I want his name to have meaning. Something strong that will always remind us of how blessed we are. Does that make sense?"

God, I love this woman.

"Yeah, babe. I get it. I've been thinking the same thing. Hear me out, okay?" She nods her head a few times, her eyes shining brightly with excitement. "The other day, I was looking up names and came across one I think will be perfect." I pause for a second and wait for her nod of approval before continuing. "So, I found one of those sites that have baby names and their meanings. There was one that means 'God given,' and babe, with everything we've been through and overcome, if this little guy isn't a sign of God giving us one hell of a blessing, I don't know what is."

In all honesty, the second I saw the name, I knew—that is my son's name. That is it. I always knew that Izzy was my blessing, my reward for my shit life. But this little miracle we made? That is OUR blessing. Our gift from God for overcoming and surviving everything he threw at us.

"Okay, well? What is it?" She is literally vibrating with excitement. She gets it. I shouldn't have doubted she would.

"Nathaniel," I reply and wait. It's a few seconds' worth of her blinking her watery eyes at me rapidly before she lets out a breathy echo, repeating my word.

"It's perfect, Ax. Our gift—Nathaniel."

"One more, babe. His middle name. I don't think I need to explain this one but I will. For too many years, I wasn't there to protect you. I wasn't there to pick up the pieces when you needed me either. But Greg was. Baby, I don't know any other way to honor that than to give Nathaniel one hell of a namesake. What do you think—Nathaniel Gregory?"

At this point, I doubt she even registers my words. Tears are falling fast and she is sobbing quietly. But after all of that, her smile is blinding. Yeah, my girl got me.

"Nathaniel Gregory Reid. I love it. Our son, our gift, and our blessing," She whispers between choked sobs.

AXEL

"Love you, Princess."
"Love you too, Axel."

THE DOCK REVISITED

"**B**ABY?"

I've been searching through the house for the last fifteen minutes, looking for my boys. I swear Axel does this just to see me laugh when I finally find them.

"Axel Reid, you come out now... I missed my boys today." Shaking my head in fake exasperation, I continue down the stairs with my soft laughter trailing behind me. "Nate baby? Mama's home. Where is my handsome little man?"

I trip over a few of Nate's toys and almost take my head off when I slip on his new favorite motorcycle from Maddox. Axel must have brought it into the kitchen to keep Nate busy while he was fixing lunch. I would be willing to bet he skipped Nate's naptime—again—so that he could keep playing with him.

My man, he loves his son.

I stop my search for a few moments to pick up the blocks that are scattered all over the floor, before continuing my mission to find my men.

I walk through out the back door, looking around the deck. Our property is vast, so it takes me a second to scan the surroundings for them. The sun warms my skin and the reflection from the lake blinds me momentarily. Now that Nate is mobile, we have been spending more and more afternoons enjoying springtime in Georgia. Today is no different. The sky is a dazzling blue, with not one cloud in the sky. The flowers we planted along the pebbled path that leads down to the dock are in full bloom.

Everything about this once barren house screams life.

Our home.

A shiver of déjà vu wraps around my spine and whispers up my back when I see movements down at the end of the dock. Sitting down with his legs dangling in the lake is my Axel. His bronze, naked back is the only thing I can see from my angle, but judging by his soft swaying, my little man is nestled tight in his arms.

I follow the pebbled path, slipping off my shoes before continuing down the wooden planks. I make sure to keep my steps slow and steady—careful to keep them unnoticeable. I'm only a few steps behind them when his voice reaches my ears.

"… and then your mommy made me the luckiest man in the world. Never thought my heart could get bigger until she told me you were coming. You don't know this now, but one day you will. Your mom… She thinks she's lucky to have us, but it's the other way around my little man. Blessed to the max. So blessed, Nate."

My foot hits a loose board that moans in protest, earning me Axel's attention. "Damn, I was trying to be sneaky," I mumble under my breath.

His smile is blinding in the late afternoon sun, his happiness is infections, and the best part is that I helped put it there.

"Hey, Princess. Have fun on your search?" His teasing tone causes my suppressed laughter to bubble out.

Shaking my head, I crouch down and press my front tight against his warm back. My legs don't even come close to falling off the side, but I can still wrap my arms around his powerful frame.

I shiver when my skin touches his.

"Hey, you. I missed my boys today." I kiss his back before looking over his shoulder at Nate. "Ax, you can't keep letting him chew on that! It's so dirty!" Reaching around, I gently remove Axel's dog tags from Nate's chubby fingers and gummy mouth. "There's mama's handsome little man."

Nate starts squirming in Axel's hold to reach me, clearly growing impatient with his father's slow transfer.

"One of these days he'll be happy just hanging out with his old man."

"Don't be such a baby," I tease, "You know he loves his daddy. His mommy just happens to have his endless food supply."

Axel shifts his position so he can pull me into his lap—holding both of us within his arms. The instant rush of safety and love that always pours out of him wraps around us, blanketing me in the world's best feeling.

I cradle Nate in my arms before bringing my shirt up so that he can reach my breast. He doesn't waste a second before latching on. I lie my head down against Axel's shoulder, and he brings his hand up to caresses Nate's soft cheek.

"I love you, baby, but right now, I'm insanely jealous of our boy."

"I can tell. And if your jealousy doesn't stop poking me in the rear, I'm taking our boy inside."

The vibrations of his laughter tickle my skin before his lips press lightly against my neck.

"I missed you today, Princess," he whispers against my skin, "What kept you away for so long?"

"Ax, I've been gone for three hours," I laugh.

"Three hours too long. I thought we decided weekends were spent at home—just us."

"We did, but you know I had to take care of some wedding stuff and Dee is always so busy that this was the only time we could get together. Then Greg came over and we just lost track of time." I turn my head, making sure he really isn't upset. Seeing the small smile on his full lips puts me at ease.

"I got it, babe. That doesn't mean I don't miss you when you aren't around. Plus Nate missed you so much he wanted to skip his nap and wait up."

"Oh? He came up with that all on his own, huh?" I laugh.

"Yup. He said he would rather pass his time building block towers."

"Ax, baby, you are ridiculous sometimes," I rush past my giggles.

"I know. So, you ready to be my wife yet, Princess?" His question warms my ears right before he nips my lobe lightly between his teeth. "You ready to *finally* be all mine?"

"I'm already yours and you know that." The argument, even playful as it always is, seems to be a daily conversation.

"Not until your last name matches mine and Nate's." His voice is firm, and I know he's losing his patience.

"I don't need to have your last name to prove anything. Especially not that my heart is yours."

"But you will," he stresses with all playfulness gone from his tone.

I know this is a sore subject, but we both agreed that it would be best to wait until Nate was born. Then we started planning and things just started taking longer. With Nate just turning nine months old, I know he's getting frustrated.

I ignore him and lift Nate up to my shoulder.

"Da-da."

"See, I told you. He only wants me to be his live-in walking re-frigerator!" I joke.

We both laugh and enjoy a few quiet moments sitting down on the dock. It's times like this when I realize just how lucky we are. Axel's right—we are truly blessed. Time spent with my soon-to-be husband and this perfect product of our love really brings that home.

I shift a now sleeping Nate in my arms and snuggle more slowly into Axel. His strong arms tighten slightly, shifting us to a more comfortable position.

"Princess, I need you to be mine." His softly spoken words break the silence.

"I know, Axel. I know. That's what took me so long today. Dee and I finished everything up. Booked, paid for, and confirmed. Can you wait just one more month?"

"Izzy, what's one more month when we've waited for this many years?" I can tell he isn't thrilled but still happy-ish knowing that it's going to be soon.

"Ax? The day I become yours will be right up there with the birth of our son as the best day of my life. I can't wait, baby."

His arms go solid for a second before he speaks. "I know." The smug tone in his voice erases all signs of his earlier impatience.

Cocky bastard.

God, I love him.

ACKNOWLEDGMENTS:

To my husband for dealing with my scattered mind and messy house while I was 'dreaming'. Thank you for all those times you watched our girls while I created this book. I love you.

To my girls, dreams can come true. Dream big and don't ever stop! This is for you. ☺

To my mom, the best damn mommager EVER!

To all the family and friends that helped me along the way. I don't think I would have been able to make Axel what it is without!

To Angela- here's to wine, cold pizza, and basement zombies. I love you! Thank you for answering my every text, email and call during this process! **Cheers to Dee**

To my 'Bookettes' for inspiring me to write this book and keeping me calm along the way. (The daily dose of half-naked men emails helped too!) If it wouldn't have been for one email that said "you should write a book" I don't know if Axel would be here. So, I owe y'all!

ALL the girls who read every single page that I wrote during this process. This book is what it is because of every single bit of help from you ladies! (A special thank you to Katie, girl I fear your frying pan skills! And Kelly for the support, hunky picture and your mad google image searching skills! You two girls, I heart you!)

Brenda, thank you so much for taking my book and making this process possible! <3

Sam, you made the editing process as painless as possible! Thank you for all of the reading, editing, and best freaking commentary ever!

My 'second eyes', Angela Cetrangola and Dana Dean. Without y'all I might have pulled my hair out during the editing days! My brain loves you!! ☺

SPECIAL THANKS TO: My BBG Pher (xoxo), Melissa (you perv...you rock!), Megan Williams, Wendy O'Hera-Perry, Allison, Tokies, Alisha, Tessa, LB, Nicky, Penny, Molly, Maria, Jolene, Andrea, Cathy, Misty, Felicia, Brittany, Deborah, Jen, Paula, Angel, Felicia, Ashley, Ruthie, Tarrinasha, Jenny, Amanda, and Ashleigh. To each and every one of my Goodreads friends and loyal supporters. Y'all never doubted me & in turn made it possible to not doubt myself. I have, hands down, the best GR friends in the world! Lastly, my IG mommas, I effin' love y'all!

If I forgot anyone, this is for you—THANK YOU! ☺

Connect with Harper Sloan to keep up to date with the next book in the Corps Security series:

You can contact Harper Sloan here:

authorharpersloan@gmail.com
www.authorharpersloan.com
www.facebook.com/harpersloanbooks
Twitter: @HarperSloan
Instagram: @Harper_Sloan

To connect a little deeper with the story and characters, visit the Pinterest boards: www.pinterest.com/harpersloan

Other books by Harper Sloan:

Cage (Corps Security, Book 2) - https://www.amazon.com/dp/B00F28ICBE

Beck (Corps Security, Book 3) - http://www.amazon.com/dp/B00H-HBU5JG

Uncaged (Corps Security, Book 3.5) - http://www.amazon.com/dp/B00IWSNSJ2

Coming Soon:

Cooper (Corps Security, Book 4) Summer 2014
Locke (Corps Security, Book 5) Winter 2014